Quiet Dawn

Quiet Dawn

Jean-Claude Fignolé

Translated by Kaiama L. Glover and Laurent Dubois

Duke University Press *Durham and London* 2025

© 2025 DUKE UNIVERSITY PRESS
Project Editor: Lisa Lawley
Designed by Dave Rainey
Typeset in FreightText Pro by Westchester Publishing
Services

Library of Congress Cataloging-in-Publication Data
Names: Fignolé, Jean-Claude, author. | Glover, Kaiama L.,
    [date] translator. | Dubois, Laurent, [date] translator.
Title: Quiet dawn / Jean-Claude Fignolé ; translated by
    Kaiama L. Glover and Laurent Dubois.
Other titles: Aube tranquille. English
Description: Durham : Duke University Press, 2025.
Identifiers: LCCN 2024033023 (print)
LCCN 2024033024 (ebook)
ISBN 9781478031611 (paperback)
ISBN 9781478028437 (hardcover)
ISBN 9781478060642 (ebook)
Subjects: LCSH: Haiti—History—Revolution, 1791–1804—
    Fiction. | LCGFT: Novels. | Historical fiction.
Classification: LCC PQ3949.2.F5 A9313 2025 (print) | LCC
    PQ3949.2.F5 (ebook) | DDC 843/.914—dc23/eng/20241021
LC record available at https://lccn.loc.gov/2024033023
LC ebook record available at https://lccn.loc.gov/2024033024

Cover credit: Frankétienne (Franck Étienne), *Untitled*, 2003.
Acrylic on Masonite, 24 × 16 in. Courtesy of the Yvonne and
Glenn Stokes Collection. Photo courtesy of El-Saieh Gallery.

For Jean-Claude Fignolé,
with gratitude for this whirld he has brought to the page.

Contents

Translators' Introduction

Kaiama L. Glover and Laurent Dubois

Let us quiet the rancor of history without denying or forgetting it and allow literature to introduce us into the eternity of its fantasies.
—Jean-Claude Fignolé (2010)

The Americas have a history problem. The Caribbean and its diasporas in particular have long struggled, that is, to fashion a historical identity untethered from the overdetermining degradations of colonialism and its stultifying (lack of) imagination. For Black peoples whose collective past has been so dramatically constituted by the relentless avarice and fantasies of racial capitalism—peoples for whom recorded history, the history of what has been deemed modernity, first emerged from the Middle Passage and the "monstrous intimacies"[1] of the plantation— possibilities for autopoiesis have been hard to come by.

Different thinkers have proposed different responses to this conundrum, to this "quarrel with history," as the Jamaican poet and scholar Edward Baugh has pithily named it. The Martinican writer and intellectual Édouard Glissant, for example, has placed the matter of history at the very center of his creative and scholarly work and has profoundly shaped the discussion of these questions over the past more than half century. In his celebrated essay collections *Caribbean Discourse* (1981) and *Poetics of Relation* (1990), as well as in his many novels and plays, Glissant exhorts his readers to embrace what he calls "a prophetic vision of the past." A much-theorized and complex concept, this generative formulation calls for reading the past against schematic chronology and toward collective destiny. It proposes looking beyond the so-called facts of history as given, and understanding present realities as the tattered dreams of the past. To look backward in time prophetically, he explains, is a process of querying and recovery that relies not on the purportedly universalist but profoundly ethnocentric "capital H History" of Hegelian chronology, but rather on a rhizomatic tangle of histories, lowercase and plural.

Haiti has had its own consuming problem with history, as novelist and essayist Jean-Claude Fignolé understands well. "History, you see, is my 'thing,'" he declared in a wide-ranging 2010 interview, "despite the fact that I'm not trained as a historian." Committed in his storytelling practice to exposing the fraught persistence of the past in Haiti's present-day struggles, Fignolé insists that "the indignity of the present that we're living is a direct consequence of the turpitudes of our History, since the very beginning."[2]

Haitian thought around history-telling reflects the unique circumstances of the nation's relationship to the empires of Europe and the United States. Ostensibly sovereign since its seizing of independence from France in 1804, Haiti has long been understood—and understood itself, for better and for worse—as an exception in the Americas and in the wider Black Atlantic.[3] This singularity has had consequences, consequences that are perhaps nowhere more robustly analyzed than by the Haitian anthropologist Michel-Rolph Trouillot. Trouillot's groundbreaking 1995 study of the practice and nature of history and historiography within the context of global capitalism, *Silencing the Past: Power and the Production of History*, is a focused reminder that stories of the past emerge in a situated fashion—that historical narratives are bound by the conditions of their production and reception and, as such, can and should be approached with a measure of skepticism.[4] Trouillot's most powerful example of this phenomenon is what he famously calls the silencing of the Haitian Revolution—that is, the Revolution's marked absence from the "official" archival record and its active erasure of histories that undermine or contest the prevailing history of white supremacy and conquest in the Americas.

A world-shattering and world-(re)making event that very literally constituted the state of Haiti as such, the Haitian Revolution was an epistemic rupture of global proportions—an unprecedented challenge to the modern world order, both in its time and in the more than two centuries since. Indeed, to this day, Haiti and its revolution remain in many ways incommensurate with desired histories of the American hemisphere and wider Atlantic world. As Haitian sociologist Jean Casimir has argued, the social and cultural structures and perspectives that emerged from 1804 among the Haitian people are still very difficult to apprehend—even for Haiti's own intellectuals—given the stubborn circulation of colonial categories and ways of thinking in the present.[5]

Haiti's novelists have largely avoided writing the story of Haiti's founding event, for reasons that speak to the Revolution's insistent effect on the nation's fate in the more than two centuries since its wresting of sovereignty from Napoleon's imperial state. As literary scholar Natalie Léger has argued, this is very likely due to the fact that the Revolution has been so cynically co-opted and deployed among Haiti's political leaders.[6] The tendency of the nation's politicians—none more notoriously so than François "Papa Doc" Duvalier—to lean on a heroic nationalist narrative with the goal of manipulating or obfuscating the country's present realities is a narrative practice that Haiti's writers are wary of legitimating.

Jean-Claude Fignolé is a rare exception to that rule. Neither a historian nor a theorist, Fignolé writes always with Haiti's revolutionary past present in his mind, a perspective that is strikingly apparent in *Quiet Dawn*. One of the very few contemporary works of Haitian prose fiction to grapple explicitly with Haiti's revolution, it pushes forcefully against the silences and silencings of Haiti's past. Indeed, despite its title, Fignolé's novel gives us a clamorous Atlantic world—a world that simply would not have been without the events of 1791 to 1804.

Seamlessly, Fignolé brings the reader of *Quiet Dawn* through several key moments in Haiti's revolutionary history, including watershed events that appear in historical works like C. L. R. James's *The Black Jacobins* and, more recently, Sudhir Hazareesingh's *Black Spartacus*.[7] Through Wolf's story, for example, we learn the history of the Swiss Regiment, an all-Black military force that played a key role in conflicts in the western province of Saint-Domingue, only to be betrayed and massacred. We discover the intricacies of the conflicts among planters, and their positions toward the free population of African descent—described variously in the novel as "freedmen" and "mulattoes," depending on who is speaking—including the executions of rebel leaders Vincent Ogé and Jean-Baptiste Chavannes. We learn about Léger-Félicité Sonthonax and Étienne Polverel, the commissioners who decreed the abolition of slavery in 1793; about their defeated royalist enemy, François-Thomas Galbaud; and about the rise of "a certain Toussaint Louverture, once known by the name of Fatras-Bâton" (page 153). We are called to witness the famous Bwa Kayiman ceremony, which launched the mass revolution of the enslaved in 1791, through Saintmilia's fervid remembrance: "Live free or die, a pig was brought out and you, possessed with hope and justice, raised your cutlass, to live free, our voices shaking with emotion, hate and vengeance merged into a single will, or die, a cry, a decision flowing from the plains to the hills, from the valleys to the mountains, to no longer be afraid, an ardent thirst, to be born, to be resuscitated, to rise up, to affirm ourselves, even if the world were to explode, even if the world were to perish, yes to remake the world" (page 151).

Quiet Dawn operates on a global stage, fully engaging with the complexities of eighteenth-century France and the revolutionary era in Europe. History is everywhere in the novel, whether or not that history ever made it into the record book of those granted the authority to account for the past. We see how the writings of Enlightenment philosophers Voltaire and Jean-Jacques Rousseau circulated within the context of Saint-Domingue, and we travel through Europe, as well, as it contends with the French Revolution and its continental repercussions. We bear witness to the counterrevolutionary war in the Vendée and its bloody suppression, to the mechanisms of the Terror, and to the rise of Napoleon Bonaparte, "the tyrant who has stolen our revolution and turned it to his own ends" (page 155). French cultural and literary history also become part of the story through evocations of the libertine writer the Marquis de Sade, the composer Jean-Philippe Rameau, and the novelist and playwright Pierre de Marivaux, and through Fignolé's humorous evocation of the celebrated Romantic writer, diplomat, and historian François-René de Chateaubriand, whose presence dominated the literary world during the first half of the nineteenth century.

This vast scope speaks to Fignolé's unsilencing of Saint-Domingue within a global frame, despite Haiti's isolation with respect to today's political power brokers. The Haitian Revolution haunts our collective human past, Fignolé insists, and he has boldly written the ghosts. He narrates the Revolution as part of an eternal return to a set of unending, spiraling histories, revealing Haiti's para-revolutionary moment as crucial to any understanding of the nation's troubling subsequent fate. In his 2010 interview, he laments that so much Haitian history has been "essentially a process of hagiography," in which "the principal actors, according to the dictates of partisan passions, are deified." Haitian politicians during the twentieth century, he notes, have led the way in "sacrificing historical truth to the lies of an excessive nationalism," leading to a tendency to refer "only to the super-heroic, quasi-divine dimension of our ancestors." Thus, while *Quiet Dawn* implicates well-known historical actors and events, it adamantly refuses any rehabilitating mythification of the Revolution. Haiti, Fignolé argues, needs a different relationship to history, and *Quiet Dawn* proposes just such a different path. It "authorizes [him] to express the human fiber of the various characters, to seize the key figures in all their weaknesses, with their qualities and their faults" and offers a way to consider the workings of Haiti's unresolved revolutionary history in a troubled global present, making plain how that history has continued to repeat itself in Haiti's at once insular, regional, and global positioning today.[8]

* * *

Published in 1990 by the prestigious French press Les Éditions du Seuil, *Quiet Dawn* is a truly singular work of literature. The author's "favorite" among his six novels,[9] it obliquely points to the painful irony of Haiti's long postrevolutionary sociopolitical circumstances through its staging in the present of events that are putatively past. Both the novel's obliqueness and its attention to the ways that history loops back on itself are reflections of Fignolé's biography and of the very particular circumstances in which he wrote.

Born in 1941, Fignolé was raised in Les Abricots, a commune in the small seaside town of Jérémie, located in the southern province of Haiti. In the mid-1960s, at the height of François Duvalier's fascist regime, he, along with fellow writers Frankétienne and René Philoctète, began developing an approach to literature and history they named Spiralism. Characterized by unresolved yet generative tension—between the insular and the global, the individual and the collective, the past and the present, the spiral enabled the three writers to embrace time's unfettered linear passage, allowing them to present—that is, quite literally to make present—Haiti's complicated past as integral to and explicitly implicated in its contemporary circumstances.[10]

Spiralism emerged against the backdrop of the excessive violence, pervasive government criminality, and absolute terror that marked Duvalier's totalitarian state. Fignolé would have been acutely aware of the imminent and awesome threat of such brutality, as Jérémie had been the site of the massacre of entire families accused of conspiring against Duvalier in 1964. In the years following, he became deeply involved in projects aiming to address environmental and economic problems in Les Abricots, and was elected mayor of the town in 2007, continuing this role through the devastating 2010 earthquake and its aftermath. *Quiet Dawn* was written during the late 1980s, a time of tremendous political transformation and upheaval in Haiti, as the country sought to rebuild democracy in the wake of Jean-Claude "Baby Doc" Duvalier's ousting and exile in 1986.

The extent to which Duvalierism transformed the social, cultural, and intellectual landscape of the nation cannot be understated. Modes of creative representation and the imaginary itself were considered the purview of Haiti's all-powerful leader, subject to his most absurd pronouncements and paranoid whims. History was shaped in accordance with Duvalierist doctrine, perverted in service to a symbolic order that gave no quarter to ordinary citizens—be they artists or athletes, journalists or priests, women or even children—who dared to call the regime into question. Many of Haiti's writers left the country during this period, having been victims of torture and other forms of repression. The Spiralists Fignolé, Frankétienne, and Philoctète, however, made an explicit pledge not to leave Duvalier's Haiti, for fear of being refused return, as had been the fate of several of their colleagues and friends.

Though the three men pursued this creative practice very differently, they were all aligned in their belief that reality has always been "lived schizophrenically by Haitians."[11] Having made the decision to stay and to write in Haiti despite the material and psychological constraints placed on the individual (and the) artist by the successive Duvalier regimes, Fignolé, Frankétienne, and Philoctète necessarily sought out ways of writing the Haitian real at once faithfully and with a certain measure of caution. They were well aware that writing subversive content into their fiction could have mortal repercussions, and so they emphasized the formal dimensions of their literary endeavors, utilizing the figure of the spiral as a platform for creating narratives that are pointedly imprecise or multivalent in time and space.

For Fignolé in particular, the spiral form provided a clear narrative structure from which to delve into an infinitely relevant and repeating past. This is palpably the case in *Quiet Dawn*, a swirling epic that amounts to a fulsome confrontation with Black Atlantic history, in all its complexity and irresolution. Switching among narrators, places, and moments in time, it is not meant to be an easy read. By constantly shifting the parameters of the present in his narrative, Fignolé implicitly demands that his reader recognize the absolute contingency and even unhelpful arbitrariness of a linear conception of time or a bordered conception of space. The present of the novel is fractured, traumatic, and multifaceted. The brutal violence of the world its characters share has broken each of them in ways more and less metaphorical, more and less literal.

This disjointedness mimetically communicates the chaos and the fissures of history without attempting to construct a single coherent, complete, or stable story of the past. Instead, that past is literally everywhere all at once. And while the narrative intends, like one of the novel's characters, to be "faithful to the rendezvous of our history" (page 128), no stable notion of what "our" history might be—of whose history is being told and experienced through the novel—is ever determined with any certainty. Alternating between and conflating the apocalyptic and the personal tragic, *Quiet Dawn* pushes the reader to perceive events without hierarchizing them, without allowing any one version to supplant any other as truth or fact. Traumatic memory, fantasy, and "official" narratives emerge as equally (un)reliable means of accessing New World (hi)stories.

The novel suggests, ultimately, that we too often limit ourselves in the ways we tell our stories, that our intellectual approach to the past little resembles the overlapping, unending, unfinished, and unwritten nature of how we live in this world. This aesthetic of the unsettled and the undone is constant throughout Fignolé's work, and it is intentional, pedagogic. His novel invites us into a different understanding of the relationship between time and place; it enjoins us to let go of what we might desire from the past. The experience of reading it thus enables a different kind of consciousness about the imbricated copresence of multiple events and our perceptions of what "really" happened.

Quiet Dawn paints an at once intimate and sweeping portrait of the Black Atlantic that is as much grounded in history as it is the fruit of Fignolé's extraordinary imagination. It plunges the reader into the time-space of colonial Saint-Domingue through the sorrowful chronicle of the eighteenth-century planter Baron Wolf von Schpeerbach; his wife, Sonja Biemme de Valembrun Lebrun; the enslaved woman Saint-milia; and her son, Salomon, all of whom live unhappily together on a vast plantation in Saint-Domingue's southern province. The tragedy of these four individuals' entwined colonial lives is set in parallel to— and eventually becomes interwoven with—the chronologically post-colonial story of the twentieth-century French nun Sister Theresa, a von Schpeerbach descendant, who has been sent to Haiti in part to do penance for the atrocities committed by her ancestors. Juxtaposing and integrating the young nun's present-day narrative with events that have taken place more than five hundred years in the past, *Quiet Dawn* is a tale of vengeful ghosts and reluctant spiritual possession, in which time refuses to keep to its proper place.

The framing twentieth-century narrative itself operates in a sort of double time. It places Sister Theresa, whose given name is Sonja Biemme de Valembrun Lebrun, at once in a convent in Haiti and in the airplane transporting her across the Atlantic to begin a missionary sojourn at that very convent. In both spaces—the convent and the airplane—Sister Theresa recounts her experiences in the first-person present of the narrative. That is, the scenes that occur in the airplane are not positioned as flashbacks; although logically they are antecedent to the events that unfold in the convent, they unfold as if existing simultaneously, so many equally present moments in the temporality of the novel. Further, it is while in the air that Sister Theresa/Sonja listens to a cassette tape given to her by her mother just prior to her boarding the aircraft. The tape is a recording of the transcribed memoirs of her great-great-great-great-grandfather the Baron von Schpeerbach. On it, yet another first-person, present-tense voice recounts the horrors that take place on von Schpeerbach's Saint-Domingue plantation at the hands or on the orders of his capricious and sadistic Breton wife, Sister Theresa's great-great-great-great-grandmother, a.k.a. the original Sonja Biemme de Valembrun Lebrun. From the moment the cassette tape begins playing, the entire narrative is resituated within the present of eighteenth-century Haiti, with Wolf (via his unnamed ventriloquist) at the storytelling helm.

As it excavates and unravels history through its imagining of these intimate tales of family tragedy and trauma, *Quiet Dawn* unfurls a breathtaking canvas and traces a devastating arc of the Black Atlantic spiral. Its depiction of the dramatic exploits of the Breton dynasty to which Sonja Biemme and Sister Theresa belong evokes Brittany's deep ties to colonial Saint-Domingue as a crucial port of the French commercial trade with both Africa and the Americas. Fignolé posits this seventeenth-century saga of the merciless slave-trafficking Biemmes as the precursor to the guilt-ridden hypocrisies of twentieth-century missionary work, thus pointing to Brittany's significance as a dynamic nodal point in the Atlantic world, both past and present. Reflecting on his initial impulse for writing the novel, Fignolé explains, "from the 17th to the 20th century, Breton missionaries stirred up all the simmering discrimination on the island, by ostracizing voodoo [*sic*], castrating the Haitians by obliging them to reject Creole as a tool of communication between each other, and inflaming color prejudice in their schools and even in their churches."[12] The sins of the fathers (and mothers!), Fignolé thus suggests, are as much reenacted by as they are visited upon their children.

Sister Theresa's crossing of the Atlantic, the reader eventually learns, is in fact a spiral echo of her ancestors' honeymoon voyage to Saint-Domingue. As such, it is at once incredible and yet somehow also unsurprising that, once in Haiti, Sister Theresa discovers an avatar of Saintmilia, also (still?) named Saintmilia, presently interned within the twentieth-century convent where she has come to reside. Consumed by "a fury repressed for two centuries" (page 3), the present-day Saintmilia lives among the ruins of her and Sister Theresa's entangled past; she remembers all the details of her ancestral suffering, and she has vowed to settle accounts. Time, Fignolé thus makes clear, most certainly does not heal the wounds of history.

Quiet Dawn is animated almost entirely by this unhealed past. At the same time (the pun is very much intended), Fignolé reveals how history's tragedies can infuse the present with transformative revolutionary power. In his depiction, for example, of the night of the Bwa Kayiman ceremony in 1791, originary event of the Haitian Revolution, he surfaces the abundance of stories that converge within this specific, pivotal episode in Haiti's history. Staging this moment as the triumphant return of the Black maroon leader François Mackandal, who had in fact been brutally executed by white planters more than three decades earlier in 1758, Fignolé powerfully invokes Vodou cosmologies to conjure the Revolution's expansive temporality: "blessed day, Agoué, the day of your rage, Mackandal rises up, a giant statue spitting fire and flames, distilling poison, Biassou cuts off heads, a tornado, a hurricane, a cyclone, Fatras-Bâton releases the *lwa*, razing plains and hills, the salt of vengeance sets fire to the cane fields" (page 178). In this scene and others, the novel spirals through the centuries of oppression, the enduring spiritualities, and the courageous imaginings of alternate futures that made it possible for the enslaved to shatter and reconfigure the political and economic landscape of Saint-Domingue and, ultimately, to create Haiti.

Quiet Dawn thus powerfully represents the gradual opening of imagination and possibility that constituted the Revolution, revealing how the nature of power shifted and how specific possibilities for action emerged among the enslaved. It captures the way the Haitian Revolution somehow accelerated time—"information seemed to travel faster than before" (page 124)—even as the events the novel relates are clearly embedded in deep and slow chronologies. The novel presents a narrative of the Revolution, and of central figures like the insurgent leader Biassou, that anticipates its own afterlives, not just imagining but embodying them. Fignolé does not create the rupture between our present and "their" past; he represents it—seeking the very most faithful rendering of the out-of-time-ness of Haiti's revolution. How, he asks, can it possibly be finished if it still so adamantly haunts the now?

Fignolé's avowal of the Revolution's imminence and immanence comes through with particular force in his writing of the enslaved-woman-turned-zonbi-warrior Toukouma, whose experience of loss and unspeakable violation starkly evinces the possible transformation of slavery's horrors into a concrete political endeavor. An avatar of such revolutionary figures as Cécile Fatiman and Sanité Bélair, among others, Fignolé's Toukouma summons to the text the many women who played crucial roles in combat, healing, and spirituality during the Revolution.[13] Whereas Haitian women writers—including Marie Vieux-Chauvet in her 1957 novel *Dance on the Volcano* and Évelyne Trouillot in her novels *The Infamous Rosalie* (2003) and *Désirée Congo* (2020)[14]—have foregrounded women's presence during and in the years immediately preceding the Revolution, Fignolé is unique in having configured a woman character so mighty as to lead warriors into battle.

Wrathful and empowered with a strength that recalls the Petro *lwa* Ezili Dantor, Toukouma rages in pursuit of vengeance both intimate and global.[15] The ferocity of the punishment she metes out to the white man who raped and beat her is proportionate to that brutalization, but also exceeds it. This is because her demand for justice extends to all the enslaved women in the novel—Maïté, Saintmilia, and countless unacknowledged others—whose bodily autonomy has been made subject to the demands of the plantation order.[16]

Not only is the reader compelled to confront the specifically gendered brutality of the colonial world through Toukouma's tragic tale, but her experiences prefigure the harshness of the postcolonial world, as well. The racism and violent encounters of the present are always in dialogue with those of the past, as is the case, for example, with the novel's third Sonja, the imperturbable Senegalese flight attendant who cares for Sister Theresa on her transatlantic and transhistorical voyage to Haiti. Sonja tells Sister Theresa about her experience of having been called a "Negro whore" and subjected to a vicious sexual assault by a group of white men in Neuilly, an upscale neighborhood of modern-day Paris. Interjected into her description of this terrifying racist attack and rape in contemporary France are the words "as naked as earthworms," a provocative intertext that gestures explicitly to words used by Toussaint Louverture in the last letter he wrote from prison (pages 160–61).[17] This rhyming of then and now suggests that in some ways the past was always already saturated with ongoing future violence.

The intimacy established between the privileged white nun Sister Theresa and the Black flight attendant Sonja is woven through the novel to multiple ends. Importantly, it allows for useful exposition: nervous and (therefore) more than a little tipsy on her first flight, Sister Theresa confides openly in Sonja from the outset, laying out the circumstances of her journey to Haiti and the long and reprehensible history that undergirds it. By no means a passive listener, Sonja refuses to let Sister Theresa wallow in self-pity, nor does she let her take comfort in any euphemistic perceptions of the past. Rather, she expands Sister Theresa's understanding of Europe's devastating toll on Black peoples across the globe by compelling her to confront the third point of the Black Atlantic triangle, the African continent. The two women argue, philosophize, and debate this long, braided history; they tell one another stories of how the conditions of the immediate and distant past have limited their personal horizons. They also flirt openly with one another, becoming ever more familiar as they pass the hours of their journey together, mutually confined in the indeterminate space-time of the aircraft. Indeed, as the narrative unfolds, it becomes apparent that Sister Theresa's feelings for Sonja are more than platonic. A subcurrent of erotic desire percolates beneath the surface of the two women's banter and becomes a portal through which the reader learns of Sister Theresa's torturous romantic and sexual relationship with Sister Hyacinthe, an older nun from her former convent in France. These queer connections among women allow for crucial, albeit fraught, modes of escape from otherwise constricted lives.

Quiet Dawn is replete with such stories of the complex lives of women—Black and white, enslaved and free, centuries gone and present day. More so than any other of the slim corpus of Haitian-authored revolutionary fictions, Fignolé's novel reminds us to attend to women's experiences, too often buried within and obscured by grand narratives of history. Thus, while the white male plantation-owner Wolf undoubtedly believes himself to be the hero of his own story, it becomes clear to the reader that he is mostly helpless and clueless in the face of women who, despite their explicit subjugation to the colonial and patriarchal order, are in many ways running the show. From his worldly and cynical courtesan-counselor, Cécile, to his unforgiving former wet nurse, Saintmilia, to his uncontrollable and viciously cruel bride, Sonja, women maroon from the world slavery has built. They make tactical strikes designed to destabilize and promptly undermine the conditions they find unbearable—so many radical bids for freedom within systems of domination, long-historical and present day. Their actions determine the course of history; they are forces of disorder, both within the novel and in the world in which Fignolé produced it. Morally ambivalent, profoundly disruptive, and in many respects unlikeable, they form no discernible sisterhood, and they are often at each other's throats. The disorderly women who populate *Quiet Dawn* highlight the narrowness and violence of the world they are driven to refuse. Desperate and despairing, they want love above all else, and they are enraged by its impossibility.[18]

"What does love taste like?" asks one of these women toward the end of the story (page 162). This question seems to run through the whole of *Quiet Dawn*. The search for tenderness, for spaces of joy and connection, is interwoven within even the most conflictual of relationships. The possibility of something else is evanescent but also ever present, spiraling through the novel just as histories of violence do. And what somehow emerges throughout is the flawed yet striving humanity of Fignolé's characters, despite—or perhaps precisely because of—the novel's risky grappling with the most disquieting human-perpetrated horrors.

It is only in the revelation of the book's final pages, a scene of unimaginable and heartbreaking brutality, that the reader discovers the original act of violence that lies at the heart of the entire narrative spiral. This scene of subjection is shown to be at once the source and the reflection of the myriad other conflicts—personal, collective, global— that structured the colonial world and that continue to take a toll on the present.[19] The novel's devastating conclusion seems to confirm the impossibility of finding a way through—or a clearing within—the absurdities of the plantation order toward relations grounded in friendship or even love.

In *Quiet Dawn*, none of this is set firmly within one moment in history, but rather exists palimpsestically in what came before and what has come since. Through his radical refusals of the conventions of historical fiction, Fignolé writes away from even the most ostensibly nontraditional literary representations of time's passage. "Histories contract and come back to life," as Fignolé puts it in the novel (page 38). He helps us experience the inescapability and oppressiveness of the past, but also offers a different kind of invitation. He asks that we readers confront, see, and feel the past as present in its full complexity. The novel proposes a way of understanding our rootedness in history as the necessary place from which to see the world around us anew, and perhaps to move forward within it. "She reconquers her past," Fignolé writes of one character (page 20), and this novel struggles to retrieve a past that has largely been silenced by dominant histories—not by narrating it in any straightforward way, but by changing the very terms through which the past is constituted and accessed. In this sense, Fignolé's novel is a radical commitment to evoking the presentness of history. It is a model of temporal instability, and as such, it raises questions about the very nature of historical time and about chronology itself.

* * *

Quiet Dawn is choral and polyphonic—orchestral, even. The novel's constantly shifting perspectives and voices suggest that its characters are at once distinct beings and nonindividuated subjects. Fignolé makes it a challenge to understand exactly who is speaking to whom, when, and where. He goes so far, even, as to bring entirely other textual worlds into the story, notably, his extraordinary 1987 novel *Les possédés de la pleine lune*, in which Saintmilia is the primary suspect in a murder mystery involving her fisherman husband, Agénor; his doppelgänger (a giant river fish named Miyan! Miyan!); and his suspected young lover, Violetta.[20]

Such disconcerting and destabilizing aspects of the novel are buttressed by a set of stylistic and grammatical choices that act as both clues and invocations. In translating *Quiet Dawn*, we have sought as much as possible to find a way to transmit the experience of reading the novel in the original French, maintaining the velocity and energy of Fignolé's breathless narrative. We adhered as closely as possible to Fignolé's punctuation, which we understand as a matter of style and rhythm. He almost never uses periods, preferring commas, to create the pacing of his prose. He also largely avoids capitalization, as a way of creating a stream-of-consciousness flow, which we have pointedly maintained.

Fignolé often moves seamlessly between the past and present tenses in ways that do not track directly with the temporality of a particular scene or dialogue, simply because time is so unstable throughout the work. Tenses often shift midparagraph, which also means midsentence, given the absence of periods. Here then, too, we followed Fignolé's lead in the original text, aware that the differences between the range and valences of tenses in French and English make this an imperfect process.

The translation of racial terminology from French to English also raises its own thorny set of issues. The French words *Nègre* or *Négresse* have always been multivalent, used in juridical and literary works as well as in daily life in different ways. This has also been true of other racial designations, such as *mulâtre*. The term *Noir*, however, was also used as a racial construct but sometimes with a different connotation. During the revolutionary period, the question of racial terminology itself became one of the terrains for political struggle. Fignolé chose to use these words variously to accord with particular voices and moments, but not in any stable or predictable way. Thus here, again, we chose to preserve the disconcerting experience of navigating these powerful and shifting terms, and we did so by translating *Nègre* and *Négresse* as *Negro* and *Negress*, and *Noir* as *Black*.

Fignolé was clearly comfortable with unsettling his readers—with creating a complex and at times difficult experience, and asking that we embrace a world of opacity, uncertainty, and shifting truths. The white eighteenth-century characters are particularly challenging, given their racism and the violence of their relationship to the enslaved. In translating the passages that are in their voices we have maintained terminology and phrasing that may be triggering and offensive in English, with the idea that Fignolé very pointedly aimed to expose the nature of the colonial and slave-holding mindset. We recognize that reading these and other passages in the novel may be disturbing and, at times, even painful but see our role as transmitting as best we can the atmosphere and experience Fignolé proposed in the original.

This commitment to unsettle his reader is also evident in Fignolé's occasional use in his novel of Haitian Creole words or phrases that he does not define for his French-language readers. We have followed this practice, leaving those same words or phrases in Creole for readers of English. Similarly, Fignolé references many historical figures, places, and literary and theatrical works without providing explicatory details, and so we have chosen not to add notes or context to those or, in the case of literary and dramatic works, to translate their titles into meaningless approximations. *Quiet Dawn* is full of such invitations to learn more, to pursue a glancing mention or travel down one rabbit hole or another, and we hope that Anglophone readers of his work will respond to that call.[21]

Fignolé describes his novel as a "universe" of meaning.[22] Unsurprisingly, then, his work aims to contain what is uncontainable—the incommensurate and the conflictual, the causal and the correlative, the possibility of love and the many obstacles to its full expression. Readers of *Quiet Dawn* must be willing to dwell in the cacophony and the chaos of this world Fignolé has built, to journey with him along the dizzying arcs of history's spiral—and to accept from word one that it will be quite a ride.

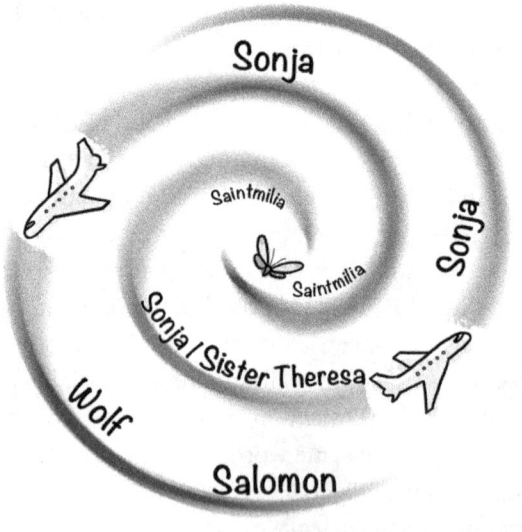

The spiral structure of *Quiet Dawn*. Illustration by Samantha Stephens

Notes

Epigraph: Kathleen Gyssels, "One Hour for Eternity: A Conversation with Jean-Claude Fignolé," *Journal of Haitian Studies* 16, no. 1 (Spring 2010): 21.

1. Christina Sharpe, *Monstrous Intimacies: Making Post-Slavery Subjects* (Durham, NC: Duke University Press, 2010).
2. Gyssels, "One Hour for Eternity," 9.
3. Alessandra Benedicty-Kokken, Jhon Picard Byron, Kaiama L. Glover, and Mark Schuller, eds., *The Haiti Exception: Anthropology and the Predicament of Narrative* (Liverpool, UK: Liverpool University Press, 2016).
4. Michel-Rolph Trouillot, *Silencing the Past: Power and the Production of History* (Boston: Beacon Press, 1995).
5. Jean Casimir, *The Haitians: A Decolonial History*, trans. Laurent Dubois (Chapel Hill: University of North Carolina Press, 2020).
6. Natalie Léger, "Partisan Politics and Twentieth-Century Fictions of the Haitian Revolution," in *A History of Haitian Literature* (Cambridge: Cambridge University Press, 2025).
7. C. L. R. James, *The Black Jacobins: Toussaint L'Ouverture and the San Domingo Revolution* (New York: Vintage Books, 1963); Sudhir Hazareesingh, *Black Spartacus: The Epic Life of Toussaint Louverture* (New York: Farrar, Straus and Giroux, 2020). There is a rich and expanding corpus of Anglophone scholarship on the Haitian Revolution that includes Carolyn E. Fick, *The Making of Haiti: The Saint Domingue Revolution from Below* (Knoxville: University of Tennessee Press, 1990), and Laurent Dubois, *Avengers of the New World: The Story of the Haitian Revolution* (Cambridge, MA: Harvard University Press, 2004); this work is all, built upon the crucial foundations of Haitian historiography, which, as Marlene L. Daut argues in *Awakening the Ashes: An Intellectual History of the Haitian Revolution* (Chapel Hill: University of North Carolina Press, 2023), also played a role in the rethinking of history more broadly during the nineteenth century.
8. Gyssels, "One Hour for Eternity," 9.
9. Gyssels, "One Hour for Eternity," 9.
10. See Kaiama L. Glover, *Haiti Unbound: A Spiralist Challenge to the Postcolonial Canon* (Liverpool, UK: Liverpool University Press, 2010).
11. Gyssels, "One Hour for Eternity," 13.
12. Gyssels, "One Hour for Eternity," 11.
13. Joan Dayan, *Haiti, History, and the Gods* (Berkeley: University of California Press, 1998); Fick, *Making of Haiti*; Karol K. Weaver, *Medical*

Revolutionaries: The Enslaved Healers of Eighteenth-Century Saint Domingue (Urbana: University of Illinois Press, 2006).

14. Marie Vieux-Chauvet, *Dance on the Volcano*, trans. Kaiama L. Glover (New York: Archipelago Books, 2016); Évelyne Trouillot, *The Infamous Rosalie*, trans. Marjorie Attignol Salvodon (Lincoln: University of Nebraska Press, 2013); Évelyne Trouillot, *Désirée Congo*, trans. Marjorie Attignol Salvodon (Charlottesville: University of Virginia Press, 2024).

15. On Ezili Dantor, see Dayan, *Haiti, History, and the Gods*; Karen McCarthy Brown, *Mama Lola: A Vodou Priestess in Brooklyn*, 3rd ed. (Berkeley: University of California Press, 2011); Omise'eke Natasha Tinsley, *Ezili's Mirrors: Imagining Black Queer Genders* (Durham, NC: Duke University Press, 2018).

16. Doris Garraway, *The Libertine Colony: Creolization in the Early French Caribbean* (Durham, NC: Duke University Press, 2005).

17. Louverture described himself in this letter as having been shipped to France "as naked as an earthworm." See Deborah Jenson, "From the Kidnapping(s) of the Louvertures to the Alleged Kidnapping of Aristide: Legacies of Slavery in the Post/Colonial World," *Yale French Studies* 107 (2005): 162–86.

18. See Kaiama L. Glover, *A Regarded Self: Caribbean Womanhood and the Ethics of Disorderly Being* (Durham, NC: Duke University Press, 2021).

19. The reference to Saidiya V. Hartman's *Scenes of Subjection: Terror, Slavery, and Self-Making in Nineteenth-Century America* (New York: Oxford University Press, 1997), a powerful study of—among else—the imbricated perversions of love, promiscuity, subjugation, and performance required by the slave order, is intentional.

20. Jean-Claude Fignolé, *Les possédés de la pleine lune* (Paris: Seuil, 1987).

21. Shepherding *Quiet Dawn* into the English-speaking world would not have been possible without the generosity of Madame Fulvie Fignolé and the Fignolé family. We are grateful, too, for the patience and steadfast support of Ken Wissoker and for his selection of excellent reader-reviewers, whose careful engagement with our translation brought welcome insights to this work.

22. Gyssels, "One Hour for Eternity," 9.

Quiet Dawn

in the morning, when I open the window, she slips into my day with her faded madras headdress, that look of a little old lady whose baleful eyes glance sidelong at suffering ever since she herself became suffering in the eyes of Agénor-the-murderer, her worn calico dress, indecent in the new light of the morning, she raises her head toward the sound of the shutters banging against the walls and further stripping away the thin layer of lime that, sign of our decrepitude, crumbles away day by day under the attack of the north wind, completely still, she contemplates the fiery path, the ordeal of ashes that led me to her sorrow and, on seeing me, a fury repressed for two centuries emblazons her face with the mark of her malediction as if the newborn splendor of the sun, illuminating our darkness, had the power to resuscitate her defunct world, to go back to her words of innocence and absolution, to an ancient (oh, so ancient!) birth, to which she regularly bears witness, in different ways, in the movement of the hours and the delirium of her bitter voice, stacked upon sufferings as old as her country, she holds out her hand in a sign of friendship, I'm not fooled by her histrionics, for in all the time she's been watching me we've already devoured our reserves of patience and indulgence, rancors, provocations, insinuations, fits of persecution, aggressions, and, beyond all of that, the pretext of madness, a lie that comes from another time, beleaguered by the turbulence of centenary dawns, endorsing one another's complaints and denunciations, constructing a coherent system out of the ramblings woven throughout her memories and so carefully structured that they betray the machinations of a lucid mind bent on destroying me, on plunging me even further into the madness of the centuries

—Mother Theresa refuses to feed me her hatred, she forces me to polish the parquet of the big house although the water crouching behind the mountains, castrated by misery, has captured the soap that will never whiten the curse affixed to our skin, this is not the first time she has made me suffer, Mother Theresa does not like us, the cruel laughter in her eyes tells us her hatred is as old as my sorrow

—liar!

—go on, dare to say you didn't steal my name! time has escaped from the cave where you walled up our words, it rants and blazes, I am the blood of the word, you have starved me

it's too much, I cannot bear it, I strike her angrily, the blows coiling around her skin, an ancient memory, images of flesh lacerated by the claw of the whip, the earth soaked with sobs and lamentations, bloodied words, she murmurs, tears rain down on my people, I continue to strike, rage colors the day with reddish streaks, covering up the memories that come back to me like the cruel part of a life buried long ago, spasms of anger, God, forgive my sins, she raises her arms, skillfully protects her face, laughs, her jeering teeth an insult to my inability to reach her, taking refuge in her madness, a carapace of feelings and sensations drowned in the strangeness of solitude, she defies my weakness, breathless, fists bruised, I cease the puerile gestures of my tantrum, she lowers her arms, revealing the mockery of a face whose eyes have forgotten how to smile, the Mother Superior never flinched, observing the incongruous spectacle with her sorrowful and disapproving gaze, her silence an indictment, a condemnation, I will not be free of this anger today, again she raises her hand, stretched out fully toward the frenzy of the light, toward that part of herself that at times bursts forth in sunny intervals of truth and reason, collapsing with laughter, crying, for happiness sometimes has its tears, playing with what's left of her blazing hair, the sun caresses her forehead, kisses her eyes, but the night quickly extinguishes her joy, the night of history sowing her dreams with nightmares, history fallen from her lips on nights of the full moon, our terror and our horror, she stammers, frightened, and she is right, yet I have no compassion for her, I hate her because of her lies, truer than her life, more singular than all those deaths from which she boasts of having returned, further away than that Africa that no longer dares to be her paradise, she raises her hand, the duration of a smile, mask and madness, as miraculous as a kiss from the sun, she points her finger at that part of my life that leans out the window, summoning frustrations more painful than my birth, offering up the darkness of my body, moaning under my simple habit, to be devoured by the light, my God! to think no more of this madwoman, of her presence as painful as the admission of a fault committed in another time, in other places, a long line of crimes, my punishment and my penitence or my redemption, the quest for an impossible miracle, choosing to go to a missionary outpost, to flee the atmosphere of a convent where every stone reminds me of the veiled confessions of the stars, to flee a history of screams, of injustices whose prolonged echo traps, within four walls, the dreams of my youth that some Madonna or other already absolved from beyond the grave, our eyes meet, smile, recognize one another: come here

—but why did you choose Haiti?

—the name evokes something familiar, stored away among mixed-up memories, imprecise, it emerged magically with a fragrance of alcohol and spice, of ripe fruit and marine algae, a thousand strange fragrances intoxicated my senses

—such words coming from your mouth, my daughter!

—an odor of sin

—quiet now, Sister Theresa!

—why, Mother? the stench of sin on the family like the

—be quiet, I said!

—a gust of hatred and death, the Marquise de Biemme de Valembrun Lebrun scalds her sleeping husband in their grand canopy bed, the scent of another woman had followed his footsteps into the marital chamber, a gust of nightmares and barbarism, her grandfather, the Duke of Valembrun, skins his valet alive for the amusement of two hundred guests to whom he had promised an unusual spectacle

———————

—enough, my daughter, I won't listen any longer!

—you will listen to me, Mama, we'll no longer have occasion to talk about our so honorable family, the Biemme de Valembrun Lebrun, natives of Nantes, of Brest, of Quimper, cutthroats, bandits, assassins, profligates, pirates, slave traders, and who knows what else hidden away in whatever memoirs, court records, legal documents, minutes from registries and lawsuits lining the shelves of some library or other

—my God! she knows

—not everything, Mother, but enough to understand that in forcing me to take my vows you are condemning me, in the name of the family, to expiate eight centuries worth of crimes, I'm not complaining, a Biemme never complains, but the cross will be heavy to bear

—Lord, have mercy on us!

—*ite missa est*, Mother! our visit is coming to an end, bless me and wish me good luck

she stiffens her arm, fist brandished like a threat, vengeance will be hers in the tenth generation when her eyes rediscover the road back to her heart, the sun will harvest the fields of rage, this will be the time of loss and of her redemption, every morning, as soon as the window opens, she raises her fist in the sole gesture that is her truth, the foundation of her existence, the justification of her hatred, the day will hesitate to enter my room as if afraid to chase away my night, I am not surprised by its reticence, this is all part of this madwoman's game, to intimidate and harass me, the hunter flushing out its prey, losing my mind, panicking, getting carried away, exploding, my irritability like some inevitable stanchion for my weakness

—I hope, Sister Theresa, that in the future you will spare us these violent outbursts, otherwise you will force me either to send you to some rural outpost or to repatriate you to France, anger is incompatible with our vocation of peace and humility

—yes, Mother Superior!

—we have pledged to no longer belong to ourselves, devoting our lives to serve the poor and the mad, fate has struck this woman cruelly, both her son and her husband are dead, her reason has been washed away by a flood in Dangluse, in the days just after she was admitted she was very worked up, even massive injections of sedatives could not calm her down, if you can believe it, Sister Theresa, she used to hide whenever she saw us and she called us all by one despicable, incomprehensible name: Sonja!

—did you say Sonja?

—what is it? you've gone pale, Theresa! do you not feel well?

—just a slight malaise, Mother, it has passed

—I'm reassured, go rest, my child, it will do you good, but wait a moment! keep in mind, we must make an effort to ease what remains of the existence of these unfortunates, do not use violence against Saintmilia, and now go! I excuse you from the communal prayer this evening

this madwoman is neither humble nor old nor unfortunate, she is certainly not mad, my intuition insists on crying out this truth, Doctor Charles laughs about it, a good joke, come now, Sister Theresa! if she is not insane then we have to believe that we are all insane here, the words gone astray on my lips belong to me, I hold them hostage, they deepen my conviction, link me to a cause for which this woman is the tool, a destiny risen up from the murky depths of the centuries and catching up to me at the end of the gangway to the 747, I expect to be snatched up into the hole of the roaring jet engines, up front under the wings they have a voice

—Sister Theresa, wait!

white smile on a black mask, white gloves, sky-blue cap, green words, brown cassette tape, rose-colored box, a veritable rainbow, my mother's message falls into my hands, the messenger does not fail to notice as I recoil, why a Black flight attendant? but why?

—play the cassette once you are on the plane, there are earphones for you so you won't bother your neighbors—Mother always thinks of everything—have pity, my daughter, and forgive me

—what do I have to forgive? I would never presume to judge you

—Sister Theresa, are you all right? we're taking off in a few moments

her face absorbs the blond sun of the north, glued to her black mask, a striking result: white teeth and chocolate candy

—I'm fine! I'm fine! thank you

the high-pitched, metallic voice of the loudspeaker: welcome aboard Air France flight 333, I press the play button, the lively bars of a waltz drown out the pained screech of the reactors suddenly turned on full force, the cabin shakes, the beast pounces, the waltz dies down and I plug in my mother in midair: this is the taped transcription of an account recorded in the memoirs of the Baron von Schpeerbach, a Swiss German, naturalized Frenchman, property owner in Saint-Domingue, the former French colony, today the Republic of Haiti, in the Abricots district, dependency of the Dalmarie parish, five thousand acres of woods, forest, plains, rivers, and coastline, twelve hundred head of cattle, five hundred purebred English horses, three hundred slaves, two thousand quintals of sugar per year, married to Sonja de Valembrun Lebrun, may her soul rest in peace, memoirs sent by the baron from his retreat in Strasbourg, just before his death on November 8, 1805, for the edification of his son Loïc Wolf Klaus von Schpeerbach, a light touch, thinking I was asleep, the hostess reached out her hand to pull up the blanket slipping from my knees, the touch of her fingers like an invasion of my privacy, a deep-blue sun flows into the cabin, I'm startled, rediscovered memories of old fears when dragons leapt out of the pages of yellowed books of magic spells to invade my nights, pinning me against the walls of distress, eating at me, white teeth trace a vague smile that has been transformed into an island Negress, sleek, slender, sky-blue cap, white gloves, beautiful to the greedy eyes of the passengers in the other rows, including to the eyes of the young man seated across from me, she sways, a fragile cane stalk waving in the caress of the trade winds

—did I frighten you, Sister Theresa? please forgive my clumsiness

she picked up the blanket that, in its fear of dragons, had fallen while making its escape, the fear of my childhood nights still visible on my face, she teased

———

—have you seen the devil, Sister?

her inquisitive smile, so calmly perfidious

—it has been a long while since he changed color, for us the devil is white

every day at that hour, the morning hour crows, the magic of the bluish air, the enchantment of the light filtering between the interstices of the window slats creates splashes of sunlight in the room, huddled in the withered shadows of the doorstep, the sight of her madras cloth crowning a ridiculous head, she leads me to images from outside of time, infant stream of water bleating in pools as wide as lakes, water lily horses leaping in the foam and the froth of the high grasses, carriages drunk with the insolent laughter of women under starry skies, my first ball, my first flustered emotions, the soundless dawn, the tight cavalcade of men and animals, who among them will escape, who will be devoured, the cruelties of a celebration whose vigilance and vanity I inexplicably shoulder, the flight attendant's white smile, black mask, white gloves, sky-blue cap, leaves to tend to other concerns, other treacheries, the devil, black eternity, might be lost in the temporary whiteness of the clouds, shifting the destiny of evil turned into goodness, I have no time to be outraged, with her passionate, impulsive temperament, Sonja flew into a blind rage whenever she was contradicted, this tendency to suddenly lose her temper came, I learned much later, from her ancestors, scattered throughout the Breton Finistère, so often in trouble with the king's law, miscreants, as indifferent to God as to the devil, they only had faith in their rapiers, always ready to assail some traveler at a bend in the road

—hey there! peasant! your money or your life!

the money fell into their purses, lives rolled into the ditches, the box opens, opens my heart to the devotion of an unexpected silence, a medallion encrusted with precious gems portrays me lying in a hammock, indolent and lascivious, my foot resting on the back of a prostrate Negress: to Sonja on her twentieth birthday, May 24, 1775

———

—Papa! Papa! oh!

misty-eyed, I chase after the hours, disjointed time, heart aflight, rain beating against the unfeeling cobblestones, racked with sobs, ultimately washed up in some doorway, my mind adrift, unknown lips press their pity against my forehead, on my cheeks, a father blown up midflight, the radio crackles, the telephone rings ceaselessly, no survivors, Papa forever sealed within an empty coffin, Papa dispersed to the four corners of the wind and me, Sonja, inconsolable sparrow, encircled within a gold and diamond frame, fixed forever in a medallion on May 24, 1775, from one first name to the other I search for the difference, periwinkle eyes, beauty mark at the corner of the right eye, thin lips, blond curls, an innocent gaze, but with a bit of hardness coiled within that extraordinary blue, a beautiful and energetic woman, her voice, dry and brittle, quickly became accustomed to pushing the Negro servants around all day long, reprimanding here, ordering there, revealing an implacable sense of authority, a rigid temperament that was an insult to common sense, she should not have been a woman, yet in the world we lived in she was my woman, a harsh world that leaves no room for the weak, as Michel Clérié and my neighbors Chassagne, Bonbon, and Saré asserted with irony

—our dear Wolf has once again purchased a slave that was being whipped, if all the officers in the Swiss Regiment are as tenderhearted as he we'll need to be careful, for they'll soon join up with the slaves

—I wouldn't be surprised, they'll take advantage of the situation to resolve the border disputes, those mountain dwellers are cunning and spiteful, say, Wolf, you aren't going to let your slaves loose on our heels, are you?

—I'm not worried as long as he's got his wife to control them

a tough woman whose inflexibility was at times frightening, I have to admit that her brutal way of managing the household gave our home an incomparable glamor, the meticulous Negroes in our service, stylish valets, majordomos with riding crops and an austere dignity that enveloped their dark features with a perfectly English composure

———

—that's ridiculous, Sonja! ridiculous, our guests must be laughing at us behind our backs

—you think so, dear Wolf! not at all, last week, after our Saint-Jean's ball, the Marquess of Fondicaq congratulated me, delighted: bravo, Sonja! we have to teach the Negroes to behave

—why doesn't she discipline her Negroes the same way?

—not everyone can be a Biemme

I envied her queenly bearing, haughty and slender, her dark lips, the curve of her legs, her smile more open this time, more open than ever, only the slightest bit ironic

—there's champagne on the menu for this flight, Sister Theresa, and caviar to celebrate our thousandth Atlantic crossing

she had turned her back to me, more than ever stripped of humanity or compassion toward the Blacks, they were an investment, ever-more expensive tools since the Revolution had broken out in France, with the English blockade preventing the refilling and renewal of supplies, whose noses Monsieur de Montesquieu's misplaced irony had judged so flat that it was impossible to pity them, she hated them and they hated her in kind, I heard them murmuring whenever she passed by

—*touffé maloé! touffé maloé*

their singsong Creole cursed her, she did not understand, did not hear the rumblings of hatred that rose up beneath her footsteps, she knew nothing of their world, and that ignorance itself was dangerous, not content to discipline them with the whip, she inflicted all kinds of humiliation, after whipping them, she would force them to kneel, to kiss her footsteps, to say

—thank you, no alcohol for me, just a fruit juice if you have it

—of course we have some, Sister, a choice of orange, apple, lemon, peach, apricot

a curious smile, a sharp little bite

—wait! don't trouble yourself, caviar and champagne

she stretched out her hand, out of surprise or regret? the plane slipped surreptitiously down the length of her finger tied to that ring with its diamond setting, which she exhibits with the indecency of a courtesan, the look-at-me of an upstart, at twenty years old, she was wild for jewelry, a devouring and exclusive passion, my wife spent hours contemplating the pale pink of a conch's spiral, the crude milkiness of a pearl, the transparent evanescence of a diamond

—I seek my soul in there, so as to better lose myself

the aisle between the seats begins to look like a parade on the Champs-Élysées, right in step, my flight attendant in her high heels with her battalions of pipe organs, Spahis, royal guards, legionnaires, Negro kings, Papa Doc, Baby Doc, Papa Bok, Big Dada, all united on the edge of her lips, exposing the double rows of her carnivorous teeth, their immaculate whiteness, polished, repolished with bleach, sparkling, my neighbor laughs foolishly, the horror! his incisors blackened by the nauseating civility of cigarettes make it harder for me to enjoy the excellent vintage of the champagne, everywhere I turn I see Negroes to be whipped, to be crucified, thieves, aggressors of lone women in the shadowy alleys of Paris, to be broken on the wheel, slowly, rapists of nuns in the Congo and yet still to be saved

—why, Sister? are they in hell?

—that's an silly question, Biemme

the director of catechism scolds me harshly, her crimson breath quickens, smells slightly of chamomile

—if you don't have anything intelligent to say, Miss de Valembrun Lebrun, then be quiet or leave

she expels me from her world, for I am no longer called Sonja, little Sonja, my little darling, the other novices burst out laughing, the little aristocrat had been brought down a peg

—a bit more champagne, Sister Theresa?

perhaps I said yes, the new weight of the glass between my fingers, and disaster! the tinkling of the crystal, the scattered breakage as if the whole cabin were reverberating with the sound of my shame

—she's drunk, a drunk nun, never seen anything like it!

the voice was more sarcastic than astonished, I let my joy slip to the floor, there are so many stars lying there inert, an apotheosis of foam, I lose my soul in them, a twenty-four-carat blue diamond stolen by the

Viscount of Biemme from Lord Gloucester one night when the Saxon dignitary was staying with him on his way to Burgundy, he was meant to negotiate an alliance between England and the Duchy of Burgundy against King Louis XI

—*by Jove! my diamond! I lost my diamond*

—be careful, milord! we're surrounded by brigands

Biemme was a clever rogue, he had stolen the diamond during a dinner given in honor of Lord Gloucester and, with the help of some paid henchmen, ambushed him the next day, attacked from all sides by raging brigands, the lord watched the men of his escort fall one by one

—how many leagues are we from Biemme's castle?

—not too far, milord, it's right there, within earshot

—can you hear us, Biemme, help! help!

and as if by miracle the barbaric gallop of hooves, the tumult of a horde rushing to the rescue

—here I am, milord, death! death! death to the brigands

like a thunderbolt Biemme, rapier in hand, fell headlong upon the pack of attackers

—fools, come feel my blade, and it slashed away, scamps, rascals, one man broke off, gave up, fled, the marauders, the cracking sound of a sword hitting a skull

—all clear, milord, the road is open unless you would prefer to return to the castle

—*by Jove, my diamond, Biemme, where did you get it?*

—on my finger, milord, where it has been since last night as payment for a debt of gratitude, I dreamed that I saved your life

losing one's soul, for good, a twenty-four-carat blue diamond, Sonja emptied the jewel boxes, the dresser drawers, scarves and frilly things, the armoire and the wardrobe, lace and muslin, she turned over the big canopy bed, found a charm bracelet and some pendants under the mattress that she had forgotten existed, felt once again on her face the tears she had abandoned off the coast of Brest in the wake of the Saint-Aignan, she summoned Carmen, the beautiful chambermaid who Alonzo called *mi dulce amor, mi suéno, mi luna llena* in his love-crazed moments, suffocating her with so many whispered kindnesses, which she fled with laughter caught between her teeth, I am not dreaming, no, this is not possible

—make her shut up

wild screams quickly broken, the dignity of silence, Alonzo astounded, disgusted but cowardly, why does he not step in, *mi dulce, mi sueño*, words, no more than words, on Sonja's orders Boto flays Alonzo's dream, blue diamonds emerge from her head, how many carats? Mistress! hate suppresses their rage, they look on, the example being made, the Blacks are excellent students, the cruelty we reproach them with is always that of the white master, their silent, aligned suffering clenches its fists, their hands seek one another out in powerless solidarity, Boto slices the skin at the base of the neck, inserts a thin stalk from a castor oil plant, which had been hollowed out earlier, he blows into it, the skin immediately bubbles, at first detaches with a kind of hiss, almost imperceptible, then the blood vessels crack, fixing the searing tear in Carmen's throat, from behind the shutters of my office I witness the agony of the flesh, like Alonzo, I do not intervene, worse than Alonzo, I hide, putting the windows between me and the horror, between those Negroes, who I will no longer dare look in the face, and my sick curiosity, Sonja rejoices, displaying a cruelty that smolders beneath her eyelids with a disturbing glimmer, the wounded sun whirls in Carmen's eyes, a bloodied sun, her skin shrieks, swells, whistles, moves, inexorably whittles down the plane of her stomach, swallows up the hollow of her navel, travels downward, plunges, the disgusted sun, her cry of agony rips through the staggering foliage of the mango trees, the assaulted sugary flesh beneath their shells is tainted with darkness, their joy extinguished, Carmen is nothing more than a ball of suffering, with diabolical dexterity a cutlass rips into two pieces her body as round as the sun, the sun of death, the flight attendant is bent over, the line of her back affixes the lustful hunger of a passenger on his way to the toilet somewhere at the very tip of her buttocks, she places the debris of the stars she has picked up into a little white bag, she will scatter them once we've arrived in Pointe-à-Pitre, so to reunite the sky and the earth, inside me it is midnight, my ancestor's voice in the earphones, in stereo, far away, staccato, interrupting the monotonous rhythm of the jet engines at regular intervals, the summer on my forehead, an icy celebration, lower the seat back, take out the earphones

—rest, Sister, the champagne has gone to your head, this cold compress will refresh your spirit

the voice trails off with the swaying of her hips, their motion sings an island lullaby, "Haiti chérie," *pi bon péyi pasé ou nan poin,* which a missionary Mother had brought back from over there along with malaria and incurable hepatitis, she died of nostalgia, they announced to the young novices, and we aspired to die just like her, exhilarated by that island song

—tan the skin, I want it dried, treated, and varnished
—what for?
—the most unique bed stool in the world
she went inside, haughty, disdainful
—the body, Mistress
—untie it and throw it to the dogs, or no! better to salt it, it will replace next week's quarter of a cow in your rations, Jésula, follow me!

go, come, indefatigable, the false joy of your smile so weary that it's a stereotype, the same, the only one, from one voyage to the next, the publicity smile plastered on the Air France posters in all the airport lounges of the world, on tour and travel-services counters across the five continents, to be encountered again one day, utterly ridiculous, at the reception area on Mars or the moon, yet when I open my eyes it babbles on my brow, the gentleness and kindness of the hand, a light caress of the fingers

—my dear, are you feeling better?
—now that you're here
—never am I loved as much as when she says such nonsense
—tell me, Sister Hyacinthe, if I die will you join me in heaven?
—there now, she's all better and right back to her delightful blunders, of course I'll join you or, even better, we'll go together
—what will Saint Peter say when he sees me with you?
—Saint Peter is a sinnerman, a great sinnerman, don't forget it
—yes, our Lord consecrated him as a true fisher of men

—how foolish you are, my dear, he was a sinnerman, not a fisherman, come now, don't sulk, you're no fool, prove it to me, be nice and give your big sister Hyacinthe a kiss, a deep one, really deep, yes, like that, ah! my Sonja, fresh as the promise of dawn

—is what we're doing a sin, Sister Hyacinthe?

—how can love be a sin when it can accomplish such marvels?

—do you love me, Sister Hyacinthe?

—of course! do you doubt it?

—very often

—Sister Theresa, would you like a fresh compress?

—no, thank you, I'm fine now

—here are your headphones and cassette, I put them in the luggage compartment, I found the medallion at your feet and put it in the jewelry box, it would be better to keep it in a purse, do you have one?

—yes, of course! of course!

—tell me, Sister, it's lovely, that medallion, a superb jewel, and a magnificent miniature portrait, the inscription says: to Sonja on her twentieth birthday

—it's not me, it's my ancestor, did you notice the date? 1775

—what a resemblance!

—I noticed, I learned of my ancestor no more than half an hour ago

—unbelievable, Sister

—not at all, the medallion, as you saw, was in the jewelry box you brought me, a message or a gift, if you prefer, from my mother, I discovered the portrait and immediately I was sure it was me, the inscription cleared that up

—why, Sister?

—my ancestor is so beautiful!

—but you are very beautiful!

—even with my squinty, watery eyes and my drooling mouth?

—stop saying horrible things, I've never seen eyes more beautiful than yours

—is that why you make them cry so often during catechism?

—during catechism I have duties and responsibilities, to shape the souls of the novices, I am a professor of moral energy

—and in this chamber, who are you, what are you, Sister Hyacinthe?

she walks off, airily, supremely elegant in her suit, white smile, white gloves, sky-blue cap, disdainful of the passengers' admiration, we recognized one another, the flame of our forbidden love shines in our eyes, weighty delights of back rooms, existing as one life, overcome by identical swoons, twin spasms, you make my head spin, Sister Hyacinthe, ah! climax! ecstasy and death!

—don't cry out, Sonja, do you want to get us caught?

she went on, nondescript, enigmatic, comfortable in her skin, my so beautiful flight attendant, her amused grin

—are you fishing for compliments, Sister Theresa?

a complicit wink, her hand once again on my forehead, but this time with a gentle breath of desire, I close my eyes, dying from this moment, when I open them again she is no longer there, she has gone off toward other caresses

—jealous, Sonja

—in my family, Sister Hyacinthe, we have never liked to share

—but I'm not sharing, my dear

—swear it to me

—does the catechism professor need to remind you that swearing is a sin?

a discreet fragrance infused her wake, my God! could it be that angels have the smell and color of the devil? my reservations toward Blacks fall away, the day rises, stretches through the passing time, the eye of the window lazily follows the fleeing clouds, some come to the windowpane and grimace, others look like my beloved and, I swear, wear my mother's devastated face

—mad, mad, like all Biemmes, so many possibilities present themselves to you, teaching in Caen at the school for Young Girls of the Lord, in the Havre at the Sainte-Marie orphanage, or at the La Providence hospice in Nantes, the Saint-Jean-de-la-Croix hospital in Brest, all of France, and Brittany, in particular, is still missionary territory, impoverished hearts to be found everywhere, the impoverished souls of the multitudes, I myself am not free from sin and if you really must save the Negroes at all costs, then start by bringing me back to God, I am going to see the Mother Abbess right now to ask that she annul your decision

—there's no point, Mother, my choice is irrevocable, I'm having trouble understanding why, after imposing a destiny on me, you now seek to prevent me from accepting it

—not when it's illogical and absurd

—my choice is logical, it's your decision that wasn't

—could I have known that? when I asked that you be admitted . . .

—locked up

—do you reproach me for having sought your happiness?

—my happiness!

—I thought I was distancing you from the curse of the Bohemian

—what curse? what are you talking about?

—Mother Mary, what have I said? she mustn't know

—what mustn't I know? quickly, speak, Mother

—it doesn't matter and it's too late for regrets

—you're right, it is too late for regrets, I'm leaving soon to accomplish or to suffer my fate, if my fate is misery then pray for me, Mother, pray for me

her footsteps on my heart, she won't have understood, shattered love, a Biemme doesn't share, neither tears nor regrets, just an immense lassitude, it's disgusting, your little hand games with the young novitiate in the darkness of the hallways, your embarrassed look, your tears and supplications in my room later, stop, don't try and use the power of your hands on me, stop feigning love and tenderness, Sister Hyacinthe, they don't suit you, her heavy steps on the cold tiles, the fear from then on that solitude is my destiny, as we arrived at the visiting room door my mother turned around, nodded her head to say goodbye, neither tears nor regrets, a Biemme doesn't cry, standing at one end and the other of the aisle with a dignity that didn't suit the circumstances, our twin sorrows, solemn and sublime, witnessed their separation, eight days later I left

—my God! my God! why have you forsaken me?

the night snivels, lamentations of the drum, from Accident Hill to Toffié Hill, the lugubrious cries of the Assotor drum call out to the African ancestors, I feel the evidence of death hovering over the room where Sonja sleeps peacefully, I take notice of the sounds that bewitch the night, groanings of the palm trees, whimpering of the mango trees, rustling of the fireflies' wings, whispers of the coffee trees, women crying in the immense disorder of the plain, sudden outburst of the drums' voices, broken, hoarse, ruffled, bitter, hostile, and these voices heat up what has become a menacing darkness, I open the windows, the curtains shudder, the air cools, the drums chatter, as if they'd only been waiting for the sudden dip in the heat, and then a brouhaha, multiplied shouts of victory, of liberation, emerging from hundreds of chests, lighting up faces licked with flames fed by Carmen's pitiful rags, it was so close but terribly far away, the flames danced, rose up, the fire sputtered, asthmatic, the flames flickered, died, a cloth wrap, the foot of a chair stirred into the embers revived their ballet, once the last madras and the last sandal had been consumed, the embers narrowed to the center of the foyer, forming a thin lick of fire, Saintmilia came forward, carefully gathered it up, brought it to her mouth, blew on it, the thread of fire hesitated and then separated itself inexorably from her thick lips, a flash of lightning, a jolt of thunder cleared the ashes from the grass, Carmen's soul was free, with a beating of wings she abolished all distance, humbled the royalty of the heat, set fire to anguish, joy transgressed forbidden borders, entered, astonished, into the infinity of freedom, into its own eternity, overcome with shame and pain, head in my hands, I listened, the house was filled with the fragrances of the bush, as if the African savanna, sweating the bland odor of backwaters, the animal odor of the jungle, had entered forcefully into our history, Sonja awoke, frightened

—what is it? what is this screaming?

—they freed Carmen's soul, she returned to Africa

—don't be ridiculous, she's marinating in the salting tub

—that was horrible and monstrous, you didn't really consider doing that . . .

—not only did I consider it but I even gave the order that her corpse be cut into pieces and salted

—I recommended it be given back to the brothers of her race

—what? you dared humiliate me?

—I saved you from adding pointless cruelty to a monstrous injustice, the Blacks held a wake for the corpse according to their Vodou faith, now that their cry has liberated her soul, it has begun the long journey of hope for their people, flying over the centuries, bearing new life

she comes to me, drawn by this new and intimate knowledge she has of the two of us, the drum coils my joy around her lasciviousness, the intoxication of the champagne like a latent hunger, she moves through my awakening, attending to each passenger with that smile whose nonchalance no longer belongs to her alone but to both of us in the complicity of happiness

—coffee, Sister?

—the cart rolls along its load of cups, glasses, teapots, bottles, coffeepots, its muted noise on the velvet carpet

—I slept

—not long, we haven't even finished the first service, do you want it strong?

black, as black as the night in the dungeons of Brittany, I take it black, unctuous, I savor it, I sip it, I lick it greedily, with the cruelty of a Valembrun Lebrun, I close my eyes at the sight of her body in the large courtyard, attached to the akoura tree, their tree of sacrifice, well then, let us sacrifice her, the blood trickles, the first drops in my throat, that particular aroma of the black flowers of the Sahara, she swells up

—we're flying over Africa, Sister, notice the gray curve of the sky, the color of the ashes of our dead, martyrs to a cause that will never cease to be

her voice vibrates with a hostile pain, returns to the memory of the drum, speaks of the first ages of man when the sun beat his wife over a handful of burned rice, glides at nineteen thousand feet, washed up on that anchor of a continent, the journey ends here, even if her smile prolongs the enchantment of Air France business class for five thousand miles, Carmen is dancing her return, at home in the deep forest everything begins and ends with dancing, the cabin roars, the voice of the bush from a continent of shattered memories, her people dispersed, scattered by the whims of avarice, she reconquers her past

—we don't understand where this absurd belief comes from, the idea that they'll return to Africa to live in the shadow of the baobab trees in complete liberty, so they seek out death by any means, poisoning, suicide, hanging themselves, self-mutilation, organizing their rituals of collective murder in clearings known to them alone, when interrogated about sudden disappearances, their accomplices, because they are all accomplices, maliciously respond *pati mètm pati pou l'Afrik*

—you don't do anything about it?

—at first, yes! but since they seek out death as a deliverance, better not to offer it to them on a silver platter

—so what do you do?

—we cut off a foot, always the right foot, thus keeping the fugitive from trying again

—you've never come upon them in a group?

—we always arrive too late, our informers tell us about the escapes two or three hours afterward, by the time we gather the neighbors and put together an armed group to go after them, pfft!! the little birds have definitively vanished into the brush, we find their *houmforts* laid out under the canopy of the undergrowth, ritual objects, drums and *assons* defy our presence and our authority in their vegetal sanctuary where light filters through the leaves and splashes onto the bloodied earth, the frightened dogs tug at their leashes, yelp, howl at death and quickly pull us away from these mysterious mass graves, upon our return, tired, aching, we can read the irony in the eyes of the Negroes, the blood is our witness, they seem to say, and protects our paths of hope, and for a long while afterward they speak of M'Bo, Dokolo, Batafou, those devilish names that I never could get used to have made the crossing, now they roar in the savanna, trumpet into the golden dusk, wail in the river basins

—the way you tell the story, Wolf, it seems like you believe in all this

—they believe it, unfortunately, and that is the source of the whole problem

—in other words?

—at the rate you punish my slaves, I'll have to close the sugar plantation and sell it within the year

—so it's my fault! it'll be my fault, go ahead and say it, I dare you

I did not dare, but she seethed nonetheless, in her moments of rage her beauty, gone vulgar, would draw on a roster of insults so vast that no Breton sailor could rival it in indecency and crudeness, she hollered like a drunkard, vociferated like a madwoman, tore at her clothes, rolled on the ground, stood up, walked outside, ran to offer the Negroes the spectacle of her body, clearly too white for the tropics

—enough, Sonja! come back in here!

she came back, on that morning, her head hanging low, she had spent the night cursing me, she had added her own curse to the imprecations of the drums, having finally run out of insults, she began sobbing in frustration, she had presumed too much of her vocabulary or perhaps of her memory, she felt humiliated, it was painful to look at her, fierce and disconsolate at once, a child, I felt ashamed, how had I not seen earlier her need for affection, for tenderness? probably because I believed she was strong, her character tempered like steel, a true Biemme, I told myself, and yet there she was, her pride wounded, shivering, she revealed her distress and her grief, I put my arm around her shoulders

—let's go in, shall we, my dear

—don't touch me

recovered from her disorientation, she pushed me away violently

—Sonja!

—don't touch me

I was shocked, turning my back on the house I quickly crossed the courtyard and headed toward Petite-Anse, I was furious at myself, I'm unable to respond to her repugnance and disdain with the indifference that would place our relationship in its persistent reality, she hates me more and more, sometimes I wish I could hate her but what would be the point of hate when the memory of love is indelible, connected to other memories that draw their importance from the vanity of men, I knew Sonja as a virgin, I was used to adventuresses more interested in money than tenderness, to wives who, upon a simple compliment, would distract themselves from boredom in the bed of some planter friend, to the young ladies of easy virtue in Saint-Domingue who, out in the fields of the coffee and sugar plantations, rushed to free themselves of an oppressive virginity, a conflation of sumptuous illnesses, vapors, humors, languors mixed up in their heads, all treatable with smelling salts, I considered myself happy beyond imagining, I had taken her home after the ball

—may I invite a savage from the islands to do me the honor of entering my modest little room

before even responding she'd opened the door, a candle flickered out, Sonja lit another, the scene felt surreal, seduced by the shining in her eyes just a few hours before I was even more overwhelmed by the sumptuousness of her body, I remember her skin, grazed by the dim light of the candle, fullness of curves and roundness, beauty trembling with desire, the caress of her pubis beneath the force of my gluttonous avidity, the tension of her hips churning like a storm at sea, her greedy mouth, her flustered caresses, the cry, the tearing, carried away on the thrust and the wave of release, we began to boil over, the joyful sweat of our loins soaking the already stained sheets, and despite our very different lives, our two bodies, intertwined, became possessed of a power emerging from the very center of the earth

—you live here alone?

—with my brother, we left him at the ball, he won't return until dawn, once he's scoured the taverns of the port, tell me, are you happy?

—and you?

—answer me first

—yes!

—look who's flattering my vanity

—and you?

—there are questions one never asks a woman, particularly in a moment like this

—oh! pardon me!

she stirred, pulled away, turned onto her stomach, a delightfully childish gesture of modesty, pulled the sheets around her, my fingers moving up to the enchanting blond of her hair, running along her back, for moments as simple as these I accept damnation, I closed my eyes, re-creating the dream and the miracle, repeating to myself that this close and beloved existence is perhaps only an illusion

—what are you thinking about?

—everything, nothing, you, the two of us

—the two of us? really?

—really! I'm thinking of this happiness that just came out of the blue

—don't reuse our clichés, isn't there an expression in the islands to describe sudden joys?

—perhaps, but since I'm not French and have been living in the islands for only ten years, I haven't mastered the subtleties of the language, especially since over there it's a bit mixed up

—what do you do in Saint-Domingue?

—I'm a colonel in the Swiss Regiment, garrisoned in the Cul-de-Sac Plain, not far from Port-au-Prince, and in my civilian life I'm a planter, a colonist

—colonist, Colonel, will you marry me?

she asked me, releasing me from my embarrassment, I was anxious to ask her the question but unfamiliar with French manners, intimidated, I had trouble finding the words, love remaining tied to dreams, I dare not say memories, because this was all too recent, of giddiness and lust, things you do not speak of to a Biemme, not even to ask if she is happy

—but will your brother consent to

—he approves of all my decisions, Wolf, do you love me?

—must I reply with some French cliché

—as long as it means yes

—then I'll reply with the most marvelous of commonplaces, I adore you

delegated by the general council of Saint-Domingue to present certain requests to the king's court, I did not come to France looking for a wife, and here destiny offers me one, the most beautiful, the most marvelous, I met Sonja at the marines' ball, in Brest, a few days before my departure for the islands, I knew immediately that I wanted her, she shone in the midst of a group of king's officers, I moved toward her, she looked at me, smiled, the brightness in her eye blotted out the little troop of admirers, they became no more than insignificant murmurings, shadowy debris in the raw light of the chandeliers, the night spoke and when the violins started up again in the night sky we danced the minuet in the company of the stars, that night we began to build our story, Sonja decided everything over the next days, the marriage, the honeymoon on the boat heading back, the construction of a sumptuous house, as soon as we arrived in Saint-Domingue, and my life became attuned to the extravagant youthfulness of my wife

—Wolf! tonight the Galbauds are coming for dinner, they'll probably bring the intendant Barbé de Marbois with them, as he's on an inspection visit in Dalmarie parish and has stopped to stay with them for three days

—Wolf! we've received an invitation from the Chassagnes, they're throwing a barbecue on Saturday at noon, and that night we'll dance until dawn at the Sarés', in the heights of l'Anse-du-Clerc

—on Sunday the king's theater company concludes its tour of the south in the village of Jérémie, with a gala evening followed by a reception at the constabulary's, shall we go, dear?

this heady social life magically ceased, she was waltzing in the arms of Paret, the captain of the grenadiers (I suspected he was whispering sweet nothings in her ear, that night, my wife was lightheaded with wine and spirits, she was laughing in his arms a bit too much for my taste), suddenly racked by a coughing fit that left her bent over, the horror! she vomited, three times, and when she stood up, her arms folded across her chest, astonished by her own fragility, she brought her hand to her forehead, spun around

—Wolf!

just before losing consciousness she called out to me, extending the echo of her suffering and shame into me, the music had stopped, the last notes trailing off amidst the general consternation, on a night that was meant to have been the most luxurious on the coast

—Wolf! we've got it, we'll have Yolan Gille's orchestra of twenty violins, four hundred guests from the six parishes of Grande'Anse, a sensational acrobatic exhibition at midnight and, as a bonus, an extraordinary fireworks display to announce the news

—what news?

—shhh! it's my secret, go, start preparing the guest list, don't forget Captain Paret, in case you have to take care of our neighbors he'll be my cicisbeo

friends, neighbors, acquaintances, we all knew the news now, she was pregnant, Paret's black leather boots were the first to hear about it and perhaps it was that which determined the course of our destiny

—on his boots, Wolf! on his boots, there in his arms in front of four hundred guests, because of you, and you weren't ashamed, I hate you, I hate this child

she closed in on herself as if the shame had been conjoined with her joy, took fewer walks in the Pandier woods, fewer acrobatic dips in the Petit-Fort creek, fewer dizzying bouts of polka dancing under the neighbor's arbor, she reproached me for having broken her seagull's flight, raised with an absentee brother in the cold tower of a castle (the wings and the center of the residence having fallen into ruin), she had wanted to devour life, alas! she had been confined to her chambers by a man's lust, to do no more than follow the development of an interior life that was not her own but in which she participated, for which she had sacrificed her dignity, she began to hate this son, whom she had wanted and of whom she was so proud that she had invented a firecracker of a name to impress her guests, to light them all up with the dazzling clarity of a birth projected way up into the sky, to give birth to a star, to millions of stars, the foolishness of a mind accumulating, month after month, without me realizing it, a tremendous reserve of resentments, an exceptional capacity for egoism

—at last! we have gotten rid of the guests and here we are alone, to exclaim our joy, Sonja, dear Sonja, why did you not tell me?

her gaze brushed over me, dull and indifferent, shame had discolored the periwinkle blue of her irises

—I beg you, leave me alone

—don't make me suffer like this

—stay away from me, I forbid you to touch me

I lowered my head, defeated by her cruel authority, I left, walked around in the emerging dawn until the voices in the fields awakened, the Blacks had drunk all night, celebrating their masters' joy, and in the morning there remained a sort of cloud of drunkenness in their eyes as they began their interminable day of hopelessness, the landscape comes undone in their loins, hollowed out with pain and resignation, in their muscles limp in the heat, they raise the hoes, bring them down in one exhausted movement, accompanying their gestures with songs that modulate their destiny to the poignant rhythm of sadness, the choruses stop at regular intervals, the simidor's call rises up from their toilings, queries the sky under cover of silence, how many secret messages are thus entrusted to the clouds to keep on behalf of a distant Africa, an imperceptible trace of joy seems to lose itself momentarily on their faces, the return to work like a condemnation, then slowly the songs start up again, driving the unbearable stench of suffering down to the very depths of the furrows

———

I lived through the darkest days of my life, bent double in pain that seeped out from everywhere because it was the pronouncement of absence, eternal, life had no meaning anymore, daily gestures lost all significance, I had only ever loved your father, I had only ever known your father, I had only lived through him and suddenly he was gone, erased from the sky, evaporated into the clouds, disturbing nature, creating the cold deity of silence within our home, that kind of suffering has no name, to whom can you speak of it? Mother, the hands that my body awaits in the darkness, the tenderness my hunger desires, the sweetness that tempts the clumsiness of my fingers, the hope of seeing the day light up my night, greedy for the communion of breaths but, for no reason, must it be for no reason, one day suffer the hopelessness of time and, especially, the emptiness, the terrifying silence of the beloved presence

—Sonja

—don't touch me, Sister Hyacinthe, go away, go away, you're causing me pain

—ah! so you still love me?

—yes, and that's why I hate you

—are you suffering, Sonja?

—don't worry, it won't be for much longer, I have lost faith, Sister Hyacinthe, I have lost joy, you can't hurt me any longer, get out of my cell

—have you already forgotten? I bring you love, I bring you joy

—you are not joy and you have never been love

—you're trying to be cruel, Biemme, I can be, too, I'll go be with the other one

—with all the other ones, Sister Hyacinthe, I don't care

I went with a Black woman, the first time out of curiosity, in the hell of Saint-Domingue (paradise is always elsewhere), a woman, no matter which one, even when she is a false hope, is always more alive than hope, she keeps us from destroying ourselves and for many among us a woman was salvation, I was seeing Cécile (seeing is a euphemism), the mistress of Monsieur de Bauduy, she wasn't the freshest cut, having wasted her youth and her charms among the men of the garrisons here and there throughout the colony before washing up in Les Abricots, she had lost several feathers, that obviously leaves a few traces, which, after the age of forty, clearly begin to look like blemishes, and yet she was "holding up" well and could, in my moments of worry, more and more common since Sonja got pregnant, distract me, diminish my doubts or transform them into certainty, I leave her house euphoric, convinced that only lust is real, infinite, because Bauduy was a jealous old graybeard, Cécile Lavlanette welcomed me once a week, on Thursdays, on the counsel of the voluptuous mambo Éliphète, who had developed a solid reputation as a poisoner by ridding Bauduy of his friends and rivals in business and politics, that was the night he spent away from home to go bury his anxieties in a houmfort where, whitest among the whites, in an orgy of rum, he communed with the lwa who protected him, notably the terrible Erzulie Dantor, leaving the field open for me, I slipped through the kitchen, led by a slender, long-legged Negress in her flared one-piece karabela dress, she appeared fleeting, elusive, gave off a sugary scent of hog plum, a sensuality that made me dizzy and that I managed to quell by plunging into the volcano that is Cécile, the night of Mardi Gras, returning from a bamboche in Bordes at Michel Clérié's house, remembering that Cécile had decided to spend carnival week in Cap-Français, I stopped at La Volière, a simple stopover to relieve a need that was becoming urgent because geographic coincidences had given it a name, Cécile, and linked it to confused karabela memories, ah! the discovery of ancillary loves! a ray of light filtered through the door, I knocked, the Negress opened it, on the first knock, perhaps she was expecting someone, she was naked, magnificently black and gleaming, sculptural, I had never seen anything so beautiful, in the half darkness of the candle the cardinal red hibiscus pinned in her hair resembled a vast bloodstain above her ear, enough to frighten you, on recognizing me she seemed scared, stepped back, I pulled her by the arm

—no, Monsieur! no! Mistress not here

her voice low, her voice serious, fear and suddenly that insistent smell of perspiration like an evil spell, I threw her nudity to the floor, she fought back, I blocked the movement of her arms, immobilized her chest, she clenched her smooth, strong thighs together, that fragrance again and still, she resisted, defended herself, I lost my head, like a coward I struck her, she surrendered, I penetrated her brutally, a groan rather than a complaint, roughly (I was half-drunk) I plowed her, tense and stiff at first, she relaxed, undulated, became wet, released her pleasure in generous and orderly movements that at times lingered at the edge of a scream, the rape of tragic mornings, panting, murmuring, the noise and the taste of words gave the silence a soul, me, a silver glimmer lost in an ebony bottle, her, supplications, invitations to plunge into an abyss, to annihilate ourselves, to push back the limits of astonishment, Cécile a novitiate in the convent! the pleasure of excess, the drunkenness of the devil, pleasure exploded in my loins like a miracle or like a defiance, I destroyed the world of the forbidden, destroying myself in the candor of night, the world changed, never again would it be what it was before, the Negress roars, deploys her sound in my spine, the bite of her scream in my shoulder, the scratches of her growling on my back, the explosion of a volcano, I was projected into the gaping heights of the night and when I fell back down, she was once again stiff, incredibly cold, intact, slowly she pushed me away, stood up, her face expressionless, impenetrable, mistress of the gift she had given despite herself, sovereignly distant, I left ashamed, a sob crossed my footsteps, I thought I heard a threat

—I will go be with all the others, Biemme, I promise you will suffer from it

a week later, the *Jérémie Gazette* reported the tragic death of Cécile's Negress (the Negroes don't have names in the obituaries), she had been found with her throat cut, the assassin or assassins had pinned a white hibiscus dipped in blood right onto her chest, the sign of Mackanda, the sign of vengeance, it reminded me of something, the enormous red hibiscus in her hair, a rallying sign, she was probably awaiting an associate, I hadn't noticed, the Negress profiting from Cécile's absence to organize Mackanda gatherings, these conspirators infuse their demands and projects with the macabre beauty of a dream, they promise a return to Africa to all Blacks who die for the emancipation of their race, all forms of refusing slavery, suicide, self-mutilation, marronage, all authorize this journey, but there was one condition, absolute, any Black accepted as a Mackanda refuses absolutely to consort with whites, and murder was the punishment for treason, Maïté (Cécile later told me the name of her Negress) had slept with a white man, it would have been acceptable had she endured violence (she would have been a martyr to the cause), but she had participated, she had enjoyed it, the Mackanda present witnessed, judged, condemned, Maïté paid, she would not return to Africa any time soon, in the soft earth of Abricots she had found a refuge far beyond the constraints of pleasure, her fear had meant something that night when I had left her, and her dignity expressed an accountability to death, she knew that I had condemned her, she had lost any chance of walking toward the light

—stay where you are, don't come any closer

she had walked into the hut, whose door opened on the night, pale with rage, following the circle of light that a dim paper lantern arranged just ahead of her steps, living spectacle of a fury that found the easiest and most ridiculous justification, I was emerging from a nightmare of unhealthy promiscuity only to enter into that of morbid jealousy, I understand immediately that in Sonja's eyes I was guilty, not of transgressing any social code, since taking advantage of the Negresses in order to appease our sexual instinct and then using our progeny as free labor is common practice, but a family code, a code of honor based on a certain idea of the Biemmes

—we do not share

from the very first moment she had decided to possess me, making love in her chambers was a selfish act, an act of possession that the wedding had simply legalized, without realizing it I allowed myself to be freed of responsibility for my feelings, she took them on quickly, with pride, by choosing me, a distant exile from the islands, rather than some local Breton second son, she had demonstrated a desire for difference that the Biemme take for the mark of their superiority, lived to the point of absurdity, above all of absurdity, thus enlisting myself in a destiny that I find myself incapable of mastering

—Sonja, what are you doing there?

I tried to infuse my voice with some authority, but it was too late and I knew it, out of a need to gather myself, to assert myself in the face of a wife who was subjecting me to the fatalism of her moods and barbarous impulses, she began with a crazed laugh, she laughed at my dangling penis, which I hadn't had time to put back into my pants, like a robot she placed the lantern next to the little Negress's pallet, planted herself in front of me and said, offhandedly

—leave immediately, there's no reason for you to be in a slave hut, Monsieur Baron

the cynical mockery, the steadiness of her gaze, the harshness of her tone, it was no longer a human voice but something dark, disincarnated, that came from beyond death as if cruelty and hatred were a voice, a coldness as brutal as a slap, all the heat in my body went to my head, I tried to find an impossible indignation to confront my wife's rage but this wasn't an easy thing, especially in my situation

—leave, or I'll chase you out with a whip

react, grab her by the arm and push her outside, but I obeyed, empty, drained, with no recourse against my cowardliness, shoulders hunched, heart heavy, certain of her victory, she gathered together and condensed her disdain and threw it in my face

—don't forget, Monsieur Baron, to tidy yourself up, you're not decent

I walked past without looking at her, I turned around in the doorway, believing that she had followed me, but she remained in place, her cruelty right there on the surface, unfurled, as if to defy me, a sturdy whip made of woven beef nerves, furious, I left, my heart stumble through the impenetrable darkness as the whip falls heavily on the body of the little Negress, turning fourteen had almost transformed her anatomy, changed the curve of her hips, awakening more than one lusty gaze

—I haven't tried her yet, Schpeerbach, she's all yours, I pay my debts sooner or later

—rather later than sooner, my dear Bonbon

—perhaps, but excessively, it has been to your advantage to wait

—she's barely worth five hundred pounds

—I only owe you four hundred, capital and interest combined

—you're the one who's profiting, you pay your debt at fair cost and rid yourself of a mouth to feed

—always running numbers other people haven't thought of

—and why not? I wouldn't be Swiss otherwise

—so what do you say?

—she looks like a good piece

—you ready to make a deal?

—I'll have to, otherwise I'll be waiting around for as good an opportunity as this to recoup my money, you've got a deal, here is my recognition of the debt paid

—thank you, do you have time to have coffee with me?

—will you drink some of this, Sister? some black coffee will help with the lasting effects of the champagne

—no thank you, Carmenta

—I'm sorry to correct you, Sister Theresa, but my name is Sonja

finally an opportunity to score a point, force her to reveal herself, to further ground our complicity in mutual understanding and, in a way, to ruin the superior nuance of her smile, her subtle arrogance taunts me and tells me in a thousand different ways: the sky is my kingdom, the ancient kingdom of Segu, the city of a hundred walls that I rebuild tirelessly among the clouds, with three continents as its borders, I interrupt her, mocking

—are you Swedish?

she laughs frankly, I thought I would shock her and expected a completely different reaction, that of outraged sensibility, but she's laughing and she's the one to score the point

—do you know any Black Swedes? my father was a chauffeur at the Swedish embassy in Dakar, he gave me the ambassador's first name, rather a pretty name, the lying mouths of men, it goes beautifully with your smile

what a girl! she was no virgin and Bonbon, the old letch, must have helped himself to her generously, she was in the hut, open and naked, handed over to Sonja's brutality

—are you happy to leave Bonbon?

—I don't know, Master, what difference is there between one cage and another for the bird's captive wings?

—there's a difference between a big cage and a little one, especially if the wings are not clipped

—but the bird is wounded every day, and the abundance of grains in a bowl doesn't replace the joy of pecking at ears of corn on their stalks

I regretted having begun this kind of conversation with a Negress, spurred on by her responses and taken with a sudden inspiration, remembering Maïté, Cécile's Mackanda, I asked with a hint of worry in my voice

—so would you like to be free?

—listen to the wind blowing in the cane fields, it is free, watch the clouds unravel and die in the azure of the sky, they are free, one of these days the Negroes will die of freedom

the first lash shocked her pride, she screamed, once, my pain! then her pride stifled her suffering, Sonja's loud breathing impregnated the night, the inexhaustible ardor of her cruelty furiously flogged the nubile breasts, the plump buttocks each of which fit into the hollow of my hands joined together, the firm shoulders, the long, delicate thighs, on that fragile, silent beauty, serene in the disdainful silence of pain

—why freedom if they have to die of it?

we walked in the blue day, her, lost in her hopes and her dreams, me, stuck in my worries, brought together for the time of a conversation but then quickly divided by a word that had the power to change the weather, we picked up our dialogue later on, through her unfinished body, language of a precociously perverse sensuality, the humidity of the night in her fingers drumming on my back, a vague sensation of expecting something else from her beyond the simple appeasement of desire, a return to the original joys of adolescence, like an aspiration to freedom, all it took was Sonja entering the hut for me to understand, in a moment of truth, that I am not free

—because . . . what's the point of explaining? you cannot understand

silence made its way between us, as deep as the abyss, crying out the truth of the injustice, more headstrong than hatred, more definitive than death, she is right, I cannot understand, I didn't stay, I didn't intervene, I didn't want to know, the plantation screamed with Sonja's frenzy, which would not stop flagellating the silence, hundreds of eyes pierced the darkness, watching and listening to the wound widening between her lacerated thighs grow, finally she left the hut, the beef nerves had left furrows in the raw flesh, which will be so many wounds in my heart, the mess of blood, yet clear is the death that seeks already to express itself, that seeks out its cry because only in the cry is the miracle, the resurrection to be found

—have you ever loved?

—stop asking questions

—might you be feeling regret?

—for having slept with Maïté, no, but for having been the direct cause of her death, yes, since I arrived here with Sonja on many occasions and for trifles I've had the feeling that something outside of me will soon push me to force the future, serious events are looming, which will end it all

—where did you get that idea?

—I don't know and yet I'm convincing myself that I'll survive that end, in these events and through these events I'll come to know myself

—I don't understand, explain it to me better

—sometimes, Cécile, everything is mixed up inside me, I wonder who I am, colonel, Swiss citizen naturalized French, plantation owner, that makes three identities, amounts to three personalities that are too often in conflict with one another, as much as about the fundamentals as about the details of life, I spend my time trying to find myself, when I think about the fact that I am also, ah! Sonja's husband, I get confused, muddled, while I chose my other roles, my wife chose me, and that turned my life upside down

—you're not being honest, haven't you always told me that you wanted Sonja?

—I thought so, but now that I know her I think she was imposed on me by the negative forces each of us carries within ourselves

—every day I ask God to protect me from Monsieur Bauduy's wild, mystical imaginings, will I have to invent a viaticum against yours?

—don't kid around Cécile, I dreamed of mastering my destiny, and I thought I had achieved that, I obtained everything I wanted from life, until I got married and returned here, now I doubt everything, even myself, what should I choose to be? every part of me buried in my conscience or inscribed in the future is merely one possibility, which the escape of a Negro or the whipping of a Negress can compromise by erasing any certitude

—were you really so sure of yourself?

—yes and my tragedy is that now I'm sure of nothing, I know my limits, the obligation I had given myself to always master the situation finds its own limits within my will, I took too long to attain my goals, I had to put too much effort into surviving in a world where luck only smiles on you when you provoke it, in Saint-Domingue everything is there for the taking, no one offers you a gift, it is a land of pillage and rape, all misfortunes should have been called Biemme de Valembrun

—Wolf! are you talking about your wife's relatives?

—you're calling me Wolf for the first time

—there's a first time for everything

my life behind me and so many useless acts, choices I should have repudiated long ago: this debilitating luxury in the midst of inclement nature, this tombstone, the inscriptions, hemmed on the secret bodies of my parents, that refuse to disappear under the heap of wild grasses attaching me to this earth in which I've rooted myself, that laugh that rings in my ears everywhere I go, which wanders even into my nights, linking them to escapades in Ti Fort creek with another rascal just like me, he and I missed our chance at the kind of brotherhood that childhood creates but that life divides, Salomon, Salomon, has the sinister cry of the woods extinguished the brightness of your eyes? these passions tamped down in the huts but fed by my wife's indifference, had you been different, Sonja, perhaps my distress would have changed horizons, the Jura with its mountains higher than clouds, me on the quest for a continent of snow and winter avalanches, of alfalfa flowering in the fields in summertime, of streams galloping through prairies of rocks and pebbles in the spring, forests transformed by the magic of autumn's russet dawns, I preferred the torture of midday in the tropics and I damned myself

—you're becoming grim, let's change the subject, say, have you been to the theater in Paris, what are the popular new plays?

—an author named Marivaux is making women's hearts swoon, in his plays he's imagined a new game in which caprices end up entrapping love

—what's the game?

—imagine that love is hidden here, but that, in order to recognize itself, it decides to search for itself through various misunderstandings, subterfuges, and tricks

—it sounds like we're reverting to preciousness

—no, no, not at all, it's lighter, more elegant, there's no longer the weight of conventions in the boudoir, created by bored coquettes to put love to the test

—in this case it's love that puts itself to the test, what are his plays called?

—the one that's a hit at the Royal Theater right now is called *Le jeu de l'amour et du hasard*

—if the play lives up to the promise of its title, it's sure to be interesting

—it's fascinating, Cécile

—ah! Wolf! that's a word I'm surprised to hear come out of your mouth

another time the barbarian within the planter had ceded to the temptation of refinement, an evening of music at the Opéra, the theater gleaming with the gold of the chandeliers, the decorations of the arches sparkling with a thousand reflections of the women, diamonds and multicolored jewels, slumped in my chair I felt shabby in the midst of these men and women in their wigs, inflated shams, in their crinolines, powdered, made up, dolled up, their voices an indistinct murmur and, from time to time, laughter fleeing some salacious joke, from the heads of the balcony to the stalls, speaking breathily to one another, whispering having become the most exquisite form of delicacy, acknowledging one another, greeting each other, congratulating each other from a distance, I drank in the women's smiles, amassing in my memory the roundness of their faces, one more expressive than the next, and when La du Barry entered, you know, our beloved king's current mistress, the murmuring ceased for a moment as if paralyzed by such grace, such beauty, such superb and prideful insolence, then they started up again, grew louder, exploded into ovations, was this the noblemen's France paying homage to beauty? no, indeed, it was the France of the bourgeoisie greeting a certain Voltaire who had entered just after La du Barry, all of Europe considered him the prince of the mind, apparently he was as witty as ten people, his many repartees filled the high society pages, they say that he had changed his name, and when the Prince of Rohan expressed surprise he responded haughtily: I'm just beginning with my name, while you are coming to the end of yours

—ah! ah! Schpeerbach, my good man, I know this, what do you call him?

—Voltaire

—this Voltaire used to be called Arouet and we were at the Jesuit school together

—he's come a long way since then, my dear Galbaud, he writes to all the kings of Europe as an equal

the first measures rang out from the orchestra pit, glided over the buzz of voices, filled the theater, hummed in my mind, I could not tear my eyes away from the aggressive and sensual beauty of the king's mistress, she exuded something so powerfully frivolous that she seemed intentionally attuned to the opera *Les Indes galantes*, the orchestra joyously carried the dramatic poem but, as if by chance, I no longer heard the words and my mind, absentmindedly, infused the melody with the rough notes of the tam-tam, a kind of barbaric chant passionately countered Rameau's words, I was the laboring Indies, savage, cruel, in my country, love is never gallant, it is always a power struggle

—even when we sell ourselves, Wolf?

—especially if we sell ourselves because here love goes to the highest bidder, and thus to the strongest

—and from you to me, my dear?

—still a power struggle, Bauduy is an old man, Cécile, I'm in my prime

—Wolf, forget the shadows of the Royal Opéra, let me feel your power

she won't be playing the whore anymore, your little Negress, the dawn paled in Sonja's voice, could she have killed the girl? I tried to grab her as she walked past

—don't touch me!

it has become a refrain, this excommunication, she chases me from her existence with words, each utterance embedded ever more deeply in the wounds of my pride, sweeping away the ruins of my dignity once and for all

—Saintmilia! Saintmilia!

she lifts her gaze up to my smiling eyes, a forced smile that attempts to greet the light, she brandishes her fist, her arm stiffened, raised in the direction of the sun, a rallying cry, ah! those victorious Blacks standing up there on the podium at the Olympic Games in Mexico, wielding their vengeance, combination of fury and hatred, apocalypse of violence and terror, to erase five centuries of humiliation, to deny hell, to reduce history, to eliminate me, leaving me Sonja Biemme to atone for the past, worse, to relive it in reverse, the future immersed in the present, the dream undoes the ages, gets carried away, the diffuse past, all frontiers abolished, histories contract and come back to life in the wildest of lies, I come back from a voyage through space while she returns from a long voyage through time, each of us enters into our own dimension

—Saintmilia!

—yes, mèt!

the presiding healer of the plantation, she brings her procession of Negroes who've come to investigate, but especially to renew, in their shared pain, the heavy chain of responsibility that will one day forge a destiny counter to our own, it is inevitable, already the Mackanda brotherhood threatens, they also say that the maroons have gathered in bands under the command of Jean-François, Biassou, and Petit-Noël Prieur, the hour of vengeance approaches, it announces the time of their freedom, the tempest roars, Rameau deludes himself, *Les Indes galantes*, a perpetual celebration? his celebration there in Paris for those libertines who, having depleted life too quickly, choose to kill themselves by leaving their history behind, as good a way as any to live life intensely, one last burst, a spasm, the last gulp of existence and the fleeting ecstasy of agony, the end, curtains, the final notes remain suspended, peaceful, immobile and then reckless and mad, drift in all directions, bringing to each countenance the elegant joy of admiration, hundreds of hands seize them, the confiscated music explodes, polyphonic, into applause that never ceases to be delighted, within me the drum sounds, outside the tropical forest assaults me right there in the middle of Paris, the croaking of toads, the sharp trill of cicadas, the groan of djondjon mushrooms digging into the earth, the wail of the southwestern wind in the bamboo, bursts of owl cries ricocheting against the trees, the smell of sound, the glimmering of sound, the taste of sound, the caresses of sound as if the night, suddenly a thousand existences, were an infinity of lives

—is that why you came back?

—yes! Switzerland is my father's country, France the country that adopted us, Saint-Domingue where I left all of myself, a world of new sensations I will never be able to deny because they've belonged to me since childhood, they are a part of my games, my turmoils, they repudiate those adult truths that change us despite ourselves, lock each of us within limits I have sought to surpass, without success, just as they concern you, Salomon, in your present, hide the past, destroy the future, Salomon! Salomon! do you hear me, Sonja has broken me, urge Saintmilia to heal the young Negress as quickly as possible, I want her to live, do you hear me, she cost me more than four hundred livres tournois

—that's a high price for one night's caprice!

he condemns me too, Salomon, you are no longer my friend, Sonja has broken you, too, I have cold hands, is that the effect of the rigors of the long Alsatian winter or just the weight of remorse, I stand up, through the window the frozen Rhine, it winds through the powdery plains with the sinuous stripe of a slug, I walk back and forth to stave off numbness, my steps oscillate between a far-off hatred, that of the Blacks who despised my cowardliness, and a present of regrets that trouble my sleep, what could I do? take the side of the little Negress against my wife? unthinkable! in the name of what, anyway? of love for justice, of simple humanity? the notion of the rights of man and citizen hadn't yet inspired the Negroes' consciousness to start making demands, nor that of the whites to have pity, Saint-Domingue is a savage land, we perpetuated so many crimes there that the cruelty of the whites seems to have inflamed the barbarity of man and amplified his bloodthirsty rage to a magnitude that surpasses in its horror anything we have known to this point

—the Negroes took it all over, the land fertilized by our tenacity and our will to tame a rebellious natural world, our husbands were initiated into debauchery by the Negresses in the filth of their huts, among the sugar boilers and the indigo basins they sowed the dust of gilded Africans who dare look directly at the sun, now they usurp our names, Sonja daughter of a chauffeur at the Swedish embassy in Dakar

—why did you call me Carmenta?

—because of your extraordinary resemblance to a girl I knew at the convent in France

—I also knew a Carmenta, I met her in Tangiers, three years ago, during my vacation

—was she Black?

—no! very brown-skinned, originally from Valencia, I think, but she had lived for a long time in Morocco, hey! I remember, she told me she had been in a convent in France

—so that's her, did you not notice that you look alike?

—people turned their heads when we passed and often I heard people whispering: they're probably twins, perhaps the resemblance was obvious to others, but not for me, the discrimination I suffered in my own country and then at the French university and in my work here make it impossible for me to ever recognize myself in a white face

—you said she was brown-skinned?

—correction, on the face of a white person

we had the same name, we knew the same people, maybe we had the same passions and who knows? the same soul, mine had traveled a prodigious distance to come die in white or Black Africa, what difference did it make if our lives have made an airplane into the meeting point of the races high above a continent that is, as archaeological digs and anthropological research make clearer and clearer every day, the cradle of the human race? I dive into myself, obsessive quest for a lost past that interests me today because it forces me to relive and to share the memories of a libidinous great-grandfather with two women

—my first name is also Sonja but they call me Sister Theresa in the faith

—Sonja! really!

—really

—Swedish?

—spot on

we both laughed the same laugh, it pulverized the metallic structure of the seat, converted this airplane cabin into a magnificent bedroom, leopard-skin bedspread, my heart freed, ready to provoke a cataclysm in the vastness of the sky, an electric shock of love, Sister Hyacinthe exploded, Carmenta torn to pieces, to please her you trampled on my fervor, the sky swallowed up, but Sonja! Sonja! doubly a survivor, to reinvent love, passion, lust

—a Frenchwoman, I don't know how far back my family has to go to connect my great-great-great-grandfather to a family tree, our grandfather plundered Brittany in the company of a Viking descendant of William the Conqueror, his name was Olaff but he was known as Olaff the Swede, mustachioed, blond, tall, brawny, blue-eyed, the sky mirrored in the deep water of the fjords, amicably noisy and with a courageousness that astonished our people, who themselves had the reputation for bravery beyond recklessness, throwing back drinks and yet still standing up long after everyone else had collapsed into the sleep of intoxication, he dreamed of having a girl, Sonja, to coax him away from his life of adventures, Sonja, a star of polar nights, a wounded star upon Olaff's brow, he had helped in a fight against the troops of John the Fearless and was now bleeding like an ox, his skull split open, intestines hanging out, he was trying to hold them in with the pressure of his thick hands
—come on, take a drink, as my name is Loïc Biemme de Valembrun I'll get you out of this and in a few days we'll be hunting deer together
he had whimpered faintly, I lay him on his back, he kept asking for something to drink (here a page is missing from Loïc Biemme's memoir), I waited all afternoon in a thicket, our men dispersed, the stench of eviscerated bellies brewed in the air above the corpses, come nightfall I put him on my shoulders, sorrow like a mass of pain, my steps slipping on the rocks, already measuring a distress that no longer sounded like a human voice

> I hear the elves running from branch to branch
> singing joyful death, the final lie
> of a life cut down on the field of honor
> sound the horn and the oliphant, by my side
> my bow my saber and my quiver
> like a great rumor, joy watches me die

Biemme, I've chosen you to set fire to my bed of dried leaves, bring the torch and don't forget to compose my saga, recount my exploits to the daughter life didn't give me but who will be yours

—hush, Olaff, you'll live to be so old that ten wives will give birth to a hundred children who will be so many Olaffs

—I don't want any male inheritors, the gods will force me to train them for war, give me a daughter, Biemme, call her Sonja, may she be all the girls of your family in memory of my mother, she let herself die of sorrow when I, her only son, left to travel the world seeking adventure

as simple as clear water and the eyes of the dawn, we bear our name like two destinies, each of them linked to events whose meaning and purpose escapes us

—Sonja! what will be the color of the dawn?

—Sister Theresa, tomorrow it will be emerald upon our bed covers

that morning, destiny decided for me, I was despicable, I knew it, I had not even a word of pity for the tattered body that had received my seed and had been the site of my pleasure, nearly five hundred livres worth, I saw the unseemliness of my remark, it confirmed my rights so as to mask my cowardice, I should have intervened, prevented a pointless cruelty for which jealousy was not even the excuse, the Blacks do not exist, how could Sonja have been jealous of nothingness

—good evening, Master, the reunion will be lovely

whenever Saintmilia put aside her usual patois it meant there was a threat not far behind, her voice refused to lisp, got stronger, tremble oh ye passing mortals, the river has reversed its course, it evaporates at its source, the ants eat the lizards, the horses revert to childishness and the dawn becomes the twilight hour, evil, evil, those nursed by Saintmilia hear her cry out

—Saintmilia! Saintmilia! what have you done with your own story?

—she is healed, Master, you can have her this very night if you so desire

I had suggested to Sonja that she go stay with Marie Andrée Josèphe, a childhood friend she had run into in Port-au-Prince, at the intendant's Christmas ball, and who had invited her to spend Easter at Pestel, too busy processing the cane before the May rains I had stayed behind to do the accounting on the most recent sale of molasses and of twelve quarters worth of sugar to the American brigantine *Missouri* heading to Galveston, despite the restrictions of the colonial monopoly we traded contraband with nearby countries, taking advantage of the better prices offered to us by Europe through them, night had fallen, perturbed by the glimmering play of the fireflies, I hadn't noticed that a servant had discreetly lit the candles and naturally I continued filing the bills

—she is waiting, Master

I walked outside, the hostile darkness, shadows brushed against the night, their movement rustling against the swaths of darkness that opened up before me and immediately closed behind me, before going into the hut I stopped to probe both the night and my own desires, the anguish of a pleasure about to be rediscovered in a body refashioned by the magic of this sorceress, pleasure like an oppressive heat, I opened my mouth, gulped down the shadows and, taking a deep breath, I went inside

—where are you? why have you not kept the light on?

I move forward, my forehead collides with legs dangling in the belly of the night, the very center of the hut, a hop to the side, to avoid the feet knocking against my head, I run into arms that push me away, a thump, the feet of the darkness, for the darkness does have feet, they strike me, a thump, toes shoved into my nose, hey! what's going on? the night begins to snort, louder and louder, sudden light, sudden, crude, dense, arms like torches fill the little room with smoke, illuminate barbaric faces, closed expressions, hostile, waiting for who knows what outcome, I saw the feet, they were the extension of a body I knew well for it was beautifully naked, placed at eye level, head tipped forward, eyes rolled into the back of the head, so young

—why are you doing this to me? you have no right to flee my desire

one night to make up for other nights, pay back more than a hundred pounds of flesh, of pleasure, embalmed in vetiver and soursop, flowing from your skin, the oils burn, sizzle in the light of the torches, Saintmilia where are you? I forbid you to take away my pleasure, the grievance of dark-haired chests, take down the body, the torches converge menacingly, my shadow shrinks, I'm not afraid, I'm no longer afraid, take her down, fast, faster, a murmur, a poignant and lugubrious chant, I'm hot, the circle tightens, pushes me toward those legs sliding down the length of the light, tumbling down, we roll on the ground, ah! dear Mother, a macabre farce, why have you done this to me, I stand up, it is no longer Nanie spanking her little master, I'm going to settle my score with you, the torches retreat, intermingling their flames, polka and quadrille, Ibo and Congo, the corpse dances, the hallucinating ground writhes, Petro, undulates, Nago, collapses, rabordaille, playacting love, playacting death, Saintmilia enters in a gust of wind, her cry extinguishes the torches, the darkness bursts into a shrill laugh, prolonged, it drills into my head, strips me of the last vestiges of lucidity, Saintmilia lights up again, I am alone, absolutely alone, I'm cold, those Black devils bewitched me, there is no more dangling corpse or torches or hidden faces swollen with hatred, Saintmilia's grimace splatters across the darkness, I'm going mad, where is she?

—she has joined the ancestors in Guinea

—don't you entangle me in your conjuring tricks, where is that dancing corpse?

—it was a reflection of your desires

—enough! enough!

I'm shaken by an urge to commit murder, to slash Saintmilia's throat, her Vodou devilry, to cut off the Negroes' heads and their laughter, which strikes me pitilessly, and then, delirious, to kill myself on their corpses, I take my revenge on Sonja and on the whole system that encourages her delirium

—it's impossible, you cannot commit a crime and remain innocent

—say rather that we are only innocent of murder committed by others

—even if we're the ones who ordered it?

—we start out innocent but we end up guilty, we're implicated sooner or later

—Wolf, watch out, you're giving in to dark thoughts, what's the matter?

—look around you Cécile, nothing is all right, something intolerable is happening, leading us into chaos, I lost my primitive innocence as soon as I started thinking about the meaning of my presence and my actions here, about the meaning of my choices, I should never have been a Swiss man in this cursed land

—what are you saying? did you not choose to be Swiss?

—on the contrary, I chose to be French, and that's even worse, as I've kept my Swiss sensibility

—the love of money?

—yes, but not under any circumstances, the passion for money is satisfied by possession, but it is never in the Jura and the other cantons, tired of life

—are you not the one who's becoming tiresome?

—I can leave if I'm boring you

—men always bore me after making love, what are you doing? I didn't tell you to leave, it's a little cold tonight, help me close the windows while I light the candles, night doesn't belong here anymore, let's throw it outside, it's giving you dark ideas

nothing to be done, the night comes thicker and heavier within Olaff, his back more and more hunched over, I wear myself out carrying it to a thatched cottage where some devoted care and a strong grog will bring my companion back to consciousness, he had traveled the world and run into the most senseless adventure, the one that cannot be beat, at the tip of some ruffian's sword, save him, Saint Michael, I promise in his name that he will go light a candle at your feet as a sign of gratitude, I know he'll try and play a practical joke, to burn your toes for the pleasure of hearing you scream but, Biemmes' honor, I'll stop him, come on Swede, tell Saint Michael that if you survive this you'll become the most serious and most devoted of the faithful, tell him about the forests that walk and terrorize the lumberjacks of your country ever since they decided to systematically chop down the trees and bleed the earth dry, sing to him of the boiling, foul-smelling waters pushing through the crust of the glaciers and let the clouds know all about the sufferings of the subterranean depths, hush dear old Olaff, do you realize that for the first time you've got nothing to say? you're as cold as the night, the silence has a constipated air that doesn't suit your good mood, pull yourself together

—your steps walk with death

—did you say something, Olaff? I see a light over there, the grasses smell of the living

I jumped on the first horse, pushed it to a gallop, hurtling down the hill at Petit-Fort, risking a broken neck, I listen to the village and its thatched houses churning in my voice, riding at full tilt, denying the suffering of the world through speed, the horse ruins the silence with his fiery hooves, the dawn breaks, echo of the drum's first yelps, sounding the alarm to waken the Negroes and begin a new day on the plantation

—who are you?

—wounded travelers attacked by brigands

a ray of light pushes the door open, it soon floods into the room, the master of the house as stocky and strong as an oak helps me lay down my charge on his pallet, he removes his hat, makes the sign of the cross

—he has gone to meet his ancestors in the land of eternal virgins and eternal peace

so ends the story of Olaff the Swede, the last, pitiful page of a book that is turning to dust, a north-facing hole dug into the earth, a few briars decorate a mound that soon will be covered over by grass, the story of a man, of solidarity, of filial love, the night over the moor is an archipelago of fog pierced by the shivering of the gorse bushes and the crude specter of a knight of the snow

—do you think he'll join his mother in paradise?

my mother knits her solitude and her young widow's destiny, seated next to the fire in a corner of the library, I hear Olaff the Swedish bull bellowing, attacking some redoubt, the clattering of swords punctuates his dreams of feints, of rapier strikes and thrusts, he dodges, strikes forward, breaks, attacked from the left, he trips, the enemy swordsman strikes in turn, a sly kick, surprised, Olaff drops his rapier, brings his hands to his belly, before he even understands what's happening a terrible shock cracks and breaks his helmet, Sonja, a murmur, he slowly bends his knees and falls onto his back, his face turned toward the northern sun, this is where the story of Sonja Biemme de Valembrun Lebrun begins, I would have preferred to imagine my father returning from a mission in the Nordic countries, bearing in his belly a mortal wound named Sonja

—beautiful love stories, Sister, are to be read in books

—are you crying? with what secret pain have you paid for a moment of joy in the arms of some Olaff?

—none, Sister Theresa, I wouldn't have let a white man hurt me in love, I would have killed him

—and me?

—you are different, Sonja, put your hand on my eyes, wipe away my tears

—my fingers pluck the leaves from images of happiness, too many emotions, I'm weeping, too, I would have thought I had run out of tears

I went deeper into the Dangluse gorges between those steep mountains that flank the sky, jagged rock walls with trees and dense vines, gouged out here and there by rocks crumbling in the fury of the winds, without my having noticed, we have left the ease of the plain, my horse was having trouble on the damp pebbles, I slowed down our pace, the dawn was already cutting large gaps of light into the night, and a cold southwestern wind rushed in between the hillsides, flattening my jerkin against my chest and stomach, the coolness of dawn, half-asleep or half-awake, penetrated me, relaxed my nerves, like a child I cried, a flood of emotions resurfaced intact, how can a broken man, arriving at the end of his life, feel so vividly a wound that marked a rupture, but that nonetheless remains, through a sensual and violent image, the connection to a land he has loved to the point of madness? absence has the capacity to amplify even unimportant memories, I'm not sure this love story was always so deep but I see how, twenty years later, he remains nostalgic for a land that could not be my future, I dismounted my horse and attached the halter to a juniper tree, removed my clothes, the first glimmers of the day piercing through the vines played on my muscles, I was naked out of a need to rediscover my innocence, to commune with nature through water, a need to accomplish something, too, but how? why? who knows, the need to exist, I entered the Couleuvre River, a tadpole jumped, fleeing the wrath of some predator, quick, I stretched out my hand

—don't touch me

—calm yourself, Sonja

—why did you order them to bury the corpse?

—could I humanely approve your decision? do you not feel the tension mounting? the Blacks are nervous, as if they're expecting something serious, what are they planning? more and more frenetic drumming assaults the night, sharpens the menace in their words, the night before last, thirty Blacks from the big house responded en masse to their call, returning only at dawn, they worked with a zeal that surprised the manager, during the midday break they gathered the slaves from the first and third huts, endless whispering and discussion, like devious conspirators, have you noticed? now they always move around with their cutlasses, why provoke them pointlessly? the punishment you inflicted on this girl is out of proportion, had no relation to the offense, if there even was an offense, she wasn't responsible for the mess in your room

I was waiting for a response, she stopped flailing about, her anger suddenly dissipated, she looked at me, stupefied, discovering me for the first time, I was a human being, capable of pity and fear, I was weak, so different from the caliber of the Biemmes, she raised her arms, an indignant protest, calling on the heavens to bear witness to my iniquity, ran to throw herself on her bed, moaning, sobbing, I turned her onto her back, she furrowed her brow, gathered a ball of spittle with a pointed gesture of her lips, spat it in my face, violently rolled over and turned away from me

—don't touch me

I no longer existed, she decided to prove it to me in the most trivial and cruel manner, in a mess of satin, brocade, velvet, so much regalia marking the scene with an unbearable strangeness

—don't touch me

Sonja's madness—it became clearer to me each day that she was mad—disheartened me, I condemned her bloody instincts, which devised the most incredible forms of torture, but was paralyzed by a kind of embarrassment (I wondered how they could be the actions of a woman, my wife), I kept myself from intervening, from opposing her, these cruelties happened so often they became banal, but nevertheless each time, something in me, wounded, pushed me to act, but a sorrow stronger than despair prevented me, faced with Sonja's unnatural feelings I preferred locking myself up in the security and discomfort of an almost admiring doubt: is this possible? is this possible?

—there is nothing surprising about this, my dear, what woman isn't cruel?

—ok, but Cécile there is no comparison between the nasty little things women do to us or to each other and the barbarity of my wife

—nasty little things, Wolf, that's nonsense, women are carnivores, assassins, we spend all our time destroying

—in love, too?

—especially in love, we only truly love after having torn apart, dismembered our prey, we feed on the spectacle of men in tatters, by intoxicating herself with horror your wife proves that she loves the Blacks much more than you think, I myself love Saint-Domingue and, because I love it, I dream of setting it on fire and soaking it in blood

—you're mad! you, too!

I couldn't understand, I no longer recognized my wife, after Klaus was born, Sonja became enraged at the slightest inconvenience, once when I took a nail-studded whip out of her hands she passed out, plunged into a comatose sleep for a week, jaw rigid, body stiff, light breathing offering the barest sign of life, day and night I watched over her, she lay there, her light extinguished, her cheerfulness prematurely dampened, her shadow tracing unreal shapes beneath the funereally white blanket, I would like to be indifferent to this life that fails to liberate me from the trap of marriage and that doesn't even leave me a choice between love and hatred, the blood of the Blacks had dug a ditch between the Biemmes' taste for carnage and the Schpeerbachs' penchant if not thirst for charity, justifying a silence that joy no longer redeemed, Sonja had once been so lively, her laughter rolling across the fortifications in the port of Brest, her adolescent braids not yet entirely emerged from childhood, her sailor's boots, a tradition in that family of corsairs, unusual for a female cavalier, our rides across the moors thick with boxwood, eight days that were an eternity of exhilarating sensations, the world sated, to the point of madness, a childish glee, eight days that connected us to one another but a whole life to regret it

—they say that the days in the islands are long, very long

—yes and no, it depends on the season

—and what is the sky like?

—bluer than here, the summer sunsets stream with gold and purple . . .

—do you spend your days working?

—definitely, that is all we do, work, battle the elements, which can ruin us in a single night, start wearing ourselves out once again

—so what's the point of having slaves?

—to work

—so if the days are long, let the slaves work, take the time to live, amuse yourself with hunting, picnicking, seeking adventure

—then who will keep an eye on the Blacks?

—tell me, are they human beings?

—the Code Noir says yes but the colonists claim they aren't

—I have never seen any, a royal edict forbids them from entering the kingdom

—you'll see some soon enough, lovely lady, beyond whatever you can imagine

—we sealed our future on the backs of the slaves, she pressed the warmth of her shoulders against my chest and I harvested the fluorescence of her lips, I know what you're thinking, you think I'm asleep, I'm not sick, I'm taking revenge on your lies, the pureblood Swiss is nothing but a bastard who has sucked the blood of a Black woman, your spoiled blood has corrupted my own and the son you gave me is somehow colored, too, I'm punishing you for having sacrificed my marriage, like a sheepish child you wait for me to come back to life, back to your life to ensure your peace of mind, you resent me, I know it, for having shattered that peace of mind, for having broken with hypocrisy, the routine of your eyes, the indignity of a masked system, hidden by the paternalism of a Schpeerbach, a Swiss German who tries to be different, I see it in your eyes, deprived of sleep, the confusion of a tormented soul, racked by regrets and remorse for having revealed the urges of these foul beasts who you want to see as human beings and who are ready to devour us, because of me, you say, yes, because of me, I know how to treat them, you tame Blacks the way you tame wild beasts, my ancestor locked them in the hold of his ship, starved them for three days, that short period was enough to destroy any spirit of independence, a barrage of lashings four or five times a day and they became docile, servile, disembarked on the docks of Brest, vile chattel, stripped of all will, indifferent to their own fate, I lied to you, one lie merits another, right? when I told you I had never seen any Negroes, I dreamed about them every night, their hideous faces like a permanent nightmare, now you'd like me to help you pamper them, I still don't understand your hatred, Sonja, too bad then, Wolf, your existence between cowardliness and foolishness, incapable of supporting my actions and taking back control of the plantation, sightless man who can't see that it's decaying because you can't control your Negroes, powerless to thwart my plans, you show yourself to be just as I predicted, weak despite your impressive build, like a bull, that arrogant and superior beauty displayed on your face like the mark and the affirmation of power, I was deceived by your eyes, they hid your soul when they should have unveiled it, Sonja, I loved your beauty, Wolf, as soon as I discovered it, I decided to possess your weakness, lost in the crowd of Breton cadets, astray among the babble of those idiots from the lesser nobility or the recent bourgeoisie, those little flirts ogling the young and naive naval officers recently garrisoned in Brest, swimming through the multitude of bizarre, supposedly Gaelic names, smelling of seaweed, algae, and herring, I smiled at your weakness, so clumsy in your efforts to approach me, I walked it through the brush, rested it at the foot of the willows and the poplars, it danced on an ocean of glimmering sadness, the ashes of the clouds like a vision of destiny

—missié, ti-vé-ti manger, the meal is ready

all your muscles extended, go, your gait weary from watching over, the despondency of regret, you hesitate at the second mouthful, your chastened child's eyes turn toward me furtively, disconsolate, as you lift the spoon to your mouth, an attempt at a lifelike gesture, I'd rather she were dead, continuing to cherish a memory, a lie, you'd have sullied it in the stench of the huts, knowing I was there, thinking I was dying, you come back to bed, to my bed, weeping not over my sickness—that's my problem—but over your own distress, which speaks to me, you don't know it yet, it speaks to me, I need it, to comfort me, it binds you to me even more than the blood ties woven through your son, the one you inflicted on me, I hear his eyelids flutter, shocked by the words that oozed from my false sleep, they broke our pact of silence, Wolf detests anything unusual and unexpected, anything that hasn't been planned by his rigid Swiss logic sends him into a panic, I've got you Wolf, why did you lie to me? you've only lived in the colony for ten years! some betrayals are worse than others, a few glimmers of the day trailed momentarily in the room and then the sun winked its eye and settled behind the hills, the weariness of sleep in my loins, heavy, like a deadly intoxication

—have you no shame?

her hand between her thighs, indecent, shameless, she was masturbating, punishing, avenging an age-old blow to her pride that had condemned me to hell, watch my fingers come, the shimmering of silk and velvet disentangled me from the presence of a dream, say it again: this isn't possible, I can't believe my eyes, might you be right, Cécile? demoniacal, the precise play of her fingers voluptuously extracted pleasure from a body that I would never again possess, the pleasure was real, more real than those nights that speak of it, so real that it awakened my ardor, as indignant as it was, her eyes were speaking to me, burning with pleasure, with rage, with soundless ferocity, the sheets were clean, the fingers white, for chrissakes, I wasn't the only white man to have slept with a Negress, not a single plantation wasn't teeming with those children whose gradations of skin color oscillated between brown and poor white, attesting to their origins and filiation, perhaps! but the other colonists weren't Puritanical, they made no claim to have generous feelings or a Christian education, he who shows no charity! blessed are the pure of heart! they acted according to a morality they had given themselves, what was the difference between skinning a Negress and raping her? none!

—shut up

—I wasn't talking to you

—I am the only white man who has to pay, in such a cruel way, for having exercised my privileges as a master

—sure, the others are bastards, but your hypocrisy makes you more vile and pathetic

I should have despised Sonja, in her solitary pleasure she appeased my own craving for pleasure, my astonished ardor beheld her, the velvet bled endlessly, dripped between her fingers, my desire was a wound in the belly of the night, I feel sorry for myself, I feel sorry for Sonja above all, she has too much pride to lower herself enough to understand, too much stubbornness to agree to forget, too much rancor to deign to forgive, I learn to live the indignity of my rejection, resigned to no longer having any self-respect, retreated into a world of interrogations, determined to save myself from her through the debauchery of Cécile, with Madame Allaud's whores, the disdainful Negresses of the plantation, they no longer recognize their master in this man with an absent look in his eye, seeking both his soul and some kind of answer to his terrors through pleasure

—Wolf, you've become someone else

—I know, Cécile, and yet I try not to think about it too much

—you seem more and more miserable

—enveloped in fog

—you're searching for something, you've always been searching for something

—in the name of certain values I considered absolute, strength, power, money, perhaps even love

—that you believed in? and now?

—nothing makes sense anymore, what are strength, power, and money once I discover they are of no use? what is the point of a love that seeks only to destroy?

—there are no answers to the questions you ask

—there have to be, I feel it, there has to be one

—probably but whoever gives it to you will take responsibility for your life once and for all, is that what you want?

—no! no! no!

—why so much violence? because you already understand that Sonja, in her way, has taken on this responsibility?

—Cécile, you always say surprising things to me, that Sonja is cruel out of a need to quench her love for the Blacks in blood, that she has already taken on this responsibility

—not only the responsibility, but more and above all the very direction of your life, do you know why? running after all the women—have you not dreamed of Madame du Barry?—you have encountered Woman in her most deceptive form, a womanchild, you didn't allow love to ripen

—that's not it, Cécile, why are you linking my problems to the shipwrecking of love? my questioning goes beyond my relationship with Sonja, this is about me, do you understand? me in my relationship with a world that was once familiar to me and that suddenly has become so familiar it threatens my future

I began to weep, collapsing on Cécile like a child, caught up in an overwhelming despair, bent over beneath a pain that was nameless because it marked a whole world of innocence that no longer existed, I was innocent as long as I did not realize that I was a participant, now that I knew this, I was devastated, distraught, calmly, very slowly, with an uncommon gentleness, Cécile caressed me, I kept sobbing, inconsolable, I don't recall at what point desire stirred within me, seeking its path through the maze of my nerves and veins, Cécile had noticed it well before I did, she rolled me on my back, while still caressing me, she opened my doublet, her restless eyes changed color, from a washed-out gray to an intense gray, she mounted me, straddled me, took full and total possession of my body, the undulations of her croup like the ridiculous yet vibrant contortions of love, she soon forgot all about me, entirely absorbed by the modulations of pleasure in her hips, she threw her torso back, arms tensed, gripping my thighs to support herself, I let myself go so as to follow her on the ascent to prodigious summits, unknown to either of us, she closed her eyes, moaned, dug her nails into my flesh, I whinnied in pain, as if possessed, I prodded Cécile's womb and, as pleasure rose up in my loins with the suddenness of a wave from the great depths, I closed my eyelids, both of us bound up in the same explosion we entered into the great silence of the earth, love had been a quality whose flavor I would only come to appreciate many days later, a very brief conversation with Cécile, during a chance encounter at Kerlegrand's yearly fair, in Bordes, she had to deploy all manner of cunningness in order to approach me

—did I give you what you were searching for, Wolf?

—it was nothing more than pleasure

—no, it was oblivion, Wolf, oblivion

she turned on her heel, disappeared into the lacy bustling of the other guests, her voice reverberated long after she'd left and, pathetically, connected her, a faded courtesan, to me, a jaded playboy, it was oblivion, Wolf, a taste of ashes on my lips, I knew and I understood, a taste of ashes and bitterness, the decomposing fervor of love

—are you still suffering?

—Sister Hyacinthe was nothing but a dream

—dreams often leave our spirit with a moment's vertigo, the flash of hopefulness

—so help me forget

—for that, I'll need to cause a different sort of vertigo within you, a new light

—what's stopping you? steep me in the magic of your people and help me be reborn

—you ask too much of love, and what if magic is powerless?

—it won't be powerless, it acts, liberating a mysterious force that leads us astray and at the same time protects us from our own madness, we are alone with a certainty that can by no means turn into suffering

—it already is suffering

—transfigured

—a suffering that does not yet know itself?

—can only be joy

—be careful, Sonja!

—you've stopped saying Sister Theresa, come closer, right up to me, put your lips on my skin, just below my ear, slowly, carefully, I hear the intoxication of their trembling, hold me, your black beauty a delicious comfort, I want to take everything from you

—because you think you can give me all of yourself?

—I don't know

—I'm not sure either that I would accept the exchange

—you're cruel, Sonja!

—don't talk that way, Sister Theresa, let us give it a try, what I take from you I'll give back a hundred times over

—thank you, Sonja, I need you so badly!

—we always need someone, Sister Theresa, to suffer and to make suffer

the monotone voice at times showed weakness, shortcomings, emotion too full with her dignity to admit that it was pain, a hushed tone, searching for the right words, often garbled them, stuttered from too much precision, gave up, my mother knew, for a long time she had believed that by being quiet she had better protected me from myself, from the inexorable fate that forges the Biemmes in violence and destruction

—what would you have done if you were her?

—how can I put myself in her shoes? maternal instinct has such subtleties . . . I would have behaved the same way, I think

—why?

—as soon as people see you, they see a wounded little girl, a woman who suffers, a living portrait of grief

—and who needs to be protected, be careful, Sonja, don't let yourself be led astray by a false reflection of the Biemmes, they think we are weak, but we defy the centuries

this goes back to the reign of Charles VIII, specifically to 1491, the year of his marriage to the Duchess Anne of Brittany, the winter glittered in its snowy finery, a wood fire crackled in the hearth and the flames, occasionally fanned up with a bellow, lick the edges of the chimney stones

—tell me, Mother, why doesn't it snow at the equator?

she opens her eyes, surprised by the candor of my question, surprised I'm talking about over there, how do you know about that? about the equator, oh Lord, protect my daughter! her knitting falls out of her hands, her surprise scatters the yarn and she swivels the seat from right to left in her effort to gather it all up

—because summer is life's only season

—are there wolves in the countries at the equator?

—no, other voracious, savage predators attack unruly children, lions, tigers, jaguars, leopards, enormous snakes, boas, anacondas wrap themselves around you, my daughter, they suffocate you, they swallow you and digest you, fearsome Jivaro Indians cut off your head, shrink it to the size of a fist through diabolical methods

—cut off your head!

—yes! you have to behave, my little one!

—so my great-grandfather was a Jivaro Indian?

paralyzed in her armchair, playing with the multicolored balls of yarn, she watched the window flicker against the surface of the night, the screeching of brakes, a muffled shock followed by shouts

—Mother, have wolves invaded Paris?

she finishes her work, right in the middle of Paris, a bird of the night traversed the silence, its faint sound entered into the library, awakening the sleeping spirit of the Biemme de Valembrun in a dozen different books, the first names given to the family members over the years weave poems in remembrance of uncles, fathers, and grandfathers who distinguished themselves through crimes, uprisings, feudal

revolts, the war in the Vendée, the sinister reputation of the Biemmes'
castle once rivaled that of the manor of Gilles de Rais, the devil's den
and the devil himself, in the form of Erwan Biemme, terrorized the
Finistère region, sometimes making excursions to Anjou and the Vendée, covering leagues and leagues in epic cavalcades, razing everything
as they went

—what do you see over there? they look like Bohemians

—they must be spies from Burgundy

—we should check, my lord

—who said anything about checking? I said they are spies from Burgundy and woe betide anyone who says the contrary, he shall answer
with his life, like vultures, Biemme and his henchmen fell upon the
band of Roma, death to the English and the Burgundians! the hurricane ransacked the camp, a few cries, moans, curses quickly stifled,
and then silence

search the caravan, the booty is ours

a bag of trinkets, knickknacks made of copper, tin, iron, kitchen
utensils, two violas and two guitars that had already been disemboweled, a few rather misshapen baubles for women, but also a strange
and magnificent brass mask, an exact replica of an old woman who
had been knocked out with the hilt of Erwan's rapier and then disemboweled by Erwan with barbaric glee

—give it to me, burn the caravan and the corpses

children, women, the elderly, and four able-bodied men all accepted
death with a resigned air, indifferent, as if they'd known it was coming, the women had attempted to flee with the children, the elderly
had looked at us without seeing, looking over our heads, their eyes
serene, the thin sun dangling above the branches, something seemed
strangely out of place in the men's behavior, strong and valiant, they
hadn't reacted, passively watching the ransacking of their peaceful
community, and that intrigued me, and then there was the mask

—Kervalou, what do you think of the mask?

—Erwan, it seems too alive

—what do you mean?

—look at it, it's as if the eyelids are moving

—you're right, the lips are moving, too, murmuring prayers that I
can hear, but whose code I can't decipher

—Erwan, the mask is cursed, it will bring us misfortune

—nonsense, Kervalou, are we ourselves not the misfortune?

gathered in the great room, commenting on the marriage of Anne of Brittany to King Charles VIII, they drink, indolent, gloomy, obsessed by the memory of this unprovoked massacre, not yet remorseful, a slight feeling of discomfort, the feeling of having been cowardly, of having fought a battle without grandeur and of having left it irredeemably vanquished, the Roma triumphed from beyond the grave, Erwan had the premonition of some terrible event with no apparent link to the death of the Bohemians but somehow connected to it by the nature of the crime, vile and heinous

—Erwan, do you think Brittany will gain an advantage from the marriage?

—certainly, we are now allies of the French kingdom, and therefore under Charles's protection

—that's one way to see it, Kervalou, have you thought about the fact that, on the contrary, we are now doubly threatened by the English and the Burgundians?

—as subjects of the king we will have certain obligations toward him, among else, to respect his authority and submit to his laws, will we keep wandering the roads, robbing travelers?

—and murdering innocents?

—why not? I, Erwan Biemme, I ask the question, why not? our only duty is to ourselves

—you're mistaken, Erwan, we have a duty to the Duchess Anne, we are her vassals, don't forget that

—ah! but then why did she decide to ruin our wonderful enterprise?

—Anne is a woman, she seeks a strong man, arms to defend her territory from the covetousness of ambitious neighbors, by allying with the king of France she has brought him Brittany as a dowry, integrating it into a vaster and stronger unit, the king is obliged to ensure her defense, she has gambled on the future

—through her marriage we have become vassals of the French king, will he assure the privileges that the Dukes of Brittany had granted to us, the right to levy troops, to defend the duchy against internal and external enemies, in return for the right to ransom them?

—ha! ha! ha!

—who laughed?

—no one

—ha! ha! ha!

Erwan raised his head, his gaze fell upon the empty eyes of the mask hanging on the wall across from him, an old woman's bitter laugh taunted him

—witchcraft!

he unsheathes his sword, pale, frighteningly pale, harbinger of the Biemmes' proverbial rage, he approaches the sardonic laugh, an insolent throat clearing that bounces off the wall

—enough!

the laughter stopped at the command, the searing flash of death, a sound of iron and fire tore through the air

—may the Biemmes be cursed! may iron and fire shatter their destiny from generation to generation until they disappear into horror! curse you! curse you!

the splintered wall collapsed onto Erwan, bringing down the ceiling and one wing of the huge grand hall along with it, the dust hadn't yet settled before serfs rushing in from all corners of the estate began struggling to remove the mounds of stone and rubble, the jumble of beams and masonry, gigantic pieces of stone, rubble under which Lord Biemme was buried, journeying from the ruins of his castle toward other ruins in a quest for some peace, there was a kind of irony in the tranquil silence of the place, despite the feverishness with which the men were removing entire sections of wall, despite the jacks chomping at the beams, the effort of muscles to hoist baskets loaded with debris, the only sound was that of the great Venetian clock, miraculously preserved, which reminded the family of the passing hours, the passing of hope, in the morning they freed Erwan's corpse, the mask glowed red, reverberated with the first light of the day, encrusted its grimace on Biemme's visage, his hands desperately clutched the copper chin, a final attempt to wrest it from his face, Sonja! Sonja! the blond one, the Black one, obscure and mysterious forces pierce the daylight, my family refuses to make like angels and the curse condemns us to be no more than beasts in brass masks, beasts without faces, for centuries infernal powers have reigned in the dwellings where we believed we had put our remorse to rest, do the sorcerers of your tribe have the power to chase away the demons?

—my family is of the Muslim faith, my grandfather was a marabout, I remember him

—don't bend my ear with stories about your grandfather, I've done enough listening to and reading about those of my own family, each one more horrible than the next

—you're right as always, Sister Theresa, in a few minutes we'll be flying over the Atlantic, would you like me to leave you alone?

—you're already talking about leaving me alone?

—just for a moment so I can take care of the other passengers

—the shortest separations are the cruelest, in the space of a moment, life ends, time takes on a particular resonance, as if broken, a crack somewhere within us, the feeling of nothingness amidst two dreams of life, the moment before and the moment after, we've been freed of a present that will never again connect the past to the future and thus join together the long chain of duration

—you're making me feel guilty, Sonja!

—don't pay any mind to whatever I've said, it's not important, I'm not thinking about it anymore, go on, duty calls

she entered the cockpit, with my eyes I followed her elegant silhouette dancing on her high heels, she has abandoned me, minimizing the anguish I felt on losing her to the banality of a conversation between a hostess and passengers, go on, Sister Hyacinthe, Sonja Biemme will not weep in sorrow

—is something wrong, Mama?

she hesitated, her painted lips, quivering bloodstain in a face suddenly altered, murmuring with a voice unable to hide her emotion

—Sonja! you're entering the convent in September

—what?

—I've arranged everything with the abbess of the Sisters of Wisdom, she's bringing you on as a postulant, you'll continue your classical studies at the convent

—but, Mother

—there is no but, this decision has broken me, but it is necessary for your well-being, I had to force myself to do it and I kept it from you, I should have talked to you about it but I'd prefer to put off any explanation till later, in any case you'll only be a postulant, in two years, if you wish, you can become a novice

—and then, if it is the desire of the Lord and of his saintly mother, I'll take my vows

I slammed the door, ran to take refuge in my room, nervously gripping my old teddy bear between my arms, a present from Father when I was six years old, I never wanted to be away from it, he was my friend during tough times, kind, docile, always available and understanding, feeling him so close was a kind of protection from the outside world, he is my beloved, he alone is Love, the inert and immobile love of my thirteen years, scorned, they wasted away, collapsed into tears as so many lucid, exasperated manifestations of my indignation and my humiliation, my mother had tossed me aside like some outdated dress she was getting rid of by giving it to charity, without even asking me, I'd prefer to put off any explanation till later, my pride is wounded, pain, rage, and sorrow, a mutilation that casts me beyond the realm of childhood and opens an abyss beneath my feet

—Papa, take me far away from here, I want to go very far away, to get lost in the forest, to die devoured by lions, strangled by boas, eaten up by piranhas

I wept, turning, turning, spinning, my teddy bear in my arms, my love, my only love, slowly, very slowly, and then fast, faster, caught up faster and faster in a whirlwind that dragged me to the very depths of a dark hole

—hello! I came back, you see, I didn't spend long with the navigation crew, I was just getting instructions for the next part of the flight

—just long enough to hurt me, you also wounded my teddy bear

—what teddy bear? what are you talking about?

he looked at me from the heights of his pity, believing he was devotedly fulfilling his duty as a husband, when in fact he's watching over the corpse of his beloved, he doesn't know it, even if he did, he'd feel no grief, he's too impotent or too cowardly to suffer

—what's happened to us, Sonja?

—you're asking me!

—yes, you! who else would you want

—your shadow, Wolf

—I've already asked myself that question over and over, I haven't found an answer

—keep asking yourself

—I sought out the laughter that used to scamper over the docks in Brest and that rang out like kisses, the joy running along the cliffs in the Finistère, sliding along while clutching the rays of the sun as it set in the waters of the ocean, paved with rocks and algae

—you should have found them, that was your laughter, your joy, and your kisses, not mine

he lowers his head, taking on the posture of a humiliated man, hiding his shame, I wait for the slap, the blessed mark of his anger on my cheeks, savage sound of love awakened at last, he stops speaking, weeps, the silence and his tears reduce to nothing my desire to reconquer a man

—what did you want from me?

—nothing, absolutely nothing, Wolf

—what are you looking for, what do you want?

—some adventure in the ferocious fullness of life, you offered me the solitude of your weakness, the mediocrity of your tenderness, a routine love, when you think you're fulfilling me you're just imposing your smiles and caresses on me, like a slow, enfeebling happiness

I hate him, he stands there with his arms crossed, his head hanging down, prostrated, just waiting to go back to those filthy pickney squealing along his path, back to those lustful creatures giggling at the sound of his footsteps and on whose behalf he asks me to be more humane

—Sonja, where does this hatred of Blacks come from?

he was searching for an answer that would help him understand, did he remember the question I asked, in Brest or Quimper, my question, what are the Blacks like? and my response, I have never seen any, I was lying, the king forbids their entrance in the kingdom, I was lying, my grandfather had ignored the ban and imported a shipment to work his land, Breton stubbornness, a corsair's temerity, a need to defy royal authority? with a Biemme you never know (our strength: the certainty that the impossible is possible for us), caught with his vile herd near Quimper he was arrested, tried, subjected to the most brutal torture, condemned by order of the king to have his head chopped off in the public square, when he appeared, pale, ragged, his beard shaggy, his unsteady walk betraying the effects of the torture, the disdainful silence of the idle onlookers darkened the day, there was a disturbance in their ranks, someone cut through the crowd, surprised the king's archers on watch and spit in my grandfather's face, can you imagine, in the face of a Biemme

—under other circumstances, you'd have hidden in your mother's belly at the mere thought of committing such an affront

there was a brouhaha, cries of hatred held back for four centuries assailed my grandmother who, against the advice of her sons, had insisted on helping her husband, she knew what she was doing, avoiding the worst, the great-uncles having decided to try rescuing their brother by force, which would have been the ruin of the Biemmes, nowhere in the kingdom would they have been able to escape the persecution and vengeance of the king, who would have ordered their castle razed to the ground

—to death, Biemme! to death! to death!

Grandfather laid his head on the block, the executioner raised his arms, ha! ha! ha! a bronze mask blew its laugh into my grandmother's face, the ax fell, my ancestor lowered his sails, lay down to die, Biemme's head flew through the air, rolled to her, smiled at her, Grandmother smiled back, some bastard painter tried to capture the tragic moment of their twinned eternal smile, but his clumsy brush turned it into a mirrored grimace that mars the noble beauty of their faces, setting the stain and leaving us the shame, a Valembrun Lebrun treated like some common thief thanks to a band of Blacks

—they weren't responsible, you should curse the rigor of royal justice and your grandfather's smuggler spirit

you trade illegally with England, you're also a smuggler and probably a slave trader, and you insult my family? traitor, I see you on the docks at Cap-Français, we had barely disembarked, the sun like a plaything in my head, a plaything made of fire, the discomfort of the climate, an excessive heat, me on the verge of fainting, you, your eyes filled with wonder on returning to the vulgar and lascivious gait of those carnival Negresses, grotesque in their cotton dresses, it wasn't the same kind of wonder that had read the changing weather to me night and day in the cabin of the *Saint-Aignan*, that one had been light and joyous, the other shady, sensually bestial, I was confused, humiliated, all I had to do was step foot on the soil of Saint-Domingue to begin hating this land that replaced the love in your gaze with lust, hating these men and women to the point of madness, of wanting to destroy their bodies, I hated you because you revealed your true self, thus justifying my decision

—she said those words, ferocious fullness of life?

—do you understand now, Cécile, that what exalts her is not life but destruction?

—she knows you better than I thought, you build but only because you need to destroy yourself, she's decided to help you achieve that, her cruelty is just a sublimated form of generosity, sublimated or perverse

—you're confusing me, I'm not trying to destroy myself, I'm chasing after what I used to be, to inhabit my memory, to inhabit the memory of my childhood

—to go back to a universe where all conflicts can be symbolically abolished, where you can resolve your own contradictions, but how can you return to who you were without destroying who you are?

—I was a happy child

—the world around you was plunged in misery

—I learned that when I began to suffer

—you began to suffer when you learned it, isn't that what you meant to say?

—perhaps! perhaps!

—so you're wrong and you're lying to yourself, that isn't the best way to resolve your interior conflicts, Wolf, you've always known, don't be hypocritical

—Cécile, I forbid you

—in the name of what? as a child you played with Salomon in the woods, you chased him all the way into his hut, the games of hide-and-seek, but did he ever drag his bare feet into your little boy's bedroom?

—I never asked myself that question

—because it would have shamed and corrupted that vision of innocence in which you have cloaked yourself while seeking a haven, as you say, in your childhood memories

—Cécile, I'm lost, give me a chance to save myself

—I'd have resolved your crisis of conscience, but I can't do that, and even if I could I wouldn't want to

—why?

—you haven't suffered yet

—I refuse to suffer

—I don't want to keep you from suffering, the experience of great suffering will be good for you because I am telling you and probably someone will repeat it to you again someday: no one knows themselves until they have suffered

—that's pretty, is it a line of poetry? by whom?

—how would I know? I won't live long enough to get a chance to learn who the author is

—but then how can you know that someone will write it?

—experience, Wolf, you forget who I am, a woman of pleasure, and thus a sister of misfortune

I had wanted your weakness, I found what was most primitive in it, most bestial, most shameful, those cries of joy greeting your return, you descended from the carriage you'd rented in Jérémie, the hysterical clan of women surrounding you, their mumbo jumbo, that mix of infantile babble and waves of sensuality, from which I recall bonjou mèt, mèt retoune nou kontan, their pidgin assailed me, repelled me, shut me out before they even knew me, when I appeared, silence, incredulity in their eyes, but more than the silence, there was your embarrassment and your reluctance to reach out your hand and help me down

—ahem! this is my wife

like a curious animal you'd show to idle onlookers coming to discover a circus troupe, what's happened to us, you ask? you want me to forgive you this affront, me, Sonja Biemme de Valembrun Lebrun, whose grandfather was subjected to the most despicable dishonor thanks to a pack of stinking monkeys, by order of his majesty King Louis, fourteenth of his name, condemning the Viscount Yann Biemme de Valembrun Lebrun to have his hands chopped off at the wrist

—you said it was the head!

—and, what does that matter!

without uttering a word, in defiance, he held out the stumps to the crowd in response to their insults and jeering, Biemme the Negro, a vile nickname, that epithet remained affixed to our name, two generations later, the students at the Jesuit school and the Daughters of Mary pension excluded the young Biemmes

—it's just disgraceful having these Negroes sitting at the same desks as us, didn't the king forbid them from disembarking in France?

we had become Negroes, the malice, the nastiness, the ferocity, their envy, if not to say their hatred, left us subject to absolute disdain, the contagious misfortune of Black blood had altered our Gallic blue blood, leaving wounds in our self-esteem that continue to bleed

—we don't want Negroes in the kingdom

—out with the Negroes!

—at first I was scared, in Marseille, in Paris, in Ivry, cries of towel-head, wog, rat, and who knows what else rang out, the French had readily forgotten that Blacks and Arabs perished on the front lines in Europe, then in Indochina, and in Algeria for a cause that certainly wasn't towel-headed, when I understood that, I resisted and I fought back

—my dear Sonja! how you must have suffered

—Sister Theresa, I am not your poor Sonja and I'll gladly do without your pity, what's more, I spit on it

—hey now, don't be upset, I didn't mean to offend you

words that the language of thugs and soldiers hadn't yet invented assailed Garic Biemme, our great-cousin, one day, thrashed him, left him for dead in an alley where some passersby found him with a broken leg, irreversible cranial trauma, he was slow-witted for the rest of his life, yet another defect that the Biemmes dragged from one corner to another of Brittany, the family idiot, all the Biemmes became thickheaded Negroes on the whim of fools, anyway, that's redundant, what Negro isn't thickheaded? when applied to us it wasn't a grammatical kindness it was

—these are things that leave a mark, Sonja! I learned to hate the Negroes in the library at the family chateau, which had been restored at the beginning of the nineteenth century by Baron von Schpeerbach, who was married to my ancestor

—the one in the medallion?

—yes, Sonja Biemme de Valembrun Lebrun, a wealthy planter in Saint-Domingue, much later, while at the convent, I learned about their exactions upon nuns in Katanga, sacrilege and profanation, I'm fully convinced that they're monsters, the rubbish of humanity

—in that case, Sister, why are you going on a mission to Haiti, land of the Blacks?

—I am taking up a challenge, we have an act of vengeance to accomplish there

—you speak of vengeance, Sister Theresa?

—does that surprise you?

—yes! I expected words of charity and forgiveness

—the path of charity does not always trace a straight line and well-conceived charity begins with oneself, I fear you haven't heard me at all, in Haiti I'm seeking the path to my own salvation, the revenge of the Biemmes against destiny

a condemnation, the foolish Negroes, the most foolish among them, Erwan—he was fortunate not to realize it—lay in the oak coffin lined with lead, his face masked with copper had corroded the brightness of the metal, all passion extinguished, his eyes fixed beyond the chapel ceiling, at the moment of absolution the dark arches lit up with green light in which drops of blood were suspended, a curse! a curse! and the cursed land remembers that Erwan's cursed soul escaped from his eyes, blazing from their enduring propensity for cruelty, they were infinity's unfathomable gaze

—why are you constantly looking at the sky?

—it will rain at dawn, it is the season of the *dékou*, I'm going home

—stay just a few more minutes, there's always time to return to hell

—hell is within me, Cécile, it's everywhere I go

—come now, Wolf! stop worrying pointlessly, stop burdening yourself with the suffering of others, living with your own misery is enough

—I don't burden myself with the suffering of others, all suffering is mine, I can't escape it, I so wish the earth would open up and swallow me

—come here

she had opened her arms, I was unfamiliar with this gesture of offering, with its whiff of repressed maternal feelings, Cécile sees in me the son that, ever since her miscarriage, she no longer awaits, in pampering the lover she in fact cradles my inner child, my full-grown child, the fantasies of the night bring our two solitudes together and, believing ourselves lost in love, we invented games in which, shattered, we drowned our dreams of the impossible

—Cécile, you are a magical being

—how so?

—every time I leave, I feel like I'm leaving a little piece of myself with you

—that's possible, I survive on crumbs of love

—you don't understand, your sensibility speaks to my own, unveils it, things become clearer, I often leave with certainties, you do me good because they prevent me from destroying myself

—don't pay me compliments or else I'll blush, it makes me look ugly, do you have any news from Klaus?

—not since the last time

—Saintmilia, hello

she's there, sitting in the same place, ruminating over a now age-less despair, she didn't stretch out her arm, she didn't even look at me, her eyes were quiet, locked inside an infinite dimension, unaware of the wild permanence of light, the blinding fears that carry sight beyond the ravine and its flooding, the overflow that coos in the pigeons' throats at the edge of the pond, the vastness of the sea that endlessly begins anew on the beach

—talk, say something, I cannot bear your silence any longer, have I lost your love?

I said the word I shouldn't have, I wanted to fix things, attempting a light kiss on your forehead, your eyes regained their fierce, icy brightness, I sensed more so than I actually saw their irritation and their rage, fate lay between us, removing any power I had over your life, projecting me far from you, I try to uncover some spark of interest in your gaze, some simple possibility laying out new projects for existence, the promise of some appeal, of a new seduction, love couldn't possibly have left us so senselessly, a detachment, an indifference that sends each of us back to a permanent solitude

—why this hostility toward me? how can your pride be so foolish and not see that solitude makes us vulnerable, in the face of the perils threatening us only love can save us, together and united in the face of misfortune?

the words had slipped right by her, pathetically useless, I am nothing, she has left, she has gone far away from me, far from any solidarity that might have connected us through work—there's so much to do on the plantation—from taking hold of the reins of our destiny, so fragile and pathetic in the light of history and its fatality, between us and within us there is nothing but a realm of shadows—you refuse to be my light—a devastated realm

—I need you, Sonja!

the effort it takes to lie is painful, I don't need her if I want to survive, ah! to escape, to flee, to refuse my own dispossession in the abdication of my principles, I realize angrily that by forcing me to approve of some of her decisions she had progressively trapped me in the ways of submission, stripping me of what, up until now, had given my life some meaning, the taste for authority, self-confidence, a vision of my future, now all of that is nothing but a joke and a shipwreck at the foot of a bed where, alone in our twin silence, we watch over the end of a dream, the prefiguration of our own death

—we have given birth to a barbarous world, sooner or later we'll have to pay, the day when God's punishment rains down

—Wolf! please don't judge our world through some kind of pastoral conscience, you spend all day feeling guilty, you didn't invent slavery, no!

—I help perpetuate it and that's worse than having invented it, in accordance with the colonial laws I've just cut off the right foot of a maroon that the slave patrol caught and brought back to me, my conscience forbade me from doing it but this world order forced me to

—and you feel guilty for having accepted law and order?

—no! I feel guilty for having told myself: Wolf, if you don't do this, soon the other slaves, seeing this bad example and sure of impunity, will maroon too, and you'll be ruined

—there's no doubt about it, so what's the problem?

—having sacrificed my conscience and the principles of Christian charity to my own interests, it isn't cowardliness, it's selfishness

—do you know of another way to succeed? Wolf! you aren't made for this world

after the incident at the ball, Sonja had cloistered herself in her room in the southern wing of the house, facing the bay, she had decided to construct two parts of the building in an L shape, opening onto a pool of water lilies, from the galleries there was a view down over the Petit-Fort creek and, beyond that, the horizon stretched from Point Digo to Cap Loko, from her window Sonja watched the sun setting behind the hills or into the ocean, depending on the time of year, a spectacle she never tired of

—Wolf! have you ever asked yourself what would happen if one day the sun stopped traveling from the east?

—what would be the point of knowing that? it will lead us nowhere

—tell me, Monsieur Schpeerbach, is that a way of avoiding answering or a means of not asking the question?

—both, I don't want to burden myself with any worries beyond the salvation of my soul

—do you believe in God?

—of course! what's the connection?

—is God a question or an answer?

—an answer, to everything

—on the contrary, Wolf! he is at the origin of all questions, in fact, he's The Question and

—in my country

—which one?

—in Switzerland we burn people for less than that, Miguel Servet knows a thing or two about that, the Swiss, too, have learned not to ask metaphysical questions

—we're not in Switzerland and you're not Calvin

a moment of silence and, without any transition, a foolish question, so candid, so sharply candid I was frightened

—how would you feel, being burned alive?

she pushes the window, opening her room and her new life to a blast of hot air, she looks over the shimmering waters of the bay, brooding over the emptiness left within her by the absence of her companions in revelry, scared that through them she would find herself face to face with her shame, her body continues its slow march toward the noble wound that will bring her back to the fullness of love and that, through torment, will make her into a new being, waiting for that day, hoping for deliverance and for a return to the life she once loved paradoxically made her feel more bitter, the more days that pass the more she fears having to face her memories, the smiles of false understanding from her friends, increasingly irritable, she refuses to see me, to talk to me, she chases me out of the house, I take refuge in an out-of-the-way cabin under the mapou tree overlooking the Coin de L'Anse ravine, from there I could hear and measure Sonja's bursts of rage whenever she reprimanded the servants, one night a scream ripped through the calm and quiet of the plantation at the hour when all were headed to sleep, I ran, Tanaké, M'Bo's little girl, was rolling on the ground, her clothes in indescribable disarray

—what's happening?

she turned her face toward me, her burned mouth was smoking, the nauseating smell of grilled flesh, that suffering emanating from her eyes, the stifling sense of horror, the unbearable logic of madness

—again, Sonja! give that to me

calmly her gaze moved from my indignation to the brand she was holding, getting ready to burn Tanaké's face with it, there was still that strange, icy glimmer in her eyes

—I ordered her to kiss my feet, she hesitated and I punished her

—I'm not asking for explanations, give me the brand

she made as if to hand it to me, then changed her mind, threw it angrily into the nearby pond, defiantly spat on Tanaké, looked me up and down (I thought for a moment she was also going to spit on me) and, disdainfully, turned on her heel and went into her room

—I punished her

what kind of society are we living in that authorizes the right to exercise such barbarism? she had punished her, that was her right, but nevertheless something inside me was offended, objected to the ease of the punishment and its obvious disproportion to the offense, had there even been an offense? she hesitated, Sonja, wasn't the offense your demanding that Tanaké kiss your feet? does the code regulating our rights and duties not proscribe such promiscuous relationships beyond those necessary for labor? does this demand not translate an unspoken need for intimacy into a mania for authority and a desire to affirm yourself by humiliating another? a kiss is a kiss, be it on the forehead, on the mouth, or on the feet, it remains an act of familiarity, of recognition between people of the same family, of the same category, of the same species

—on the foot, it is an act of submission and allegiance

—explain that to me, Cécile

—the explanation is within you, Wolf

—how so?

—I don't know myself, it must reside somewhere between your wife's need for love and your powerlessness to respond to this need

—she always pushes me away

—she's waiting for something other than tenderness

—I can't possibly take my wife by force

if I had raped Tanaké (I'll surely do it one day in the name of the right of the first night) I'd have felt no remorse, but that my wife, without the slightest regret, had discovered the resources and reflexes of our cruel practices in Saint-Domingue made me feel as much despair as fear, a calamity, this would neither be my first scare nor my last moment of despair, Sonja had an inexhaustible capacity to renew the rites of horror, her sadism (apparently that is the new word made fashionable by a certain Marquis de Sade as a way of naming a certain disposition, pleasure taken in making and watching others suffer) surpassed anything our imagination had already come up with in matters of ritual cruelty

—how can you do this, Sonja?

—how dare you? Monsieur Schpeerbach, I recall having forbidden you to enter my room

—I heard screaming

—would you have worried if you had heard your horse neigh?

—I would have asked the groom to check

—perfect! send your groom to go get the Negress and bring her to the women's quarters, now leave!

the door slammed violently in the face of my shame, something final, the certainty that I was entering the age of terror and that the end was near

—I did not walk in the righteous path of the Lord

—you came here to tell me that?

—I need to talk to someone, Cécile

—go find a priest

—you know perfectly well that we converted out of self-interest, not conviction, in the French kingdom, after the revocation of the Edict of Nantes, my family chose Catholicism to save their property

—come into my arms and forget your emotional crises

—ah! Cécile, I'm too weak for the world I live in

—stop thinking about it

I woke up at dawn still engrossed in my own moodiness, it had rained during the night, the slope was slippery and I had to hold fast to the reins to prevent the horse from panicking, the drums anxiously disturbed the silence, some news was circulating, taken up from one drum to the next with a certain jubilation, the taut leather exalting with a different kind of sound, it was no longer sadness or lamentations of resignation, but a sort of power in its brutal, savage, bloody explosion

—Wolf! do you hear that?

—yes, Cécile! it's different from what we've heard before

—I'm returning to Port-au-Prince

—I had a feeling, has Monsieur Bauduy gotten some orders?

—yes, I'm relieved to be leaving, since Maïté's death I have been scared

—everyone has their fears, Cécile, but why worry, you've always been good to your Negroes?

—you too, but is that enough?

—you're the one asking that question?

—you've asked it so many times that you've ended up making me doubt

—it isn't enough to be good to the Negroes, you have to see them as human beings, I fear that now it's too late, which reminds me, does Bauduy know the reasons for his new posting?

—yes and he's not happy about it, Biassou and Jean-François and their troops have switched over to the side of the Spanish

—a catastrophe! Spain is forming alliances with the Negroes? it's the end, Cécile, it's the end, the colony is lost

—and the English?

—they will also forge alliances with the slaves in order to crush France in the Americas, after which, they'll turn against the Negroes to crush them in turn

—what's to be done?

—we must fight on all fronts, I'll certainly see you again in Port-au-Prince

—on what occasion?

—I'm taking back my command of the Swiss Regiment

—finally a cause worthy of you

the drums accompanied the horse's exhausted steps, spreading the news to the Negroes and calling on them to rally around the Spanish flag, as soon as I returned to the plantation I sent a message to the government to ask for my reintegration, Alonzo and Salomon will have to redouble their vigilance, to prevent any unrest and to keep my Negroes from fleeing, if it weren't for Sonja I would leave unworried, the news is serious but less alarming than what we're hearing from France, the Revolution is triumphing, the king and queen arrested at Varennes, locked up in the Temple and later decapitated, their heads tossed aside in defiance of all Europe, the rights of man acknowledged and proclaimed, Danton standing tall, towering like an exterminating angel set on destroying the future: better the colonies perish than a principle! I condemn Sonja's excesses and the whole of the colonial system in the name of principles, and now principles are triumphing, but I fear that the outburst of passions will lead us to the edge of the abyss, I always fear violence, especially if it is the violence of the masses through which history is made, at the price of how many broken lives! of how many annihilated hopes! curiously, prey to all kinds of anxieties, I wanted to hold on to hope, the drums stopped, the day rose serene, from the heights of the hill at Gros-Caye I take in a vast panorama all at once, from Bambou to the Lonmon plateau, to the south, the Castaches hills, extending all the way to La Hotte, mark the edge of the horizon, just before me, the white-capped waves of the sea rise in the east wind, between that and the mountains, there is the plain of Les Abricots where the smoke rises from the sugar works, the first fourth of sugar will be ready soon, a light fog floats over the valley, it's so reassuring, there was such an atmosphere of peace and serenity that for an instant I thought life had stopped, we are at the very origins of the world

—in the beginning, Sister Theresa, there is water, the peaceful harmony of the ocean defies time, dilutes space, and creates a coherent whole, we are a part of that whole
—is that what Islam teaches?
—before the arrival of the Prophet, the griots already knew about the relationship between humans and the universe, between us and nature, this knowledge is true
—it survived neither the arrival of history nor the spread of Islam
—that's not true, Sister Theresa, it survived and only Hegel in his stupidity could believe that prior to the colonial era Black Africa was shrouded in the black color of night
—you surprise me, Sonja, you know Hegel?
—with all due respect and whether Heidegger likes it or not, philosophy is not a privilege of the white world
—it gets better and better
she cast a sidelong glance at my amused smile, an airline hostess philosophizing midflight, citing Hegel and Heidegger with the same ease that she might speak about hunting antelope, she lit a cigarette, closed her eyes, inhaled, a voluptuously fragile gesture that made a swell of emotion rise up within me, we moved our heads closer together, in my mouth the velvety taste of Rothmans, which was also the taste of love, she pushed aside my tortured hand already brushing against her flesh, in the beginning there is water, the water was within me, fresh and anxious to know Sonja, it flowed, torrents of gold and azure in the luminous splendor of the day

I decided to turn off toward the plain and inspect the Kòbô bayou, I had just crossed over the river when a drumbeat announced a set of strange chords, what's going on? the Negroes don't play the drums during the day, out of a superstitious fear that their soul will crystallize in the azure and become a reflection, nothing but a reflection, it only blossoms at night, ready to be transfigured, to complete all its replenishing travels, so what is it? I spurred my horse to a gallop in the Nan-Jouissant plain, pushing on up to the hillock at Chatelin, from there my eyes fell upon a group of Negroes gathered around an almond tree at the entrance to the ravine separating the Kòbô bayou from Fondlin, what were they plotting at this hour? they should have been at work in the sugar mill, or perhaps not, this Friday the overseer should have brought them to catechism at Nan-Poste

—to what end, Wolf? those people have no soul

—because you yourself, Clérié, no longer have one

—inevitably, my dear man, a buccaneer who doubles as a slave trader believes neither in God nor the devil, threatened from all sides by English or Spanish grapeshot, I seek my salvation either in battle or in flight, not in an act of contrition

—the day when a cannonball shatters your head

—I won't have the time to think about God or pray to him

—but you'll have to

—in the meantime, I couldn't care less

—Father Aloïus thinks the Negroes are men like us

—he is either naive or dangerously subversive, we know it, affiliated with the Society of the Friends of the Blacks he constantly demands more humane treatment for the Negroes

—he's right, don't you have your Club Massiac over in Paris lobbying for your interests?

—in the name of God

—don't joke, Father Aloïus is also protecting his interests, in the name of common sense, the better you treat your slaves, the more they work

—allow me to laugh, my dear Schpeerbach, your slaves don't seem like a great example

—I have learned not to demand too much of them, I let them work at their own rhythm, the results aren't that disappointing

—that's not what Madame thinks

—I know, but can you deny that until very recently the number of runaways, suicides, and self-mutilations was lower on my plantation than it was on many others?

—the golden age, huh!

—you can mock me, to prove it, I can cite Bréda as an example, he treats his Negroes kindly, he even taught one of them to read and write, Fatras-Bâton, who has become his right-hand man, manages his stud farm, trains his horses with such perfection that the neighboring planters call him the centaur of the savanna

—what fervor and vivacity! a magnificent argument but you won't convince me

—because you're a slave trader counting on the survival of the system, you can't live without the enslavement of the Blacks

let us take a closer look at this, I'll demand an explanation from Father Aloïus, he reprimands me if I don't send my Negroes to the catechism, but when I release them he allows them to just disappear into the bush, and if they decide to maroon permanently will God pay me back? I tumble quickly down the slope, to surprise them, identify them, they heard me coming, they didn't run away, on the contrary! they lift their arms and heads up toward the almond tree, their eyelids shut, faces transfigured by the simmering ecstasy, eerie, chants and lamentations, prayers and sobs, music and incantation, I, too, raise my head, subjugated, bewitched, atop the almond tree the Negress Toukouma, pregnant, likely the work of the overseer, twirls in the morning light, dancing with ease as if in the plantation courtyard, jumping from one branch to another, writhing, exalting, stamping her feet, possessed, might she be sunstruck? she looks down, sees me, immediately stops her farandole, ceases her movements, runs out onto the most fragile branch, a sudden panic, to my surprise I shout no! no! that Negress costs me a hundred and fifty guineas in upkeep per year, ah! Cécile, always these references to money, you once joked that I have a gold coin where my heart should be, could you be right? if it's a boy the child will start working in four years, we need hands, no! don't take another step, stay where you are, that's an order! you monkeys, go up and get her, help her come down, they continue with their nonsense, still in ecstasy, subject to the senseless fascination with death as deliverance, they'll be the death of me, these apes, she moves forward, her foot weighing on my conscience, on the gold louis I'll lose in a poker game where the Negroes' superstition rubs off on the good cards, ignoring my shouting stop you fool! she keeps moving forward, my life cracks, my life shatters with a crash that bursts my eardrums, her hands reach out as if to grab hold of the void, she whirls around in the autumn wind, I close my eyes, surrounded by the sound of dry, crumpled leaves, punctuated suddenly with a salvo of thunder, the drums let loose all around me, and the shouts and the cheers and the hurrahs, the sun a demented clamor in my head, Otovi agate la misèchita Agoué batala deliverans, I open my eyes upon a spectacle of horror! no! not possible, I burst into nervous laughter, indecent, hysterical, Toukouma is carrying her belly like a barrel of joy, stamping the ground with her bare feet, her eyes bloodshot, ugly, fierce, shoulders slack, disjointed, detached from her head, which rolls around, forward, backward, forward again, nostrils quivering and, louder, more guttural, more brutal than all the other excessively open mouths, Agoué batala délivrans

—Cécile, those Blacks are solid, yes! she'd fallen from a height of almost forty yards, a pregnant woman, imagine that, and she was alive
—that surprises you? not me, with the Blacks, life no longer makes sense, it has never made sense, how did the others react?
—Toukouma directed them to leave, imperiously, they passed before me, their eyes expressionless, heads high, they moved stiffly, as if controlled by an external will, some faces seemed familiar to me, guess who I saw? now don't keel over from the shock, Maïté
—Maïté!
—yes, in the flesh
—that's worrying! it seems to confirm a vision I had ten or so days ago, it all makes sense now, it was neither a vision nor a hallucination nor a dream, I was napping in my hammock between the soapberry trees when I heard someone say Mistress! Mistress! I opened my eyes, I saw Maïté, she was turning the corner of the plantation, Maïté! she stopped, smiled at me, a hint of menace in her voice, and shouted: beware! beware! I rubbed my eyes, realizing and proving to myself that I was truly awake, I wanted to call for help, but no sound came out of my throat, paralyzed by fear, I was speechless
—I called out to Maïté, she didn't hear me or pretended not to, I moved toward her, with the firm intention of restraining her, was I being deceived by some extraordinary resemblance or was this an effect of their extraordinary magic? I wanted to grab her arm, a shock to my chest, stars in my head, the prodigious light of the sun burned my eyes

—mèt, you reckless, Toukouma's band is a band of zonbi, contact with them not good, I'm going to prepare a bath for you

—Saintmilia, do you believe these stories?

—we don't talk about them, Master, they bring bad luck, I'll run and pick some artemisia and guava leaves to purify the water, take off your clothes, they've been infused with bad spirits, give them to me, I'll burn them, if you keep them on any longer they'll start playing with your mind, their miasmas are deadly

—I just can't believe all these stories, if there were a zonbi in the plane, Sonja, how would I recognize it?

—Saintmilia, you're wasting your time, none of what you are telling me is serious

—it's very serious, Master

—she forced her medicine on me, I found myself in a bath, the water tinted with leaves, apparently I fell asleep in there, a ruse on the part of bad spirits trying to avoid leaving, Saintmilia whipped me with a little branch from a lemon tree, they finally left while muttering threats

—you'd notice its steady gaze, robotic movement, sleepwalker's manner

—is it true it can resist bullets?

—of course! if it's already dead then who can kill the life within it?

—I'm trembling, and if one crosses my path?

—it'll pass by without seeing you, Sister Theresa, unless it was sent for you

—so they can be conditioned, programmed?

—you were almost zombified, Wolf, if Saintmilia's medicine hadn't worked, you never would have woken from your slumber

—is this the first time they've attacked a white person, Cécile?

—no, remember how they found Father Kor at Moron a few days after his death, he was in a complete daze, his Black housekeeper suggested they give him salt to eat, he recovered a bit of his mind and recounted how he had been following along with every detail of his funeral, but it was like he was paralyzed

—I find the Blacks' plotting disconcerting, they're planning something, but what?

—have you finished your shift?

—the first one? yes, I have an hour to rest, I'm going to go join the flight crew

—don't leave me alone, there might be a zonbi in the plane

the water swishes, shimmers, the water ripples, howls, troubled water, beyond the window and for several days the overflowing presence of water, a passive witness to Sonja's intimacy with the temptation of death, presence of the inexhaustible patience of life that persisted in holding her back, though drawn closer by the ordeal, we were absent from one another, I no longer recognized those eyes that made the brightness of the chandeliers at the naval ball seem dim and there was still no answer to my question, how and why had we gotten here? I no longer chase after her youth as it scrambles across the ramparts, tripping from one stepping-stone to another, hesitating at the edge of the machicolation, she turns, deliciously provocative

—one more step, Colonel, and I'll throw myself into the void rather than be soiled by your embrace

she is kidding, of course, but her voice vibrates with such determination that I stop, vaguely worried, has she really decided to sever me from such unexpected and surprising happiness?

—stop, my beautiful lady, I beg you not to do anything (my joy, already, sounded a bit broken)

—on the condition, Monsieur, that you stop pursuing me with your assiduous attention

—I promise, my lady

—on your honor?

—soldier's honor

—close your eyes

laughter cascades along the steps leading to the moat, hey there! I don't have the heart to play with you anymore, meet me down below, I don't have the heart to kid around, come on, come down, don't make that face

—if you had stepped any closer I would have thrown myself into the void, do you doubt it?

for a brief instant the dazzle of the fall, as if in slow motion, Sonja twirls, her hair loosened, a final trail of splendor, the muslin sails, a whirlwind of color, diaphanous, the horrible sound of the body slamming into the ground, and the superimposed sound of the howling sea as it climbs the walls of the defensive towers

—I am sure that at that very instant you would have jumped

—what would I have proven?

—that you don't love me

—fool! on the contrary! I love you enough to hope that you would have jumped after me, joining me in death, dying together, reinventing love for the time of a fall, Héloïse and Abelard admired by the crowds, creating for ourselves a destiny beyond history, beyond the centuries

that crystal laugh has already gone off toward the heights of madness, what does Sonja want? to test me? to test my brand-new love? was it necessary to threaten to destroy us, to provoke a tension between us that builds, that grows with the absurdity of whatever intentions or challenges, that becomes absorbed into this fear that holds me captive and leaves me defenseless in the face of her caprices (I thought of them as such), against the infinite reserve of cruelty that pushes her to thoughtlessly torture those she loves

—the journey is long, Wolf

—ten days more, if the trade winds keep up, and we'll be there

—I'm bored to death

—you surprise me, I thought you had imagined making this journey into a honeymoon, an incredible celebration of love

—there would have to be two of us

—but there are two of us!

—you think so? Wolf, I am alone, absolutely alone, it's not enough to wake me each morning by telling me: the dawn is the color of your eyes, for love to be reawakened, or to listen to the captain's insipid conversation with my head resting on your shoulder, to be entertained

—but Sonja, we were limited by

—of course, there was the matter of space, but it was also a matter of feelings, yours are tiresome, do you know how I've been passing my time to protect myself from their tediousness?

— . . .

—I imagined I was stabbing a sword into your heart, but instead of blood a kind of resin poured out, I am stuck because of you, Wolf the sea is nothing but tears, the wind keeps up at six knots, tears of mourning a love, I wonder who made the dawn weep in Sonja's eyes that morning, she opens the porthole, the nakedness of the sky and the ocean floods into the cabin, envelops her body, she locks herself up in her tears, her smooth skin becomes transparent, I can't make out the color of her blood, she swims, dives, resurfaces, the sky now drowns within her, completely, in a few moments she'll drift toward the thin ray of sunlight peeking between the door and the frame, to sunbathe, she'll say, her way of seizing, of capturing in the reflections of light, the tiny bits of the European sun that never cease to nourish her fantasies, her frustrations, her fears of being devoured by the great uncertainty of the islands, hotter, more searing, brighter, naughtier—does it not spend its time cursing in our minds—than all the suns of Europe combined, I loved her tears

—Wolf, forgive me, I'm being dreadful, I feel like I'm suffocating in this cabin, the open sea calls to me but the water imprisons me, forgive me, you are so good and patient

I was drinking my tears, drinking the ocean, a taste of the sky, a taste of bile, love like a wound to my pride, did I forgive her? I wouldn't have known, in the last days of the voyage I wore a mask of indifference that was the expression of my hopelessness, here I thought I was passionate but my feelings were tiresome, I had gotten in deeper than what my body could handle, too much attentiveness, tenderness, understanding, her endless caprices, her puerile jokes, enjoyment at being the complacent husband of the little baroness, as the passengers put it

—Wolf, find me a seagull

—I would be happy to offer you one but where will I find it?

—look, a few cables' lengths behind me there's a flock of seagulls following us

—I see the birds, but how do you know they are seagulls from this distance?

—because I'm telling you they are, ask the captain to stop the *Saint-Aignan*, they'll catch up to us and you can capture the prettiest one

the captain's laughing face, big brown hands slapping my shoulders, his drunk, mocking voice and the astonishment of the ship's officers wondering what enchantment had driven me mad, I was embarrassed, ashamed, destroyed, an object of derision in the eyes of these men who had previously greeted me with respect, greetings, Colonel von Schpeerbach, and who now clearly considered me a fool manipulated by a woman who was really still a child

—ah! Colonel, it's not a seagull you should offer to your wife, so young and so pretty, she wants the impossible, try to give it to her, the impossible has a name here on board, in the solitude of the cabin

—Wolf! you were stupid to let yourself be so readily impressed by the captain's potbelly and the red faces of those brutish officers, truly, I don't recognize you

she furrowed her brow, but her anger blunted itself in an expression of stubbornness, dissipated quickly, I was looking at myself in the cabin's mirror, there was such turmoil in my eyes that I felt an almost childish joy in turning away, to no longer have to contemplate my degradation, much later, recalling this memory, I will tell myself, Wolf, that's the day you started to lose faith in yourself

—look, Sister Theresa, another flock of seagulls?

—my other story, renewed

—the pilot will probably swerve a bit further to the left to avoid them

—the past became familiar, like an image to be captured

—sucked into the jet engines, they often cause accidents

—to transfigure one's reflection, the incredible made magnificent

—fortunately . . .

—don't let your madness revive me, Sister Hyacinthe, we are false lovers

—in our days

—melancholia is neither a pretext nor a refuge for me

—after the acci . . .

—the extravagant sickness of happiness

—dents of the first Comets

—my father blown apart, in full flight, because of these creatures? I don't believe you, Sonja

—the investigation confirmed it, seagulls had obstructed the airflow into the jet engines, provoking

—headed off toward other shores, other joys, aspiring to happiness in an indefinable relationship with death, everything's changed, what do I have left to lose?

she held out her fist toward a silhouette leaning out the window and that looked at her without surprise, not at all astonished to see her again, just as she did every morning, prostrated in the corner of a doorway, again tracing that gesture of hope without understanding that her skinny arm bears the hopelessness of her entire life, a silhouette carved out by the oblique light of the morning, I am called to that other existence I know of through my mother's sobs, returning to a mangled, tortured story, an existence made my own through Saintmilia's tenacious hostility, a link to the outraged image, to the damned figure who refuses to die in her memory, rooted in what remains her history, our history is unfinished, she repeats, prolonging the echo of a scream that never changes over time, emotional energy dangerously contaminated by madness, she is no longer life, she is no more than a ghost awaiting a vengeance that will finally bring her some peace, bring her to the truth of her madness, that will lead her, miraculous flight through time, to her final dwelling, that mythic Africa haunting her mambo nights, she rises, still brandishing her fist, a club, a shield, a cannonball, threatening me, me, in an almost sensual symbol of youth, me, truest representation of death, attentive to what will, to what must happen, already filtered through the evil eye of hate, certain of its strength and its powers but, determined to resist, I have freed myself from the truth, there will be neither sacrifice nor atonement, anyway how could I atone, the crime was wickedness, I'm not to blame, with a single word she eliminates all responsibility and all guilt, doubtful of her own actions, despite everything, befouled by irrational bursts of anger, slightly remorseful at having let herself be so trapped by the deranged eyes of a madwoman, she sees herself as both guilty and innocent, divided, tugged at, torn apart, above all uncertain, insistent on seeing herself in the image of another self, destroyed by history but reassembled through all these stories told by Saintmilia's madness and the cold wisdom of an ancestor made to feel guilty
—sorry
—Sister Theresa, you have condemned us to wretchedness
—did I desire your misery?

—it was born from the disaster of my race

—allow me to be your friend

—to help me deny my suffering?

—I don't know your suffering, it has fled my century

—in that case, what am I supposed to do with your regrets? the suffering of my race belongs to all centuries

—well then stop nourishing the misunderstandings between us, Saintmilia

—another one of your inventions designed to ridicule me, Sister Theresa

here we are standing face to face in the torpor of the morning, the silence quickening our heartbeats, linked anxiety, the same exaltation, the same decision, to fight once and for all and be done with it, both awakened from this nightmare, each of us regaining clarity, here we are, mute, weighed down by so many stories that warp the different passions of our lives, separate them, bristling hatred, life's only principle, coagulated silence, our only law, in the silence, however, a pressing need to speak, not to communicate, but to confront one another, to go back to the beginning, back to the irritation of words swallowed in one's throat for fear of the whip and of torture, back to this stormy violence rolling through our hearts, back to this need to debase by first degrading those who debase, back to the necessary confrontation that one fine day leaves us not only in our own presence but that forces us to face ourselves, women alone accepting a singular destiny, delivering us from the curse of hatred, fist ever brandished, the shock of sun on my forehead, the mark of centuries, a hollow of suffering radiating out in long, slow waves through my flesh, its unsettled patience, my gaze opened excessively onto a void that I gradually fill with the blurry vision of a mutilated body, horribly lacerated, torn apart but immobile, attached to an image way down below, immutable in the silent rays of light, jagged, fevered, twisted, perpetuating the unbearable atmosphere of violence she has carried within her for two centuries

—*ayi loko! pati bra dèyè mon dé krétien vivan kontré*

she is neither Christian nor living, she is death and vengeance, determined to survive beyond guilt and forgiveness

—how will the uncles react?

—Grandmother's surprising end will ruin all their plans, they will curse themselves for not having acted earlier and they will also curse the central power of France, a tradition long anchored in the family, the Biemmes regularly arrange to be members of the opposition even when their sympathies and interests direct them to vote for the government, they were rebels against Mazarin, joined the Vendée resistance to the Revolution, were Royalists against Bonaparte, republicans against the Restoration and the Empire, Communards and Royalists against the republicans, Gaullists under Vichy, socialists under de Gaulle

—it would seem that our family lacks conviction?

—on the contrary, my dear, the Biemmes only have one conviction expressed fully in hatred of authority

—who must I hate, Mother?

—God

—Sister Theresa, you never cease to surprise me, how can one hate God?

—by scorning him, scorning his works, refusing the destiny he has prepared for us, by commanding nature, destroying

—why do you always speak so violently?

—because in nature only violence is real

—so you don't love anything or anyone?

—what a stupid question! I love you for everything that's unique about you, I love all women for what is eternal and irreplaceable in them

—rather, you like the idea you create of us, admit it, you're laughing

—the way you surprise yourself is unique, you're right, I don't love you, I've finished loving a moment with you, the great joy of the world like a divine song, Eternity

my words make no sense, faced with the permanent aggression of this woman, they protect me, my father torn to shreds, in my ac-cumulated memories, sewn back together, to reconstruct an airplane where my desires pass through, the splendid flowering of the clouds splattered with the bloody fragrance of hibiscus, the delirium of an invention worrying over itself, to re-create the world out of the orig-inal sin, spasms of agony, rebellious solitude and, more destructive than the flood, a need for a love that has neither the language nor the face of love, each hour the ecstasy of sorrow, unconfessed madness, my mother so used to her pale memories still doesn't manage to die, her sweaters, Papa's pullovers, his tics, Papa's warm socks, his moods, Papa's burning stockings, only the deathly cold of winter reflects his heart, since that fatal day the radio brings only sad news, drought in the Sahel, famine in Ethiopia, bombings in Beirut and in the heart of Paris, the lynching of a Black man in the New York subway and of an Algerian man in Marseille, Negroes and Arabs are all bastards, Negroes, get out, let's blow them up, they took our women, they confiscated our language, they're even talking about the biggest twit among them, a certain Senghor at the Académie, bastardizing the race, Biemme is ours, mine are the light cavalry and the musketeers of

—Sister Theresa, wake up, wake up

—I'm not sleeping, Mother Superior, I saw Saintmilia at the head of an army of Negroes invading Saint-Denis and crowning Baby Doc the king of the French on the tomb of Saint Louis

—thank God, the French will finally learn some respect for authority, I remember how they caricatured the general, now they'll really suffer, no more of this rebellious spirit, no more complaining, quarreling in the public square, no more multiparty system, political schemes, all those avatars people believe are the privileges of democracy, Papa Doc said it was all shit, am I shocking you dear child?

—not at all, not at all, in my family we're used to all kinds of disagreements, the general will be happy, when he was alive he didn't spare his compatriots and called them all kinds of names, dogs, cows, idiots, bastards, it's even said that one day he told Baudin they all deserved to be fucked up the ass

—yes, yes, stick it to them, skewer them, make them

—like we did with the Negroes in Saint-Domingue when the militia caught them running away, they were impaled on a burning stake, without any kind of trial, my Mother, do you think de Gaulle had slave traders in his family?

—of course, which Frenchman, which Englishman, which Spaniard isn't a slave trader, still today Europe is built on the sweat and blood of Negroes

—do you regret it?

—what makes you think that? I love the Negroes too much (my presence in Haiti is proof of that) not to recognize that they've been useful, even necessary for the progress of capitalism and Western civilization, was it not in the colonies that we perfected and tested out both racism and fascism?

—so we were right to enslave them

—in the name of God and men, yes, even if God condemns us missionaries to atone for the injustices of our white brothers in the hell of the tropics and the equator

—speaking of the general, do you think he was a slave trader and a racist?

—getting involved in politics always leads to betrayal or to selling someone else out, just as there were French Negroes or Negro Frenchmen, the general, playing the game of alliances and in the name of matters of state, had to buy and sell a few of them, racist? he had to have been, otherwise why did he hate Gaston Monnerville so much? do you know he refused to shake his hand during an official ceremony? he turned his back on him and, making as if to bend down, shouted with a booming voice: I shit on your hand

—impossible! are you quite sure of that, Sister?

—I heard the story from a Martinican nun, who was proud of it

—why?

—because of the response, imagine, the Negro, instead of getting flustered, was witty enough to reply, with feigned disappointment: what a pity that the ass of such a great man is situated so very low

—what did the general respond?

—he was furious, he sent Sékou Touré packing that very evening and chased Guinea right out of the French community, leaving the Negroes to themselves, to their tribal conflicts, to their primitive poverty

—why Sékou Touré?

—because he applauded Gaston

—Guinea must be the ultimate mission territory, a challenge to live up to, Mother Superior, let us show our humanity, how generous the white world is

—alas! Sister Theresa, Monsieur Touré chased all the missionaries out of Guinea, calling us colonialists, can you imagine that, colonialists, when all we wanted was to save the souls of the Negroes?

—they're all ingrates, my ancestor always claimed they were too black to have a soul

—that's true! but shhh, they've become so sensitive, don't repeat that because if they hear it and they get angry they'll certainly put an end to our vacations in their country

—Mother, are we going to the Schpeerbach cousins' house this year?

—Frau Rommie has begun to ramble on, her stories of white Negroes in Saint-Domingue bore me

—she promised me she'd tell the story of my great-great-grandfather

—I'm sorry, Sonja, we'll go next year

—Sister Theresa, excuse the abrupt change of subject, but do you know how to ski?

—I learned in Switzerland

—with your cousins?

—yes, one day I saw a Negro ski in Mont-Aigoual, a tiny black stain in the infinite whiteness, it was spectral

the news should have surprised me, but it didn't, I felt relieved, blood rushed to my temples, the brief dizziness of anguish as if the world might fall on my head, and then calm, a great internal peace, everything back in its place, I had been wrong to torment myself, I had always been ready for what was happening, no more qualms, I know what my duty is now and it would have been too beautiful or too simple to reconcile what I am with what I was, too bad, there can be no hesitation now, accept the horror, it controls all of us, we cannot escape it, I am damned

the horse's gallop drew me out to the courtyard, what was the bad news now, the mill had broken the night before last, delaying the rolling of the cane, a boiler had exploded the week before and caused the loss of a quarter of the sugar cane juice, now don't tell me the oven has exploded, Alonso had assured me it would hold until the end of the season, what! an urgent message from Bonbon, he had dismounted, the poor guy was trembling, visibly afraid, what sudden event was producing such fear in his eyes, I was immediately alarmed, what could have happened to Bonbon to justify sending a message with a courier riding his horse, a horse that no one but him usually mounts

—is there a problem, Djoko?

—a big problem, a pregnant woman leading an armed troop has invaded and pillaged the plantation

—a pregnant woman! is her name Toukouma?

—those who recognized her called her that

—did your master put together a defense?

—he gathered the Negroes and the female house servants, the Negroes in the workhouses fled when Toukouma approached, the overseers and the masters tried in vain to stop the surging horde, the bullets from their muskets went right through those freaks without even wounding them, stunned, the master and those loyal to him barricaded themselves inside the house, I jumped on the fastest horse and ran here to ask for your help

—Alonzo, quickly, Salomon, gather eight men, join me on horseback at Bonbon, with weapons and ammunition, hurry, there's little time

from Cassé Damme-Jeanne Hill I discover the first glimmers of the fire, too late, I told myself, I'm arriving too late, sobs in my throat, whipping my horse, I forced him onward, expecting him to collapse beneath me at any moment, he galloped like lightning, with me, pitched forward over his neck, my head aflame and exploding with questions as we pressed on, how had Toukouma managed to outsmart the vigilant overseers and leave her plantation? why attack Bonbon, ten kilometers away, and not me? was it true that bullets did no harm to her accomplices? I crossed the river, bypassing the path leading to the cove, and turned up toward the heights of Ti Source, from there I'd have a view of the entire situation, it was a staggering spectacle, the slave huts were burning, the indigo works and the depot were in flames, the tobacco fields glowed red right up to the edge of the horizon, running toward the sea the flames kept climbing, licking the clouds, coloring the immense curl of smoke darkening the sky in a deep crimson, fortunately the central house seemed intact, spared by the fire gnawing at the land and advancing inexorably toward the superb wood-and-stone building, I rushed down the hill at full tilt, fearing the worst but with hope in my heart that Bonbon had managed to hold out until my arrival, but that was asking too much of the Eternal One, Toukouma and her band had already sown death and desolation, corpses were strewn all over the ground, their heads and members cut off, some of them merely disemboweled, others completely eviscerated, the air stunk of intestines, of blood and excrement, terrifying carnage, I looked for Bonbon, his head had wandered far from his body, his eyes wide with terror, and, supreme indecency or extreme refinement, his blood-soaked penis hung from his mouth as if his executioner had sought to give him the countenance of the sexual beast that, during his lifetime, my friend had claimed to be

—don't you understand, Wolf, that the assassin—was it an assassin or an executioner like you said—autographed the murder? what horrible vengeance! do you remember (no, you were completing your studies with the Jesuits at the time), your mother had loaned out Toukouma, at twelve years old, to Suzanne Bonbon to help her servants during a ball, she kept her for a week, praising her precocious skills as a cook, no one knew better than she how to prepare the pork griot or the smoked fish stew, Suzanne was so taken by her that she allowed her to sleep in the little room adjoining the kitchen, on the last night, hearing screams, she ran and found her unconscious, awash in her own blood, Bonbon had penetrated her with unimaginable cruelty, carving a burning crater between her legs, she had bitten his right cheek to defend herself, leaving that badly healed sore he covers instinctively with his hand whenever you look at him, the bite enraged him, he struck Toukouma so savagely he broke her pelvis, taking away any hope of her ever having a child

—I can imagine the spectacle

—what planter would boast of never having caused just such a spectacle? brought back to life through the care of Madame Bonbon, the little Toukouma couldn't walk, a few days later, her burning genitals were swarming with maggots

—misery!

—indeed, even for a Negress! Saintmilia's science put her back on her feet, Maïté told me that the day she began following in the healer's footsteps, the two women fell into each other's arms, crying hot tears, Toukouma swore she would avenge herself, every year, on the anniversary of the rape, her stomach swells, just ask her, she'll invariably answer: I'm pregnant with Bonbon's death

the ceremony I had witnessed at the entrance to the bayou was preparation, Toukouma had gathered her band together to ready them to carry out their task, on the date of the anniversary, pregnant with my fear, the rape gave birth to death, I don't hesitate, everything is perfectly clear to me, I know my duty, the mutilated corpses of my friends command me to round up my troops and pursue the assassins immediately, a crime premeditated for ten, fifteen, twenty, thirty years, what do I know? if the slaves have given themselves permission to seek vengeance, what destiny are they planning for the whites other than what they've done to Bonbon? with or without a clear conscience, I'll assume responsibility for vengeance, Wolf! in the name of what? in seeking a response that justifies vengeance, there'll only be new crises of conscience, for the response would itself justify Bonbon's murder, would be to enter further into the logic of hatred through the obligation for vengeance, Toukouma avenged herself, it was her right, the colonists' justice could never claim the contrary, I see the apocalypse coming, in the name of the whites' collective responsibility, sooner or later the Negroes will be right to avenge themselves, and woe betide us on that day

—Wolf! you're scaring me

—me, that's ridiculous! these days we should be scared of our own shadows

—yes, in a sense, that is, from her point of view, Toukouma was right and I wonder why we went after her, sowing carnage in the stupidity of rage, nothing is clear, it's all become so confusing, ah! Cécile, why weren't you there to help me?

—at your service, Monsieur von Schpeerbach, the Negro millworkers who had run away are starting to come back, they'll take care of the corpses, the assassins don't have much of a head start, Salomon picked up their tracks, they're still fresh, if we go after them immediately we'll catch them within the hour

—there's only ten of us, Alonzo

—about thirty, Monsieur, Chassagne and Saré have joined us, along with twenty or so well-armed men

—where are they? I don't see them

—they are scouring the Petite Plaine, picking up the tracks

—then let's not waste any time, onward!

we found their tracks, they were leading upward in parallel to the riverbed, wading through the swamps of Petite Plaine and then climbing the foothills of En-Bas-la-Rivière, Toukouma hadn't sought to erase or muddle them, they were easy to see, taunting our stupidity, our complete absence of discernment and judgment, they led us right to where Toukouma wanted us to go, to her lair, it was a trap, we walked right into it, the road to hell

—stop!

—why, Schpeerbach? they're on foot and aren't very far ahead of us, let's go on and we'll catch up to them in a matter of minutes

—look around you, the tracks are more recent and they stop here, it's worrisome don't you think, cliffs on one side, the slopes of the mountain on the other, if Toukouma wanted to ambush us, there'd be no place better suited than this basin, between the sky and the water, we're trapped, what do you think, Chassagne?

—that's what I think, too, I'd hesitate to go any further, though if we turn back we might never capture these assassins

—let's be even more careful and send out scouts

a wild cry followed by shouts and screams, a maddening din, like a sudden tempest, Toukouma's band clambered down from the rocks and trees, attacking our flanks, cutting off our retreat, closing off the path in front of us, charge! Saré, Chassagne, charge! forward, Alonzo! but the cries of the zonbi amplified by the raucous sound of the drums frightened the horses, pushing them into each other, we heard their whinnying mixed with the terrified screams of the overseers, plunging to their deaths along the cliffs, anticipating all our maneuvers, the Negroes had us trapped, Toukouma's relentless laughter, we raised our heads toward a clearing among the rocks, there, just above us, at the peak, Chassagne shouldered his rifle, took aim, fired, the bullet ricocheted off her laugh, struck Chassagne full force, his arms flailed, his horse reared up and threw him off, he collapsed, struck down, Alonzo was fighting a Black devil, opened his skull with a strike of his machete, split the torso into two parts that soldered themselves back together under the effect of some powerful magic, the Negro stretched out his arm, grabbed Alonzo by the hair, and with one violent shake snapped the vertebrae in his neck, the sound itself pained me, full of rage I dove into the heart of the battle, bringing my sword down on skulls that refused to break, a Negro snapped it right down to the hilt with a powerful blow from his pickaxe, grabbing my horse's bridle, he held firm, Salomon, help me! here I am, Master, he was also disarmed, powerless, the two of us stuck on some quiet beach, as if excluded from the tumult and the battle, Saré fell in turn, stabbed over and over, a large cutlass sticking out of his back like a decisive affirmation of death, the surviving overseers abandoned the fight, begged for mercy, but Toukouma's zonbi, blind and deaf, continued their work with methodical violence, cutting off heads, arms, legs, with the precision of butchers, soon it was all over, the zonbi disappeared and their laughter remained suspended for a moment over Salomon and me, then stopped, a menacing silence, death in its triumphant brutality, I close my eyes, it's over

—you partook of Saintmilia's milk, that saves you today and will save you again tomorrow but not forever, tell the whites what you have seen, the army of shadows is on the march, nothing will stop it

silently, Salomon and I inspected the battlefield, the scattered torsos, severed hands, legs strewn about like in the macabre images of other scenes of horror prescribed by the rules of the colony, perpetrated in the name of the law, a slave caught stealing, hand cut off at the wrist; caught running away, leg severed; with weapons in hand, decapitation, breaking on the wheel, burning at the stake, the future burst into the present, dark, frightening, do we have a future? it is fully inscribed in the present and we already know what that is, the good times are finished, the whites no longer decide between good and evil, life and death in Saint-Domingue, we believed ourselves to be good in all our luxurious splendor, our prideful wealth, the insolence of lust, not knowing that in the eyes of the Blacks there was no mystery to our evil, unlike their Vodou, shrouded in secrets and prohibitions, in the absolute evil of crime and madness, for we were foolish to have exploited their fear, their weaknesses, their naivete, in fact we were more naive than they, how had we persuaded ourselves that the hell we'd built on their rage and on their despair would guarantee us the eternal security of paradise?

—Salomon, I didn't see Chassagne's or Saré's heads

—no, Master

—let's find them, we'll ask the militia to come get the corpses, we'll have their funerals at the same time as those of the Bonbon family

—and the Blacks?

the sudden anguish in his tone, according to Vodou beliefs the unburied dead are condemned to wander eternally, their souls never knowing peace, having lost any chance of returning to Africa they sharpen their hatred for the living, tormenting them until they die of despair, the question surprised me, a touch of bitterness, like a reproach, his eyes on me, anxious

—send some carts to pick up the bodies

his face relaxed, a subtle joy, likely restrained because of my sadness, Salomon had never liked the overseers, but he felt a solidarity with them, based on the ancient African legends, between the whites and the Negroes the savagery, the depth, the timelessness of Africa remains present, we haven't been paying attention, this continent will consume us

—Master, they took the heads as trophies, Alonzo's has disappeared, too

as trophies? the word was put out there, full of troubling significance, the defeat of the whites, the victory of the Negroes, we were able to enslave them because our bullets, our cannonballs, our ammunition assured us a superiority that compensated for the weakness of our numbers, today their magic has responded, it triumphs, Toukouma carries around the head of defeated whites on a pike, the Blacks will learn that they can beat the whites, that we are not invincible, in this truth lies the end of the system, the Negroes will no longer be afraid, if they find a leader capable of exploiting their hatred, of channeling their fury, of organizing their revolt in the name of liberty, not one of us will survive

—the army of shadows is on the march, nothing can stop it

we dismounted our horses, our boots becoming stuck in the thick brown blood already decomposing in the sun, the flies and horseflies buzzing around and circling incessantly, attracted by the acrid smell of the corpses, I recognize Chassagne's corpulent chest, a machete had traced a furrow through clumps of hair, nearby, Alonzo, his skin black from having been grilled by the stultifying Caribbean or Mandingo sun, I can't remember which, the other white man had to be Saré, all three of them reduced to their torsos, chests and bellies mutilated, nothing left but their trunks, they left their homes this morning, as if to go for a stroll, straw hats, light jerkins, rifles slung over their shoulders, the only thing missing were some hunting dogs and the countless wranglers tasked with flushing out the wild pigs or maroon steers, they left full of life with that ardor of a "young" maturity that required them to show off their strength and courage, faced, unfortunately, with the Negroes and with death, Saré often laughed (though that morning he had held back) about my curious mania for wearing patent leather boots even to work, he was a bon vivant who took pride in how well he hosted friends and guests, from his terrace his laughter cascaded across the gorges of Terre-Rouge, awakening the sleepy echoes of L'Anse-du-Clerc hill, flying above the little bay and, amplified by the cries of the pelicans, mixed together with the laughter of the ebbing tide, modulated in a thousand different ways, then hit the cliffs at la Croque, came back and died quietly at the foot of its master, staggering!

—listen to the water singing in my head, come, Schpeerbach, put your ear against my forehead, move down, a little lower, there

his intense, childish joy bursts my eardrums, a crude joke, I had let myself be tricked, everyone burst out laughing

—I am a force of nature, just ask Schpeerbach, what other planter here can boast of merging his laughter with that of the woods whenever he wants?

Saré's laughter would no longer burst out like a fanfare in the heads of his guests and Chassagne's trilling voice would no longer resound through the logwood, his joyous habit of vocalizing to calm the bees so he could gather their honey in complete safety, it's stupid but I cry for them, for myself, so much carnage, my illusions shattered, a fragile balance destroyed, the malignant eye of the sun blinks in my mind, knocks forcefully against my temples, Dante, could you have been right? abandon all hope, ye who enter here

—let's go, Wolf, let's get out of here

he had put his arm around my shoulders, friendly, the world capsized in his voice, a complaint, a plea, a secret pain I felt as my own, the certainty of an imminent separation, inescapable, all those things we both loved and shared, that we should have enjoyed together, the landscapes of our joy were crumbling, by what miracle was our childhood still alive, bringing our hands together? our fingers, an understanding between men, a friendship we no longer understood and that we were no longer used to

—Salomon

—yes, Wolf!

—why? tell me, why?

—for everything

he had responded in a low voice, without passion or hatred, almost ashamed and embarrassed to have had to express in my stead what I secretly believed, I had always known what his answer would be, it was the source of our shared impulses, sometimes shattered our fears, sharpened our worries, in asking for explanations I was trying to figure out whether Salomon felt as implicated as the other Negroes, particularly the maroons, whether he wanted to be involved, and what to conclude from that involvement, he had fought by my side out of loyalty and I thank him for that, he had probably been warned of Toukouma's power and knew how the confrontation with the army of shadows would end, he shared the risks with me, at several points had found himself between my horse and the pack of zonbi, protecting me, it couldn't have been a coincidence that this kept happening, he had protected me and, strangely, also seemed to be seeking out death, torn between two loyalties, one to our childhood and one to his race, Toukouma had understood that, by sparing both of us and entrusting us with the same message, she was predicting what would become of us, loyalty has its limits, in Salomon's place would I have been loyal to our childhood? for a brief moment we had walked together, hand in hand, two scared little boys, frightened by the destiny that weighed upon our shoulders, lost in Lonmon Woods, seeking out a path through the undergrowth and thickets, scratched up by the mesquite trees, the call of the conch shell got us moving again, picking up the sound of terrified loved ones in the cries of the drums, Salomon traced a path by following the voices of the tam-tams

—don't be afraid, Wolf, we'll find the way eventually

—I'm not afraid, Salomon, but I'm worried we're turning in circles, look! a piece of your coat hanging from this logwood branch, we already passed this way

—let's go in a different direction

—why don't we split up? you go right and I'll go left, and the first one to find the path will call to the other

—that's a crazy idea, no! we'll get out of here more easily together, imagine if you ran into the devil of the Lonmon Woods by yourself?

—my mother says that in our family all the men are devils, so I'm not afraid, everyone knows that devils don't eat other devils

—it's also well known that big devils kill little devils, so as to cut down on competition, you're a little devil, Wolf, let's stay together

we kept turning in circles until finally, exhausted, we sat with our backs leaning on a mango tree, the juicy fruit delighted our hunger, sated, drunk on the juice, even more tired than before, shoulder to shoulder, head to head, we soldered our dreams together, the night enveloped the day, the battle of light and shadow, fierce and unfettered rays of sun, we resisted the invasion of the darkness for a long time but, exhausted, we were getting ready to give up when bursts of light, like so many holes in the darkness, rushed in to rescue us, we were saved, my father

—you rascals, you had me worried

—we heard the news, Colonel Schpeerbach, my men and I await your command

hearing my officer's rank said out loud was a torture, a colonel defeated by a woman leading a band of zonbi, defeated and still alive, shame slipped in between my skin and my shirt, a carapace of shame, thick and cold, I wanted to crawl underground, to avoid Paret's look

—unfortunately you have arrived too late, Captain

—I see you're here alone with your Negro, where are the others?

—Salomon and I are the only survivors

—impossible, that woman and her band of slaves got the best of you?

—they massacred Bonbon, his overseers and domestics, why did they not also take our lives?

—let us pursue them, Colonel, it's too much, the insult must be avenged immediately

—your indignation honors you, Captain, but I doubt it will wash away my shame, try your luck against Toukouma if your heart desires, she is probably still in the area, but if I were you I would take care of the dead

—you are not wounded, at least?

—worse than that, my dear man, Salomon and I are both walking dead

his false concern was directed only at me, but I chose to include Salomon in my response, to finally make him present in my life, embrace the friendship, embrace our childhood, that rebel part of me that refused to die, dips in the waters of Petite-Anse, horse rides to the sugar refinery and beyond, way up at Dangluse, Sanglant, that magic tree at the confluence where the stream meets Fanel Spring, Marcorel and its wounded fields, red stains on the slopes of barren hills, Pavrette and the audacity of its great path plunging down directly into the widest basin of the Seringue, joyful landscapes like so many happy scars in my memory, unlimited horizons, an appeal, an aspiration toward freedom, to escape ourselves, we were free, living in truth and in communion with nature, to be Wolf and Salomon, not knowing if he was white, if I was Black, testing ourselves with fantastic rages, epic battles, decisive battles the adults knew nothing about, which of us would jump first from the top of the Morne-Tranglé rock, which of us would open the crab cage in the grasses at Maro, who'd share the news of an American ship anchoring at Petite-Anse to spend the night unloading contraband? futile pursuits more important in our eyes than the parish mass on the first Sunday of the month, a mass that created a barrier in our childhood friendship, in the chancel, the front rows were for the whites, the back ones for the Blacks, the free people of color in the middle, we looked for each other amidst these adult stupidities, when we finally met beyond the multitude of curly or kinky heads, we told each other—no one else heard and that was the magic of childhood—that they'd better hurry and wrap up their foolishness soon, meet up under the quenepa tree at Belle-Roche

—promise?

—promise!

testing ourselves despite the morbid fear we had of Saintmilia's medicines, bitter locks of hair, acrid, gummy, bizarre mixes of mombin bata, milkweed, Kulimbé, cerasee, palma Christi oil, snake plants, Keezhanelli leaves, garlic, onions, wormseed, shallots, first-order emetics, known laxatives, fabulous dewormers, excellent against all sorts of illness, malaria, intestinal parasites, indigestion, flatulence, flu, bronchitis, endless dry heaves, bent over chamber pots filled with our interminable droppings, multiplying the echo of our tormented intestines, backfirings and expectorations from stomachs brought back to their most basic capacity, that kind of knowledge, could there be any hatred capable of snatching it away from us?

—Salomon!

—yes, Master

he disentwined his fingers, the childhood in our looks cedes to our adult fears, I looked for hatred in his eyes, I read pain there, an immense pity, we each saw our own truth in ourselves, we feared the future and pitied ourselves, our destiny traced in our tears

—Salomon, we were wrong to ever leave our childhood

—but we had to, Master, what would we have gained by refusing to confront our truth?

—to dismiss it

—that would have been a hypocritical deferral, the world of adults would have broken us sooner or later

—my father's death split my life in two, before that I wanted to grow up very quickly, enter into the strange world of adults, responsible for themselves and to themselves for their actions, afterward I would have rather not grown up, remained a child, pampering my teddy bear, talking to it, finding through him that indispensable and necessary compromise that foils life's traps, creating a universe where joy is the rule, incommensurable and beautiful innocence

—foolishly childish

—why foolishly?

—well, because!

—we are all children, luckily, Sonja, the part of us that remains a child is the strongest, preventing us from becoming totally adult

—can adulthood not create joy?

—joy is like love, it is only true once, adult joys are just lies, there is too much calculation in them, the child is foundationally happy, one might say, the adult seeks joy because of a need to be happy and that need spoils everything, between one age and the other is adolescence, where innocence gets perverted

—I don't agree, adolescence is often a school where we learn innocence

—an innocent adolescent is at best a simpleton, at worst mentally retarded

I was categorical, my mother raised her eyebrow, surprised that her daughter the nun, so ignorant of the facts of this world, was so easily handing out condemnations on subjects unrelated to Christian morality, she looked at me, suspicious

—what do you know about the innocence of adults?

Sister Hyacinthe emerged, her thick habit brushing against my mother's leg, startling her, the three of us laughed, a falsely candid happiness, will I reveal to my mother that Sister Hyacinthe's intrusion is not innocent? so much perverse intention in this touch, so much provocation that I was jealous, Mother will not understand, she lags behind, her spirit stained with the memories of a husband who was father to both her and me, my mother has become a child

—what did she see in you, Carmenta, that I didn't offer her
—a dream
—we often spoke together about the shape and color our dream would take
—the shape of a hummingbird, the scarlet color of night
—but night is black
—she found me beyond the night, at the very heart of the flame that burns inside me and consumes me
—what motivated her, her hand playing on my breasts, to listen to the beating of my fire?
—the desire to understand an icy fire
—so I burned her?
—the cold blazes but it does not burn down, I kissed her
—I remember her music like the harmony of the world
—you should have done what I did, pluck out all the harmonies from her, sate my hunger, sate my thirst, love like a trap, I put your illusions in a cage
—my dream, my hunger, and my thirst, my love and my illusions, why did you take them from me, Carmenta?
—how many times must I repeat that I'm not Carmenta?
—get rid of my tears
—perhaps! you possess nothing of Hyacinthe's life, she was a mirage, I'm offering you the chance to forget her, am I not right here?
—how would I think about a flash of lightning?
—I ask only to be grasped for a blink of time
—the lightning will strike me down
—and then won't our only hope be to destroy ourselves?
—Sonja, don't tempt me
the airplane bounces about, incomprehensible mood swings, the day lacks clairvoyance, the sun splutters so far above us, Sonja's malicious

eyes study it at length, seeking answers to silent interrogations, preoccupations linked to the needs of an existence that love itself hesitates to reveal to me, she knows everything about me, all she has to do is come close to see herself in my troubled gaze, I recognized my desires in her voice, but the echoes of their distant rumbling soon abated

—Sister Theresa, the devil isn't to be tempted

—even if the devil is named Salomon

—have you the audacity to justify the

—looking at it carefully, my ancestor was right

—because one doesn't refuse the love of a Biemme

—did she love him?

—undoubtedly, otherwise why would she have provoked him?

—Grandfather didn't say

—it is not what he said that matters but what he believed, why is he so insistent about Salomon's loyalty and faithfulness?

—out of surprise that Salomon tried to protect him at the risk of his own life

—you're naive, Sister Theresa, Salomon had refused your ancestor's advances and he expected the worst, he had the choice between becoming a maroon or dying

—why didn't he become a maroon? it was so easy

—and what if he loved Sonja? death was the definitive solution to his torment, does Schpeerbach not recount that in the days before the events at Bonbon's, Salomon seemed troubled, tortured, he avoided his masters' presence, especially Sonja's, clear signs of a deep internal confusion

—how do you know? don't make me laugh

—you finally found the jewel

—I'd been looking in the wrong jewelry box, I'd left the devil's eye in Marie Andrée's, she sent it back to me with Paret when he returned from an inspection tour in Pestel and Corail

—and every day you put your feet down on the bedside rug without any regret, without any guilt?

—don't fill my ears with your reproaches, Wolf, go see if Salomon has saddled the horses yet

—he's already been waiting for you for some time

—why don't you come with me today?

—you know perfectly well that I'll be busy overseeing the bagging of the sugar

—take a bit better care of your wife, Wolf

—patience, my dear, I won't be long

—ah!

—what's the matter? are you feeling unwell?

—no, a sudden glare, I thought I saw God, come, look at the sun raising a screen of light between Salomon and Brito, the effect is striking, he's magnificent, eh! he's beautiful

—who? the horse?

—come now, Wolf, don't be a fool! Salomon, I'm ready, bring Brito, he seems nervous to me

—he ate too much corn and hamo branches in the past days, once you've tired him out a bit it'll be fine, just start easy with him

Sonja had established a certain camaraderie with Salomon different from her customary brusqueness with the other Blacks, especially the overseers, did she know of the ties that bound us? in introducing him I had merely said, this is Salomon, my right hand, he had taken a step forward, bowed his head slightly in deferential greeting, she had looked at me with questioning eyes, what should I do, Wolf? I turned my head away, pretending not to understand, she furrowed her brow, looked haughtily at Salomon and then, smiling

—hello Salomon, my name is Sonja

—hello, Mistress, welcome to the plantation

the very next day Salomon took charge of Sonja, I was busy checking accounts with Alonzo, supervising here, inspecting there, putting my finger once again on the pulse of my affairs, I had confided my wife to the person who, despite the idiotic prejudices of an idiotic society, I can now consider my brother, a sort of foster brother, my mother had never recovered from childbirth, five days after I was born she died, my father looked for a white wet nurse nearby but he couldn't find one, desperate, he resigned himself to confiding me to Saintmilia who had given birth to a boy two weeks earlier, no idea who the father was, some claimed Salomon might have been the son of the overseer Zaka, or of the former manager Arétiste, or even of my father himself, rather reddish at birth, his skin became increasingly brown and, six days later, had become completely black, jet black, which ended the gossip about

Arétiste and my father, but at no point did Zaka claim paternity, much later there will be other rumors when a man named Agénor, a free man of color from Dalmarie parish, a fisherman, begins coming by Saint-milia's hut on nights of the full moon, it will be remembered that he has known her since time immemorial and that their destiny is to lose one another, to search for one another, to find one another, and to lose one another once again, and that they will finally be united once love has triumphed over hatred and a certain fish Miyan! Miyan! will stroll around the plaza in Les Abricots on the arm of a virgin named Violetta in the middle of the day, they're just a bunch of old stories from the past, the kind the Negroes tell each other on moonlit nights, their laughter accompanied by the sound of the drums and a few sips of rum until the cold southwestern wind forces them back to the warmth of their huts, how many times, hanging on the words of these minstrels, had Salomon and I seen the pale ghost of a fish floating over our heads

—try to catch it, Salomon

—how can I catch a ghost, Wolf?

—you're stupid

—and you're ignorant

I sense a fight coming, we're both strong and well built, of equal strength, but those extra two weeks on Salomon gave him a birthright that I was wary of, any time we fought and Saintmilia found out, she whipped her son, even when I had been wrong to provoke him, she explained

—you're older than he is, you have to protect him

one day he would reveal the real reason and it was only years later that I would understand all the implications

—Wolf, you're the little master and Mama told me that you have the right to thrash me, I don't have the right to give you "what for"

—even if I want to kill you

—you have all rights, even the right to kill me

—so stick out your neck and give me a cutlass, I'm going to cut off your head

—yes, Master!

he had hesitated, a hint of panic in his eyes, but he handed me the blade

—don't be stupid, Salomon, I was only joking

—how can you joke about such things, Little Master?

that was the question, I was posing it to myself when Salomon held the bridle and helped Sonja mount Brito, he swung up on Ti Brun's back, they began trotting toward the gate, once they'd passed it their laughter and their joyful *boula* stirred up the dust on the path

—you should have known how this whole affair would end

—nothing happened, Cécile, I'm sure of Salomon's loyalty

—the whole drama came from the fact that as far as we knew nothing had happened, in fact, Salomon's presence had provoked a storm in Sonja's soul, your wife hated the Blacks too much not to love the only one among them she had the courage to accept as a human being

—is it you, Wolf, who put these absurd ideas in Salomon's head?

—which ones?

—he told me that one day soon the Blacks will be free, that everything is building toward their freedom

—he reads Voltaire and, no more than a week ago, the abbot Aloïus loaned him the latest from Rousseau: *Discourse on the Origin and Basis of Inequality among Men*

—what! he knows how to read?

—of course, Sonja, here, compare, this one is Alonzo's account book, this one's Salomon's, he takes notes every day, they allow me to expose certain irregularities in the numbers of that rascal of a Spaniard

—your Negro is a phenomenon

—I'm glad to hear you say that, for a long time I feared you'd hate him, too

—so you wanted me to love him?

—I desperately wanted the two of you to be friends

—you see, Wolf, she had penetrated your most secret intentions

—don't say silly things, Cécile, how can you possibly think I wanted to make my wife Salomon's mistress?

—to share the same joys, Wolf, to share the same joys and once again inhabit the childhood you two shared

—I hate you, Cécile

—if we were talking about someone else I would have rejoiced, hating me is still the best way to love me

every day, Sonja rode Brito in Salomon's company, roaming the Abricots region, marveling at the beauty of the landscapes, surprised to hear familiar names ringing out everywhere, Nouvelle-Touraine, Havre, Saint-Michel, Montreux, pieces of France re-created here and there according to the whims or the nostalgia of the landowners, she covered several kilometers worth of road, devoured vast spaces, explored shady inlets along the rivers, savored the sprawling, sun-filled beaches among the cliffs at Bois-Duval, Brito returned, sometimes exhausted from having outpaced a storm at a vertiginous gallop, he trotted happily when Sonja patted his neck, long before my departure Salomon had chosen him, a magnificent chestnut, and trained him, reserving him for the wife I would bring back from France

—Master, come back with a mistress

—please, Salomon, stop nagging me with your demands and I forbid you to call me Master, to you I am Wolf, have you forgotten or are you trying to forget that Saintmilia suckled us both, both sitting on her lap and each of us latched on to one of her breasts, do you want to deny that she bathed us in the same basin and that water from our bodies irrigated the same vegetable garden, do you pretend not to remember the tales she reeled off to enchant our sleeplessness, during each season of tears the north wind fights a fierce battle with the sun, beware, any little boys it comes upon at midday in the company of its enemy, it places them in the shade, for the north wind hates to feel the pricking of the sun on its skin, it places them in the shade, ties them up, blows a cold wind upon them, transforms them into statues of ice and salt that will melt in the first December storm, surely she heard that story about the salt statue during a catechism class and we were convinced of that when Father Lazenaec initiated us into the mysteries of faith, but, back then, she threatened us with it as an irremediable calamity that would strike us if we kept playing blind man's bluff under the midday sun, have you forgotten how our teeth chattered just from hearing about the evil spells cast by the sun, could you forget this past that is our innocence?

—and now?

—what does that mean: and now?

—now, Master, every day there is the blood of my brothers between us

—are you accusing me of having spilled the blood of Negroes?

a howl cut short my indignant questioning, a chopping block rolled to
a stop at my feet, Nkoli's fakery! I forced myself to be impassive, no,
Master, I won't maroon again, spare me! this plea went straight to my
heart, I try to catch Salomon's eyes, he turns his head away and spits,
conspicuously, why did this simple gesture deepen my determination,
you denied me your understanding, if only you had looked me in the
eye, my God, Wolf, what are you doing? don't let them destroy you, I
would have recognized my shame, your disdain pushed me into confusion, solitude, I didn't even feel my own pain, let's go, and may this
serve as an example, the foot flew off, once we began to apply the hot
peppers and the rum to cauterize the stump and avoid infection I left
straightaway, followed by the cries and groans that had become nothing short of torture for me, I was bereft, you abandoned me to myself,
you knew I was suffering but for an entire week you avoided me, there
was the blood of your brothers between us, you were right, but could
I have done otherwise?

—only you can know, Wolf, but I wonder, do you doubt that one
day the spilled blood will demand justice from the whites?

—those are subversive words, Salomon, you know the rules, for
your own good, I've heard nothing, I'm leaving in an hour, at nightfall,
don't ruin the joy I'll feel when I think of my return, of seeing you again

I did see him again, he welcomed me without any real joy, accepted
my wife without much enthusiasm, received without thanks the presents I had put so much effort into choosing and buying, green velvet
pants, a belt with a large buckle, a white cloth jacket

—you are dressed like us now, Salomon

—I would have preferred not to wear your rags

—you didn't like my present?

—you promised to bring me books

his kinky-haired head bent over the grammar book, one finger hesi-
tantly following the letters, identifying the words, the joy of reading
for the first time, the drive to learn, a certain hypersensitivity any

time we talked about Fatras-Bâton's intelligence, a constant need to exchange ideas, a curiosity steadily awakened, a catastrophe, I had forgotten my promise, I lied

—you demanded I come back here with a wife, so to remember the books! you understand

—you'll buy some for me next time?

he deigned to smile, not at all fooled by my little lie, he still awaits his books, luckily he seems distracted by Sonja's company, if they agree to talk about books all the better, they leave earlier and earlier, sometimes at dawn, returning at dusk, this life of freedom, out in the open air, pleases my wife, the sun has colored her cheeks and her shoulders a red copper color, as if, using some old Indian recipes, she had daubed her skin with achiote, in the evenings at dinnertime, her eyes shining and sated with landscapes, excited, she told me of her extravagant rides, half listening, distracted, lost in my worries and my misgivings, Alonzo stole from me, force him to confess, send him away

—Wolf, I'm speaking to you

—I'm listening, dear, I'm listening

—are you aware that you're neglecting me?

—don't be unfair, try to understand, I've got a lot of worries, I get the impression that . . .

—leave your impressions aside, I need certainties, can you explain to me why all the Negroes, even Salomon, insist on wearing short, skintight pants like underwear that, rather than hiding their body, offers it to the eyes of the whole world?

—to save money, my dear, the Code Noir requires that they be given two pairs of pants per year, but since it doesn't specify the length, they are made as short and narrow as possible

—they're indecent

—here, white women ignore the indecency of the Negroes

—why?

—they see them as animals, do you notice Brito's nakedness?

—Wolf, with Salomon, it's not the same thing, he was swimming today and I . . .

—of course it's not the same thing, Salomon isn't a Negro

—I don't understand

—uh! I meant to say that I never thought of him as a slave

—why don't you free him?

I was going to reply when thunder struck, coming between us with sinister vehemence, I leapt to my feet, knocking over a chair, ran outside

—Salomon, did you close up the stalls for the horses and cows

his voice distant, full of the agitation of the other Negroes, blurred by the chaos of the wind

—done, all good

I put my hands around my mouth to amplify my words, a foolish attempt to prevail over the commotion of the elements

—as soon as you're done, come join me

to share my misgivings with him, with an open heart, misgivings brought on by him contradicting me, to return to that conversation where, choosing not to reveal anything further, he had adroitly slipped in this proverb: the eye of the master suffices to fatten his animal, which made me more suspicious than if he had kept talking

—here I am, Master

his voice emerged from the darkness, friendly and warm despite the hint of obsequiousness he tried to put into it

—let's go in, shall we, in a little while it won't be nice outside

—thank you, Master

—you were right, Cécile, for the first time I invited him into my house

—what was his reaction?

—naturally, he showed no surprise, he went in, I let him go ahead of me

—Wolf, that's simply not done

he hesitated to cross the threshold

—Master, your wife is right, one doesn't make way for a slave

—he said that, Schpeerbach, ah! he is intelligent

—I wasn't fooled by the false humility of his tone, Salomon is a mountain of pride

—we can talk on the porch, Master, otherwise, till tomorrow morning

—come with me into my office

—bravo, Wolf, you passed the test with flying colors in front of Salomon and certainly Sonja must have understood

—Wolf!

my name struck me right in the back, aggressive

—yes, Sonja!

—we were having a conversation

—we'll continue later, there's no rush

—in fact, yes there is, it cannot wait, Salomon was disrespectful

—how so?

—he dared to see me naked

—how is that a mark of disrespect? you're aware aren't you! whites bathe naked and hide none of their secret charms from the Negroes

—he was indecent

—I don't really understand

—it doesn't matter whether you understand or not, I demand

again the crash of the thunder as if the sky was exploding everywhere, falling on our heads, the gusts of wind blew back the doors and the shutters on the windows, simultaneously blew out the candles, plunging us into an opaque darkness, hurricane season had begun

—that he be publicly castrated

did I hear that right, the shuddering of the thunder tore through the silence, my heart stopped, unthinkable, she's all sugar and honey with Salomon, she can't suddenly hate him, he was indecent, what did she mean by that? Wolf had heard and understood perfectly well, the storm surges in his head, the darkness amplifies his unsteady steps, they resonate and crunch on the paving stones, he knocks into the furniture, moving in front of doors and windows to block them, reconnecting with the sound of a dead feeling, the light, crackling and flaming at the end of a match, I feel too light, the slipping of his feet is so unpleasant and futile even as the wind improvises rites of rage and madness as it slams against the house with an incredible fervor, disrespect, indecency, the excessiveness of a secret blown outrageously out of proportion, speaking the language of my frustrations, calling me to other and new dissatisfactions, the violence of the blood against my temples, Salomon vibrating, he lied to me, had only lived in the islands for ten years, whereas he was born here, he sucked Black milk, he is Black, my son is Black, a Biemme de Valembrun Lebrun, a curse, the idiotic Negroes, he encouraged the rabble to turn on us, debased, degraded his own family, I listened to the memory of storms in Brittany, a little girl terrorized by the wind whistling through the slots in the ramparts, the roar of waves smashing the groan of the schooners against the cliffs, the sailors' fear, an ordinary occurrence repeated season after season with more or less intensity, cries and tears depending on whether the seagulls returned to port with their sails hanging or their hearts in turmoil, in Saint-Domingue everything is different, an unspoken dream, monstrous, every sensation becomes exaggerated, hallucinatory, the night snaps its fingers, suddenly a tree dies with a racket that seems to precede an immobile silence and is then immediately pierced by an uproar rolling with apocalyptic force, a herd of cattle thrown into the air, their bellowing echoes against the flashes of lightning, squalls of water churn the sea, the doubled violence of the sky and the ocean is at its peak, mind intoxicated, heart impetuous, I open myself up to all these sounds unknown to me less than a moment ago and, suddenly sensual, mortally perverse, madly exciting, liberating all the disorder of the barbarous Valembrun Lebrun blood within me, I shouted and, frenetic, I was nothing more than a hurricane

—Sonja, the plane is shaking

—don't worry! we've just fallen into an air pocket, we'll be through it soon

—a disagreeable sensation, my stomach is in my chest, I thought I was going to pass out

—the air turbulence pitched the plane into the void, it was like being sucked in, we suddenly dropped about a hundred feet

—my God! I'm still shaken up

—a little cognac to help you get over your fright?

—certainly not, my experience with the champagne was quite enough

—Sonja, dare a little, are you not seeking the ferocious fullness of life?

—yes, but I'm not looking to embarrass myself in front of everyone

—by becoming a nun you are dead to the world, so what does it matter?

—let's not get into these monastic discussions

—thus, love

—not at all, after such a fright, I would like to get drunk on happiness, why didn't the plane flip over in its joy?

—I've got a profusion of joy in store for you, today is carnival, the Negroes are organizing spectacles full of

—no! no!

—afraid again, why my dear?

—Wolf! in my family carnival is a baneful joy

—in Saint-Domingue the Negroes will hunt . . .

—in Venice! in Venice, Jehan de Biemme, imprisoned by the Italians after the debacle of François I's campaign, initiated himself into the customs of carnival, a captive (but what kind of captivity was it that elevated beauty and love, music and poetry?), captive, this fine flower of French knighthood discovered a life of luxury, byzantine luxury, Greco-Latin culture, the refinements of a civilization becoming reborn, he learned Italy and brought it back, to this side of the Alps, a carbon copy, from one castle to another it was all Italian theater, balls, concerts, poetry recitations, madrigals and sonnets calling on us to enjoy life and, during the carnival, three days to forget our troubles, to hide our anxieties behind a mask, to hold on to pleasure with both hands

—I'm tired of dressing up as a pirate, as Othello, as a Turk or a Persian, tonight I'm going to wear the gypsy mask

—you're mad, Jehan, don't speak of that cursed mask, it brought misfortune to this family

—we are not condemned to live under the threat of a curse, tonight I will exorcise it beneath a shower of wine and confetti

—stop kidding around, the mask is the

—I'm not kidding, I already tore it off my ancestor's face, at this very moment, Gaston, the new butler, is cleaning it, the family's superstitious terrors don't bother him

flurry of stars, farandoles, confetti, fantasias played on the viola, dark-sounding guitars, and shrill chords, a drunken Jehan exhibited the false gaiety of the mask he was wearing, a limping devil, he hopped from one foot to the other, there was something macabre about his pirouettes, something diabolical, the terrified noblewomen sensed damnation crossing their paths, Beelzebub's deathly aura, one after the next they inexplicably felt lightheaded, they fled his bitter laughter

—you're scaring me, Sister Theresa

—when he removed the mask the morning after the ball, his scream turned the blood in my veins to ice, I stopped at the top of the stairs and turned around, his back was turned to me and he was looking at the big mirror in the trophy room

—you frightened me, Jehan

—he turned slightly, turning his head toward me, brought his hands to his face, I heard him sobbing bitterly, he dropped his arms in a gesture of exhaustion and despair, I saw him and it was horrible, his face was pocked with holes as if he'd been gnawed at by smallpox, only his eyes were alive, the last remnants of tattered skin were just peeling off, so much shimmering dust, a thin trace of green light shot through here and there with a few bursts of scarlet, a nightmare, Sonja, his face soon had no more skin on it, and right there next to me was a skull like the one you see on the flags of pirate ships, a real skull, I screamed in horror

—where were the others?

—my brother Théodore ran over, sword in hand, you know how hot-blooded the Biemmes are, he thought I'd been attacked by some insolent country squire who, despite our vigilance, had been hiding in the attic, he stopped in his tracks, the sword fell from his hands, he was trembling

—I understand, enough to drive you mad

—Jehan ran up the stairs four at a time, pushed me aside as he passed, went to the central tower and, before Théodore could stop him, threw his leg over the window and threw himself into the abyss

—what did you do with the mask? burn it? bury it?

—it's unbelievable, Cécile, but no one knows, during the funeral, right when he was being lowered into the ground, rain was pouring down, even though the sky was clear, it flowed over us in thick, heavy streams of water, not a cloud above us, was it the end of the world, claps of thunder detached from the sky, striking down the soursop tree across from the graveyard, our surprise and the squall had us scattering into the nearby houses, once the storm had passed we came back, total shock! the skulls of Chassagne, Saré, Alonzo, completely fleshless, bleached as if they'd been washed with lime and placed right there in the coffin, announced Toukouma's newest provocation, they looked to be snickering, not even covering the massive coffins with dirt, the terrified Blacks cried Vodou! Vodou! they fled and scattered among the caves, a wind of horror blowing over us all

—Wolf, let's leave! let's go back to France

—don't tell me you're scared, Sonja

—if you really want to know, it's not that I'm scared, but I realize these curses are depressing me, let's go on holiday, let's go to Port-au-Prince for a month

—what would we go looking for there? nowhere will we be safe unless we change the system

—yet I feel safe here, Wolf

—because Bauduy gave you six soldiers to guard you?

—of course, even though you weren't far, I felt so alone in Les Abricots, so alone

—now you aren't anymore?

—I won't answer that question, see this ring, a Negress will bring it to you, follow her calmly and you'll be brought to me

—by the ring or the Negress?

she hadn't recognized me, how could she have anyway, we'd never met before, an abyss of centuries between us into which her memory foundered, the melancholy look in her eyes was opaque and didn't even reflect the suffering of old age, she had placed a veil of modesty between her eyes and the world, overwhelming sadness against which all our questions butted up, I immediately recognized her faded madras just as it had last been seen by my ancestor, she was running on the waves, vomiting in an unknown patois, her native language having recalled the memory of words, countless threats, heaping a new volley of curses upon the Biemmes, the blood of her son between us, blood cannot be redeemed, as their spiteful proverbs say, yet it will have to, from one generation to the next we've paid, now that I know, I've decided to atone, for the last or the first time my ancestor's father had noticed her at the Croix des Bossales, how old might she have been? seven or twelve, nine or fifteen, bent over, wrinkled, memories of the torture of the hold in her vertebrae, chained to a destiny she wished had been different, having crossed through hell from Dahomey to Saint-Domingue, she ruminated on her sufferings, seated facing the sun, her eyes, still filled with dreams of the bush and the savanna, refracted the fires of the New World, a birth she will remember, she was waiting, seemingly indifferent to the bargaining happening all around her, her thin body curled up around her fears but startled by each outburst from the commissioner driving the auction with arguments and shots of rum, ladies and gentlemen, for there were ladies there to give the spectacle the air of a social event, ladies and gentlemen, take your pick, highest quality ebony wood, healthy gums, full sets of teeth, from the Ibo tribe, this one here, with the impressive build, ideal for replacing the cows and mules turning the mill, with him you won't have to worry about processing the cane, and this girl here is Yoruba, take a good look, she's probably a virgin, a rare virtue in this island of pleasure, who's tempted? we'll have to see about that, a voice snickered, trivial and salacious, we'll have to see about that, I'll give her a try, come closer, her nudity, freshly washed on the docks, instinctively recoiled, believing she might protect herself from some obscure and imminent danger, she'd felt a sharp pain the length of a foot in her back, a sharp nudge sent her back toward the danger and the danger held her fast while a finger, or perhaps even a bamboo shoot or a branch from a logwood tree and, who knows? the channeled anger of Ogoun Ferraille, penetrated somewhere within her, a glimmer, a burst of suffering layered over other sufferings, breaking with an old order of innocence, she opened her mouth to scream, the scream died in her throat, the finger advanced very far, as far as it could, tested, groped, foraged, inflaming the pain, my flesh torn, the vile laughter of that finger in my face, a drunken, nauseating laughter, I closed my eyes on so many sufferings and humiliations, come on, ladies and gentlemen, make your choice, you've all seen it, she's a virgin, impeccable teeth, no skin diseases, perfect for domestic service, day and night, priced at a hundred pounds, a great deal, I hear a hundred and twenty, I'm at a hundred and fifty, I see a hundred and sixty, a hundred and seventy-five, going once, going twice, I offer two hundred, the bidding is still open, two hundred, still open, going once, twice, three times, sold

—cover yourself with this karabela, the mistress won't like seeing you arrive in this state

she had understood neither the words nor the gesture, rediscovering the use of her hands she'd grabbed the piece of cloth but didn't know what to do with it, Boutoug, she would learn his name later as they worked together on the plantation, under orders from the master, Boutoug wrapped the cloth around her skinny body, signaling to her to sponge off the blood between her thighs, he bundled her up with some other purchases, then once they were all tied together he led them neither roughly nor gently along paths like those of the lowlands of her native Dahomey, but she was entering another universe, orderly, governed by codes whose rigors she would learn bit by bit, she swapped bodies, pierced now with a wound that would never heal, she changed histories, no lions roared in those of the whites, try as she might to raise her head and catch sight of an elephant's fate amidst the flight of vultures, the sky remained silent and deserted, worse, she changed her name, no longer is she Ti Mèmè N'kedi, wild flower of the savanna, the first time they called her she failed to hear Boutoug's order and was punished with ten strikes of a leather whip, two sharp smacks will teach your mouth to respond, in truth she hadn't done it on purpose, how could she have recognized her name, songlike and so poetic, in this Saintmilia, baptized by the Blessed Family of the Christ Child, yes, tell me, Boutoug, how could I have? now I have a soul, an old white man in a white cassock convinced me of that, I must save it, prayers, songs, confessions, communion, and whatever else is there to change? she washed the piece of cloth, leached the blood of the second misfortune, the first one being my capture at the edge of the forest by rogue Congos, she made it into a singular madras scarf and crowned her head with it as if to anchor in her mind, every day and every night, the memory of her first contact with those who would be her masters after they'd determined the course of her life, as if to create a barrier between herself and the sky, hoping that once weathered the cloth would take on the color of the air, renewing the connection to the innocence of the *shoungo*, sacred virgins possessing from childhood the secret of healing, of commanding the rains, of reading the present and the future of the water, on that day, I, Ti Mémé N'kedi, I learned to forget, I learned love in order to lose myself, struck down, Agoué batala délivrans, she is still there, in the refraction of the light, so black she is blue, the gray sun of tropical hurricanes

—still here and, despite everything, still alive, our family is indestructible

—in fact, Sister Theresa, according to what you've told me, you are the last of the Biemmes, the name will die with you

—that is precisely why I have to atone, and refuse hell and damnation

—you seem to enjoy the role of victim?

—I conjure the past and redeem history

—what does it matter! if there are no more Biemmes to know about it and live like Christians

—on the contrary, it matters, we will live again elsewhere

—in Africa?

—everywhere people suffer

—have the Biemmes finished imposing misfortune on other people?

—we will have found peace

—you're more of a Schpeerbach than a Biemme

—Sonja was the only survivor of the Biemmes, there were no more male inheritors to perpetuate the name, the last one, a corsair, was captured by the Portuguese, they hanged him from the highest topsail of a boat in the port of Lisbon, or so the reports say, thus she insisted that her son Klaus add the Biemme patronym to that of Schpeerbach, two branches sharing the Schpeerbach inheritance, that of Switzerland, those are my cousins, very stiff people but they could not be more kindhearted, more like peasants than aristocrats, endowed with all the virtues that make the Swiss what they are, honesty, a sense of thriftiness and hospitality, a spirit of tolerance that allows them to easily preach Calvinism while serving as bodyguards to the pope, generosity and openness in their hearts

—generosity? yes, that's how they earn forgiveness for helping the tyrants of the world despoil their own people

—I spent my vacations with them, the first days were happy but soon came boredom, the Swiss are too methodical and meticulous in both their business affairs and in their daily life not to be boring, ultimately

—the exact opposite of the Biemmes

—yes, the opposite of the Schpeerbach Biemme de Valembrun Lebrun who are the French branch of the family

—and of whom you are the last representative, born in Saint-Domingue, the Schpeerbach Biemme branch will come to an end in the native land

—in such torment, Sonja!

Port-au-Prince had changed since my last visit, there was the usual feverishness along the port protected by Fort Islet and in the lower part of the town, the business zone connecting to the market at Croix des Bossales, perhaps the largest slave market in the world, but faces were tense, there was anxiety in everyone's eyes, the altercations between whites and free people of color constantly degenerated into brawls and only the vigorous intervention of the militia prevented them from turning into pitched battles, there was extreme agitation, a firecracker exploded and everyone panicked, rushed home, barricaded themselves inside, abandoning the streets to the violence of foreign troublemakers, like the Italian Praloto, that damned soul in the service of the Count of Caradeux, who openly called for racial hatred between whites and free people of color, conflicting interests were bringing about an inevitable confrontation, Port-au-Prince was settling into a state of horror, the very night of my arrival a patrol discovered the mutilated and terribly disfigured body of a mulatto in the Delmas woods, he was later identified as a distant relative of Lacombe, one of the most ferocious extremists in the camp of the freed people, for good measure, the next day Praloto's militia found one of their men hung from one of those rude hooks butchers use to hang quarters of beef, having split open his chest and stomach, his assassins had taken out his liver and heart, the factions armed themselves and Monsieur Barbé de Marbois, aiding Governor Blanchelande, had to deploy real diplomacy, use all his authority, even threatening to deport Praloto, in order to bring the two parties back to reason, a good thing, too, otherwise I would have missed my rendezvous with Cécile

—ever mysterious, you made me change coaches twice on the way to your house, are we in the Heights of the Marquis de Sant?

—I'm hosting you in my country home, you had to come here in his carriage so as not to raise suspicion, you haven't kissed me, Wolf?

—apologies, I've been so caught up in these twists and turns that I've forgotten the conventions of love

—I was happy to see you, you know, it's reassuring to cling to a solid piece of the past in the midst of so much worry

—six months have changed your way of speaking, you're becoming rather priggish, if not to say pedantic, Cécile

—neither one nor the other, Wolf, propelled by the nonsensical logic of their self-interest, the whites are leading us down absurd paths, whenever we rediscover the emotional path we must let our hearts speak, I am inspired by joy

pink moonlit nights, blue mornings, violet dawns, orange afternoons, flamboyant life in the shadows of giant mapou trees, parties swirling in the clearings of surging waters, *barbacoa* on the feast day of Saint-Jean, late-night celebrations from Christmas to the Epiphany, butterfly-catching tournaments, Rara carnival balls and festivities, a hodgepodge of sensations, a jumble of delights, the joy of defying old age and death, renewing time through the intoxication of the *koudyay*, each person crazier than the next, but the grimacing of death, discovery of my vulnerability, our vulnerability: a Negress has been murdered? our universe has become fragile, reminds us we are dancing on a volcano; a Negress decides one morning to return to earlier moments of her life? our guardrails are falling, the kings are naked, defenseless

—is Sonja here with you?

—she stayed on the plantation, traumatized by Saré's death, she insisted on returning to Port-au-Prince, where she stayed for two months, she returned disgusted, she vowed never to set foot there again

—will you stay with me?

—in fact I can't, though I'm happy to see you again, Governor Blanchelande has accepted my request to reorganize the Swiss Regiment, I've already begun my service

—why do they give that name to a regiment of Negro guards?

—because of the Schpeerbach, my father created it and was its first commander, but more generally as a reference to the pope's guards: soldiers straight out of a comic opera

—and out of a masked ball, my dear, their purple tunic falling over the baggy olive-brown pants contrasting with their black skin, it's ridiculously extravagant

—as of yesterday they wear a blue uniform, they're no longer marionettes dressed up to march back and forth in front of the palace of the governor and the intendant, I'm preparing them for war

—against whom?

—against the troublemakers, extremists of all kinds

—you mean against the hyper-reactionary colonists like Galbaud and the leaders of Negro insurgents like Petit-Noël Prieur

—you said it

—you will never cease to surprise me, Wolf, you are training Blacks to fight whites in the hopes they will help the latter, if need be, massacre other hotheaded Negroes

—it's not exactly that

—what is it then?

—I'm allowing them to be the arbiters of a situation that will soon get out of control if we aren't careful, they'll learn to fight this violence and align themselves with the moderate camp that

—nonsense, Wolf, and you know it, if you use violence to fight violence will they not become violent themselves? how will they benefit from supporting the cause of the moderates, and anyway do moderates exist in this powder keg brewing with all kinds of passions?

—their interest is clear, they will go from the condition of slaves to that of soldiers whose upkeep is the responsibility of the population

—I don't see the difference, as slaves they're already taken care of by their masters

—they will become part of a new group of overseers responsible not just to their masters but also to themselves

—since when have overseers not been slaves? Wolf, you're offering these poor Negroes a fool's bargain, I expected more of you

—are you criticizing me for trying, by any means, to save the fragile equilibrium of our society?

—I am criticizing you for losing yourself without realizing it, you think you're working for good but you're still mentally imprisoned by the evil that infects the colonial world, your calculations are cynical, playing the Blacks against the whites and the Blacks against the Blacks to the certain profit of the whites, I'm trying to discern even the slightest bit of generosity in your machinations, I can't see any, I once told you, Wolf, you're a hypocrite, perhaps you don't realize it, but you are fundamentally a hypocrite, and your hypocrisy is dangerous

—well, what have I done wrong?

—and naive, to boot! you haven't done anything wrong, Wolf, you want my opinion? I'll speak to you in a language that, as a Protestant, you'll understand

—I'm Catholic

—another illusion, your mentality is that of a Protestant, so think about what I am going to tell you, the evil is within you, to save yourself you have to free yourself from it

—is that all?

—almost, and please don't get angry, but how are things going between you and Sonja?

she had heard the carriage, seated facing the ocean, caught up in the interior dreams she has been dwelling on since the time of her pregnancy, lost in secret thoughts from which she excludes me and that constantly lead her back to her demented and cruel family history, head lowered, she waited

—hello, Sonja!

on leave for a month, I took the opportunity to return to the plantation, to return to myself, to the tranquility of a life swept up in the swirl of events, spirits are heating up even in the smallest villages, mulattoes and whites getting stirred up and fighting one another under the watchful eyes of the Negroes, in promulgating the Declaration of the Rights of Man and of the Citizen, the revolution in France made the freedmen of Saint-Domingue aware of their dignity, they demand their rights with increasingly inflammatory and threatening petitions, taking note of the conflicts among the propertied classes, the maroons plan and attempt audacious attacks on the plantations, bands organized and armed by our Spanish enemies strike along the border with Hispaniola, we're going to have to fight on all fronts, pulled into this attack on the country that had adopted my family, I'm not sure which camp to choose

—that of your own interests, Wolf, you're a planter, don't forget it

—I'm not forgetting it, but I do wonder if my interests are the same as yours

—why not, you walk with us, my dear, the Revolution is liberating us from the constraints of the colonial order, let's move toward autonomy for Saint-Domingue, for the freedom to trade with our neighbors and with Europe, from now on let our motto and rallying cry be: everything by and for the planters

—Monsieur Moron, allow me to share my concerns, we are demanding too much and too fast for our sole benefit, let us think of others, liberty must be for all of us on this island or for no one at all, your motto bears catastrophe within it, it singularly limits our future because it closes off the future to the mulattoes and Blacks

—Monsieur Schpeerbach, I'm willing to believe you're a liberal but your remarks are, to my mind, the words of a deserter, do you intend to abandon the cause?

—what cause, Caradeux? I will maintain my loyalty to France to the very end, but take heed, the next time you call me a deserter I'll shove those words down your throat

—gently, Colonel, just understand that I don't share your point of view, there may have been a bit of humor in what I said, I had no intention of angering you

—I want to believe you, Caradeux, but you must understand I am speaking to all of you in the language of reason, the mulattoes were born free, some Blacks have bought their freedom, together they make up the class of the freedmen, economically powerful, they already own a third of the plantations and a quarter of the slaves, is that right?

—yes, according to the latest census we did to establish the dossier of grievances to present to the Estates General

—with their economic power, what could be more natural than their demands for civil and political rights

—I'm going to stop you there, Schpeerbach, do you know what it will mean if they get them?

—yes, they will be our equals

—you see, Schpeerbach! I don't know what your idea of the mulattoes is, but despite their golden skin they are Negroes and, as such, their place is in the pigsty

—nonsense, you're spouting nonsense, the freedmen are asking to be our allies against the slaves, by rejecting their offer we're pushing them to ally themselves with the Negroes and against us, don't you see the danger? they outnumber us and the Negroes will pillage our properties, we will lose everything whereas by granting the freedmen the rights they're asking for now we save everything

—you're talking nonsense, my dear man, you bet your life if I ever see a Negro owner of my plantation, I'd shatter his head with a bullet

—if he didn't decapitate you first with his machete and take your pistol off of you

—might you be on the side of the Negroes, Schpeerbach? your plea on their behalf is quite suspect

—you haven't understood me, I realize now I'm talking to fanatics, reason is always suspect for people like you

two days before my return to Les Abricots, I learned that Ogé and Chavannes, two mulatto agitators freshly disembarked from France, had been put under house arrest in the Cap region, their activities deeply worried the colonial authorities, for they were aiming to assemble the freedmen and demand the application of the March 18, 1790, decree granting all people the right to vote and be elected

—it says people, Schpeerbach, nowhere does the decree specify men of color or emancipated Negroes

—a vicious exception, Caradeux, be careful not to fall into the trap of words, your decision is unjust, don't frustrate the mulattoes even more than

—they have no right, Schpeerbach, I'm telling you

the mulattoes were arming themselves, ready for a new confrontation with the whites, they had fought alongside the royal officials against the autonomist colonists in a proxy war, the white rosettes against the red rosettes, and they made all the difference, but Colonel Mauduit's arrogance compelled them to leave the coalition

—Colonel, we are asking to be incorporated permanently into your regiments and to wear the white cockade of the king's troops

—the descendants of slaves cannot wear the same insignia as the whites, if you want you can adopt a yellow cockade

two weeks later, Monsieur Mauduit was assassinated, when I first heard the rumors I thought it was Bauduy who had been killed and rushed to offer my condolences to Cécile

—we are taking a wrong turn

—you'll have to choose soon, behind which side will you put your Swiss Regiment?

—they will take action in accordance with the orders of the French revolutionary powers

—always loyal to the mother country

—that's being loyal to myself, Cécile, you cannot call me a hypocrite this time crossing the newer neighborhoods in Jérémie, I could see the same tension on the faces of the whites and the mulattoes, information seemed to travel faster than before, the news of the hanging of the freedman Lacombe in Le Cap had preceded me, as had that of the assassination in Petit-Goâve of the white man Ferrand de Baudières, who had supported the demands of the mulattoes, the writing is on the wall I told myself on seeing the regional quadroon militia in Source-Dommage, its commander, Lanoux, who used to sell me his cane harvests sometimes, pretended not to hear my greeting, he proceeded menacingly at the head of his fellow soldiers, all of whom were trying to look more martial than was necessary, in other times it would have had a comic effect but today it was sinister

—I am not your enemy, Lanoux, come over and drink a grog with me next Sunday

I desperately want to escape this tense atmosphere and return home, back to the quiet dawns that bathe my plantation in a serene light, the great peace of violet dusks over Lonmon Woods, but I am worried about my wife's welcome, she had not deigned to respond to any of my letters, the special delivery I sent to her was returned to me bearing only Salomon's message

Master,
    everything is going fine on the plantation, though not as well as if you were here, the sugar mill is working and although the rains in November and December lessened the sugar output, we still produced a sufficient amount, as for the house I won't say much, when you get back you will see for yourself, I hope you are not too bored in Port-au-Prince, above all don't endanger yourself, come back alive
                                            salutations from Salomon

I almost didn't recognize her, six months had been enough to transform her, my absence had changed her, she had gained weight, puffy rolls of flesh overflowed her hips, thickening a silhouette whose svelteness I could no longer recall, the features of her face, slightly broadened, accentuated the brightness and harshness of her eyes, in vain I looked for the sketch of a smile on her lips, truly I didn't recognize my wife in this precocious matron, yet she was in front of me, intact, complete in her intransigence and hatred, unchanged but physically she had mutated, I confused the sight of her with the image I had carried with me for years like a taste of joy or like the scent of cruelty, she stood up, I moved closer, kissed her on the forehead, embraced her, she stiffened in my embrace, I should have taken offense as in the past, but instead I opened my arms, relieved that my reaction was what I expected, I then understood that I had changed, I was weary of the battle I had been fighting against myself, it would only make sense if I'd found my old self again, the innocent gaze I bestowed on all things, I'm deluding myself, it would only make sense if I broke with the man I had always been and who felt such guilt in his desperate desire to be innocent, the veil had been torn, Sonja sat back down, and pointed to an armchair made of woven palm leaves

—coffee?

I didn't respond, there we were, face to face, I opened my mouth, to reestablish the connection between us, to experience the deepening of the light together, there's no point! why must it be that foolishness and pride are greater than love between us? I hear the silence, it's bitter

—Sonja, what's happening?

the sounds crackled, bursting through the speakers, flooding into the cabin on their disordered waves, the worrying clamor of a crowd, the dull hammering of feet on the tarmac, the wild eruption of joy as if thousands of unbridled instincts were exploding in the metamorphosis of an enchanted, unreal afternoon, the airplane pitches, a maniacal trepidation as if taken with madness, I'm suffocating from the shock

—my God, what's happening?

—don't panic, Sister Theresa, keep calm

some grotesque music invades me, heats up the little world of the passengers and their astonished, worried faces, it flattens me against my seat, oppresses me, I thought I would faint, then very quickly the noise came together, the drums were ringing out at the top of their lungs, exalting the sensual intoxication of life, their voices sustained by the strident caterwauling of electric guitars, punctuated by the whirring of the bass the background of a harmony exacerbated from time to time by the epileptic interventions of a trumpet

—I thought I was going to die, what is it?

—carnival, Sister Theresa, we have entered Haitian air space, the pilot decided to surprise you by playing a local radio station for you

—it's madness, this Haitian music

—as mad as jazz or reggae, bearing the creativity of an entire race

—Haitian carnival music? what I'm hearing now?

—absolutely, listen to the improvisation of the trumpet, it's the soul of tens of thousands of people, they live and dance in the streets, the rhythm of passion, jubilation, madness

—madness?

—the madness of living, a kind of revenge against the mediocrity of their existence, they're releasing a thousand and one frustrations

the airplane swayed its hips, the music churned in its blood, it cackled, the passengers stood up all at once, stomping, open arms raised above their heads, the magical play of feet, they wriggled, leapt about, shouted, jostled one another, slapped hands, exchanging laughter and glances, we are masks of madness, shaken up by the exuberance of a people that has chosen to forget its misfortune

—control yourself, Sister Theresa, you're becoming obscene

such big words, Sonja! if I have to save the Haitians I should at least experience their temptations, share with them a community of life, sin together

—fasten your seat belts

the command descends upon our joy without chilling our enthusiasm, we latch our laughter onto one another, our gaiety bound together, reinforced solidarity among fools, the joyful aircraft traces the path of two wide curves, descends quickly, lands, bounces on the runway three times, the electronic autopilot has gone off the rails, the pilot and copilot, laughing, stop right at the end of the runway, welcome to the land of carnival

—they celebrate carnival all year long

—bloody, Sister Theresa

—oh yes! the Tontons Macoutes?

—they are poems in their own right, sparkling and tragic

—who?

—the perverse side of their history

—now you're speaking in enigmas, I don't follow you anymore

—almost two centuries ago, they were our honor, our glory, the joy of all Black peoples

—but the joy remains!

—in what state?

a banner greets me, Haiti, the pearl of the Antilles, wait, I thought that was Cuba, I'll check in my travel guide, a second banner declares Long Live Difference, which kind? I have just arrived, it's true, I won't be able to understand it immediately, what is different? the tiny airport, the idiotic sun for tanning, the denuded mountains, the miasmas, decomposing tropics, for sale, the same thing everywhere in these outdated countries that manage their poverty with the insouciance characteristic of the dispossessed, what will tomorrow be like? my eyes seek a response from Sonja, she is no longer there, disappeared, she has already abandoned me, our gazes burned with the same fire for the brief time of the journey, our lips kissed the dreams we'd silenced, without ever intertwining, our hands caressed desires on the edge of vertigo, my impulses held back by the seat belt, despite everything had I tasted fervor and passion fulfilled?

—Sister Theresa, have a wonderful time in Haiti

she was waiting at the bottom of the steps, smiling, perfectly fulfilling her final role as a hostess, she turned her gaze away from mine, refusing the confessions I had hidden there, the buried tenderness, the words like a hint of modesty, my shame, the fear of new suffering, without you knowing it, we went on the most beautiful of journeys together, I loved you with the complicity of the clouds, combining the blue of your cap with the azure of the sky, the two of us soldered together in the intimacy of the pleasure we will explore one day, the time has come for separation, I have never known how to say farewell, have a good stay, thank you, a simple word, I would have liked to kiss you in front of the shocked and indignant passengers, I didn't dare hold out my hand, with the slight pressure of my fingers, cry out the pain of losing her, did I ever possess her? she is no longer wearing her gloves and her black hand stains her dress with the dried blood of the Biemmes, I flee, rolling my suitcase behind me, it laughed outrageously, I turned around to give her laughter a smack ha! ha! standing under the idiotic sun, Sonja was laughing, too, she had let her face fall to the ground, a mask of copper or brass, what do I know? looking at me, destiny's inevitably mocking expression, even closer, dozens, hundreds of devils perched high on the roof of the airport were waving their arms, handkerchiefs, and hats, the whiteness of their teeth crystallized on their black faces, the beauty of the devil, sovereign heat, sticky, coursing down my skin and wetting my clothes, hell and malediction, my bag like an overflowing locomotive wagon lagging behind, breathless I let myself fall to the ground and kneeling on the burning cement, hands clasped together, I pray, expiation has begun

—a malaise, Sister Theresa?

Sonja's voice, nothing like a caress, the metallic voice of the mask, a smell of sulfur, I stood up, frightened, scampered off without asking for my due

—the devil! the devil!

she has certainly recognized me, I know that now, she closes her eyes on the vision of the resurfacing past, protecting herself from the despair she had not been able to exorcise and that has haunted her for two centuries, faithful to the rendezvous of our history, she waits for me, rigid in the permanence of her sorrow and hatred

—you took my son from me

—keep my life in exchange

—you stole hope from us, will you give it back to us when you are once again as you were when the mask gave birth to you? I will wait as long as it takes

—I have made you wait a long while, but why have you arranged our rendezvous at the very site of our memory?

—did we have a choice? do you remember your slap, it knocked two of my teeth out, look, my mouth exhales a rotten odor, the gangrenous gums hesitate between violet and putrescent brown, look, those were my wisdom teeth, the others, after them, fell out during childhood, I must have lost my wisdom, since my friends in the madhouse sarcastically call me crazy, do you share that opinion?

—the mask falls onto the head of the king, come now, Biemme, you're a rascal, you cheated, you are mistaken, sire, I did not beat your highness in a poker game

—do you remember the iron stigmata on my back?

—why were the other slaves branded with the initials WdS and not you, Saintmilia, or your son?

—ah! you remember: Boutoug, brand her immediately, and you Boto, right now, bring the son and brand him too

—go tell your master that we are here by the will of the people and we will only leave at the tip of bayonets, I exult, my grandfather defying the king of France right alongside Mirabeau

—and then there's that infusion of hot tea you threw in my face, scalding me from head to shoulders, I almost lost my right eye because

—because what? in the end, your memories bore me, tell me instead about

she unwinds the surplus of her history, so many histories hanging by the thread of her memory, she pulls at it, pulls at it to the point of losing herself, of losing me, Wolf and his regiment of Swiss proceed with a brilliant (her way of insulting me) about-face maneuver, surrounding the white colonists in a cane field, setting it on fire (could Wolf really have done that? he surprises me) and offering victory to the freedmen on the Pernier plantation, his principles triumphed, liberty, equality, fraternity, but the slaves? Wolf, in a hurry to return to his wife, left the freedman Lambert, a Negro who'd mysteriously arrived from Martinique (oh! these Black white men of our history, Lambert, Borno, Duvalier) to negotiate liberty for the Swiss Regiment with the white colonial authorities, but betrayed by the Martinican, who declared his complete indifference to their fate, they were all killed on the pontoons at Môle Saint-Nicolas

—Sister Theresa's hands, Mother Superior, are soaked in the blood of the Swiss, she sold them to the planters

—Cécile, how could she?

—through the intermediary of Paret who warned Bauduy and Blanchelande, she pleaded with them to eliminate the Swiss Regiment because after their victory they presented a threat to all the planters

—I don't believe any of it

—it doesn't matter what you believe, she achieved her goal, to blame you, for the rest of your entire life you'll reproach yourself for having murdered your own soldiers by leaving Lambert in command

—diabolical

—what are you going to do?

—reconstitute the Swiss Regiment and commit myself resolutely to the cause of those fighting for liberty

—you want to become an outlaw? the Swiss Regiment has been definitively dissolved, on the order of the governor

—without telling me?

—what would that have changed? go back to your plantation, Wolf, let the white and mulatto politicians tear each other apart, one day the Negroes will bring them back to reason, trust my experience

—Cécile, I should put a bullet in my head

—why?

—in less than two years, two stains have tarnished my honor as a soldier

—your death won't resolve anything and won't give you back the honor you think you've lost, go home, a more urgent task awaits you there

—which one?

—to save Salomon, to save your memory and your childhood, to prevent the shipwreck of your life, otherwise

—otherwise?

he didn't dare speak, he didn't dare look at me, but I assumed he had learned the truth, Cécile, that whore, informed him, the letter I intercepted leaves no doubt, unfortunately the date it was sent is not mentioned, so I won't know with certainty for how long he has known about my activities

> dear friend,
>
> things are happening, strange to say the least, on your plantation, as soon as you get back, try to come see me quickly for fuller details
>
> yours,
>
> Cécile

what is he waiting for and why? he's probably trying to find the right words, between anger and pity, hesitating about what decisions to make, I know him, incapable of hating he loses himself in conjectures, inventing explanations and reasons to exculpate me not because he thinks I am truly innocent but because he's trying to preserve the image he has of me, the image of his happiness, forests, groves, laughter, promenades, kisses, embraces, spices, sugar, rum, tobacco, the ordinariness of a life with nothing appealing about it, a dream of mediocrity that I sought to shatter from the beginning, but he's holding on to it, a peasant's stubbornness, forcing me to always go further in my intent to open his eyes, to finally break him, to impose myself on him just as I am, the way I want him to see me, to see humility and admiration in his eyes, and then to cherish his weakness and to rebuild the ancient pride of the Biemme upon it, why else would I have come to waste away in the islands, surrounded by the promiscuity of these strange-smelling Negroes? to whip them, knock them about, use them to excess, exploit them even more, in service to my best interest, I already rebuilt our ancient and venerable dwelling, sculpted on the front wall of the dungeon, as a kind of defiance of time and history, the curse of the mask and the Bohemian

—explain all this to me

—there is nothing to explain that you don't already know

—still, I would like to understand

—what for?

the question took me by surprise, Sonja was right, what for, in truth? to force her to admit she was guilty, to try to understand, to find excuses for her? is that necessary? Sonja had assimilated the principles of the Biemmes very well, outside of all morality, her actions found their justification within themselves, solely on the basis of the interests of the clan

—contraband is illegal and dangerous, isn't that so?

—of course, I admit that my Christian conscience disapproves of such tactics, and does not allow me to render unto Caesar that which is Caesar's due, but since free trade is a sacred right in Switzerland, I figure . . .

—are you a Swiss citizen or a French citizen?

—the question is irrelevant, commerce has no nation

—or much morality, Wolf, let's admit, but let's leave morality aside, can I make a suggestion?

—I'm listening

—do you think it's profitable to maintain business relations only with Captain Percy?

—certainly not, but what other solution is there? the Royal Navy is watching, and potential clients avoid taking too many risks

—so Captain Percy pays us the prices he wishes

—would another offer us any better?

—you would compare and choose

—that's easy to say, but where to find this good Samaritan?

—be at Petite-Anse at midnight, an American ship will anchor there, raise and lower your lantern three times, the ship will respond to your signal, a dinghy will bring you a good client

—you surprise me, Sonja, who is this good client?

—don't ask questions, I'm watching out for your interests, as you negotiate, bear in mind that it will also benefit my family

—what does that mean? aren't I your family?

—how and from whom did she find out? did you not assure me, Mother Superior, that this woman is mad?

—obviously I am mad, that's why I stole his eyes from the night, I see the hidden corners of his soul, break down his joy and pain, penetrate their secrets, do you hear the drum's heartbeat? it announces the arrival of the American, Sister Theresa, why are you hiding from the Negroes who embalm the sugar and rum, turn blue from the indigo, snow underneath the avalanches of cotton? why do you lock yourself in your cabin to write a letter that you'll give to the overseer Ouzog? for your mistress, you murmur, for no one else, if the master is present, the missives weep in the drawers, the writing heavy and fat, they sulk and the mistress is unhappy, why is that? the moon knows the answer, it enveloped me in its brightness and the night spoke to me, passing through the porthole, I surprised Sister Theresa despite her vigilance, landing right on her nose

—Saintmilia, you! a black butterfly!

—a nighttime metamorphosis! anticipating your move to chase me away, my wings carried me far out of reach of your hands as my eyes continued frolicking about the cabin, where did your hair go?

—gathered at my neck in a braid

—a worried wrinkle crossed your forehead

—the royal corvette *Le Vigilant* and its thirty cannons is patrolling close by

—the flash of lightning in your eyes singed my wings

—I didn't do it on purpose

—it was definitely her, Mother Superior, I was not lying, we have known each other ever since the first days of creation, I am the water and she is the fire

—that's Ericq, my twin brother, the last male descendant of the Biemmes

—you hid him from me?

—what do my family matters have to do with you, Monsieur Schpeerbach?

formidable Sonja, she had sought financial independence by setting up a shop selling tafia in the village, organizing the daily routine in the house and the maintenance of the slaves as she wished, curiously, she had found a way to reconcile her taste for luxury and her pronounced thriftiness, very quickly she had made a small fortune, which she invested in purchasing and arming a small ship, her brother was the brawn with the contraband, she was the brains of the operation, receiving lengthy reports, accounts of sales, purchases, and investments, and in return she dispatched her instructions, which proceeded via side roads, dismayed by the heavy responsibility, Ouzog threaded his way through the brush, glided through the low foliage, stretched or flattened himself between two rock flats, frightened of his own shadow

—one day, for no real reason, she sent for Ouzog, Sister Theresa, do you remember, cruel one

—tie his hands behind his back

—you grab his throat, he moans, drooling, his eyes popping out of his head, his tongue protruding from his mouth, your razor abruptly silenced him for good

—did I have any choice? only the mute don't speak

—the dead do not speak either

—he was useful to me alive

—cruel one

—no more than you, slandering me all day long, distorting the facts, intentionally ignoring the most important thing, recount how

I rewarded Ouzog, the nicest hut, a little bit of land, presents after each journey, American pants and vests for him, dresses and toys for his wife and children, the only happy Negro family on the plantation, occasionally I gave him a little money, if he saved up, he could have bought his freedom one day

—what was the price of his silence? he loved to laugh, and you made him sullen and taciturn, he loved to tell stories, our memories collected in a corner of his mind, you murdered our memory on his lips, there he was, condemned, by your revolting generosity, to the silence of the tomb

—more of your ridiculous stories, why do the Negroes take so much pleasure in listening to you?

incomprehensible, unimaginable, they flood out from the northern gate of the cemetery on the outskirts of town, white-skinned, black legs, portly and plump, chubby and hairy, the bystanders confirm that they are zonbi raised by Toukouma, exterminating angels vomited up from hell, but why then those white woolen masks that make them look like a procession of saintly hermits, they stroll unctuously along the funeral street, swaying their hips like vulgar prostitutes, the Vodou initiates hold back their laughter as they rush to put on their ceremonial garments, they cross the plaza facing the cathedral, stop at the little market, sprinkle their fleece with a fine dusting of charcoal, bleat provocatively, as if to declare the triumph of Black over white, take up their procession again, climb the hill at Bel-Air and end up at the sentry box of the governor's residence, the first one stands on his hind legs, the second lies down with his belly in the air, the third lowers his head and clears his throat, as for the fourth, he begins a speech, blathering on about liberty, equality, fraternity

—he never finished, a bullet passed through his thick sheep's head

—the whites, who we despise, have consigned to their record book, for the benefit of history, that one of Beauvais's soldiers admonished one of

—Praloto's artillerymen, the latter lit his fuse and fired on the crowd of sheep, for in an instant they were thousands of black beasts unleashed on the upscale neighborhoods of Bel-Air, the result, Wolf, fire, with a lick of its tongue, spread through the houses, rolled right through the hills and its fury laid siege to the clouds, torrents of flames roared, hissed, rumbled, turned angrily upon themselves, poured into the ravines at Saint-Martin, which drained their devastating madness into the ocean, the muskets rang out, cannons blared, punctuating the screams and terrified voices with their alarms, the punctured air quivered, everywhere the whistling of bitterness, blind hatred, the clash of prejudices, disdain and vengeance, blood

—despite the Concordat de Damien?

—the massacre of your Swiss Regiment has called it into question, delivered from the fear of Black troops, the whites became arrogant again

—Cécile, if the mulattoes have learned anything, they will have already sealed an alliance with the enslaved, the logic of events compels them

—rather, the folly of the planters

—you're right, all of our folly, the colony is now a powder keg that the tiniest spark can detonate

—you're lying, Sister Theresa

—the nerve of you, interrupting me

—impudent one, you distort the truth, none of those sheep navigated through the bay of L'Anse-du-Clerc, the thunder shook the air, the fiery boat passed by Bonbon Point and the sand from Petite-Anse filled Boutoug's eyes, his hair, and even his dumbstruck mouth, a ball of fire, four times bigger than his fist, slammed down four fathoms beneath his toes

—Salomon! quickly! a horse and pistols in the saddle holsters

—I won't let you go out alone, Mistress

—come with me, gather the Negroes, tell them to wrangle all the mules and horses they can to pick up the merchandise

—you had wings, Sister Theresa, you flew toward yourself, toward another existence, at once other and part of your own life, which played out its destiny each time, lost between the sky and the water, it sustained your dream of reconquering hope

—hope lost forever

—the night carries me ahead of you, the night my friend from the old days gleaming with joy on the savanna, it opens my eyes and sings into my ears, more thunder, the foremast, you are surprised I know the language of your family, the foremast, broken almost level with the deck, collapsed in a tangle of ropes and folded sails, the portholes of the ship opened up, spat out portside, pivoted, veered windward, vomited flames to the starboard side, the grapeshot crackled, smashing into the wood panels with a sinister crunching sound, swept away the deck of the ship and its agonized pleas, struck the deckhouse in a direct hit, blowing it to bits, razed the afterdeck with the precision of a metalworker, carrying away your head, Sister Theresa, far above the inlet, placed it in your arms at the very moment you set foot at the top of the cliff at Trou-Fol, later you'll claim that the Negroes had clouded the day with their magic

—were you crying?

—yes, Wolf, I was crying for the first time in my life, crying out of rage at the stupidity of fate, it hounds and condemns us, ruins our projects, I thought I was up to the challenge when I put four thousand leagues between that curse and us, using up my energies to rebuild a name, a fortune, but it didn't work out for us

—Sister Theresa, between love and hate, you chose hate

—and vengeance, I was wrong, Wolf, I should have loved you for what you were offering me, I took advantage of you to settle my scores with a past too full of ugly stories, here I am at the edge of the abyss, alone with my mourning, custodian of an inheritance that I cannot renounce without falling short

—shall I reveal, Sister Theresa, that you unraveled your only braid, buried your head between the roots of a giant akoma tree while Boutoug nailed a grimacing mask on its trunk, during each season of the north winds you screech, the crime rolls across the backs of the centuries, such a need for carnage reflected in your savage eyes, a heart eaten away by violence and, more than anything, the tragedy that will bring us from one calamity to the next until the end of my days

—do you hear me? overtaken by your worries and regrets, you travel far from me, inventing ways to save your name from disaster, to repair my shame, trying not to add an even greater dishonor to this series of dishonors, defeated soldier, felonious leader, smuggler and, on top of all that, slave trader

—not that, my God, not that

—what? Cécile didn't tell you? I'm in the business of selling Negroes

—I know that you used my seal to order Lambert to sell out my Swiss Regiment to the English in Jamaica, to the Spanish in Cuba, because you hate the Negroes or out of a need to ruin my career?

—it was for the love of money, it's as simple as that

—you could just have asked me for some

—ask! ask! and be dependent

—but you are my wife, Sonja, what would be shameful about

—I am the wife of a certain destiny, Wolf, not of a man, never forget that

I know it, I, Saintmilia, queen turtledove of sleepless nights, you had chosen Salomon, he should have been your first victim but he uncovered your trap, it was a mistake to ask him about the Negroes on the plantation, about their habits, about the maroons and their hiding places

—would you like to live their life?

—they are free

—a hunted freedom, threatened each day

—it doesn't matter, they have chosen it and that is what makes them free

—why do you not join them? you know where they're hiding, right? so go, since you like their freedom so much, go, no one will stop you, least of all me

he had smiled, it was childish, of course he knew their sanctuaries, you could do your best to follow him at a distance and find the few traces they leave behind to mark the path for those they've conjured, Salomon wasn't fooled and he was suspicious of your kindness when, feigning to pity the fate of the slaves, you applauded the escape of a Negro, against your own interests, you who hates us so! was that not surprising? and then, why those repeated visits to Clérié when the master wasn't around, why didn't the slaves who disappeared ever reappear in the ranks of the fighters at Trois-Mamelles? the drum calls them to the assembly in vain, our voices sojourn in silence and there is no echo, even Toukouma didn't enlist us in her regiment of zonbi, so tell me, Sister Theresa, where did you put us

—look in the two caves at Bonbon when the ocean beats against the flanks of the cliffs, lamentations and wailing filter through the cracks, tonight you won't hear them, my brother already packed up a shipment that he'll sell in Louisiana, unseen and unknown, the drum wails, the conch shell blows, none among the living respond, Africa is severed from one possibility: the renewal of its myths, only the shrewd intelligence of the Biemmes triumphs

—so it was a good idea for me to meet you in this isolated village, Jérémie is a town of dust and swamps, unhealthy in every season

—you're mixing up your memories, in the Grande'Anse loop the climate is even, and constant all year round, a real paradise for tourists, are you on vacation? did you bring Carmenta?

—I am alone and I agonized over you

—I don't recognize you without the blue Air France logo

—because it is the color of African skies and it suits me?

—truly, you are here! it really is you! I'm dreaming, Sonja, tell me I'm dreaming

—not at all, I'm here, Sister Theresa, in the flesh, I'm seeking, seeking our memories, you left me in the plane with my feelings

—shh! lower your voice

—unfulfilled

—be quiet, we are no longer thousands of feet above the sounds and ears on the ground, here, even silence knows how to listen, you wouldn't want Saintmilia's unhinged world to come across our secret, would you?

—too bad, what would be the problem?

—love, according to one of their songs, is a disease that is hard to cure

—a commonplace

—eaten away by sadness

—but do you still love Sister Hyacinthe? she's kept your gaze aflame in her heart, and when I gave her your message

—which one?

—how am I supposed to remember if you've already forgotten?

—Sonja! I'm so tired, I feel like I am coming back from far away, so far away

—Sister Theresa! Sister Theresa!

—Sister Hyacinthe, don't shout, your voice hurts my ears

—you don't recognize me?

—Mother Superior, I do recognize you, of course I recognize you

—you were sick for a long time, the very day of your arrival the sun was playing in your head

—I have no memory of the taste of a kiss

—you bear the mark of one on your forehead

—he hurt me with love, the sun, oh, the sun

—Sister Theresa, are you feeling all right?

—I'm happy to be the wife of the sun, sorry, of the Lord, but my head is a little heavy

—that's the effect of the sedatives, Marie Auxiliatrice, with the help of her girls, has brought back Sister Theresa, let us thank her and bless her works

—Sister Theresa, why in your delirium did you link my name to Saintmilia's, Wolf's, to a litany of Africans and Italians

—a family history, tell them

she locked herself up in a disconcerting muteness, diverting my questions in advance so as to better sound my silence and force me to be prudent with her, to show a restraint that she probably saw as weakness, we held ourselves stiffly, pallid, not knowing how to begin the necessary conversation that would finally bring us to our truth, naked, diluting the false image of one another we held on to out of some need to preserve whatever emotion we had left, linked to the fragility of memories, the sun is already low on the horizon, it is no longer hot but not yet cool, as if the temperature were hesitating to make a decision, I sought out Sonja's gaze, her transparent yet closed expression, the wrinkles visible beneath the thin layer of fat on her jowls, the recent events have aged her, she lowers her eyes, dusty boots, worn leather, they had covered many miles, their shine now foreign to this man, he himself a true stranger to everything ever since he learned of the massacre of his soldiers, he was attached to them because they were his dream, a project of moderation in the midst of torment, the future rescued through clairvoyance and wisdom, I clipped the wings of his dream and his silence holds me accountable, I beg of you, Wolf, don't look at me, I, too, have lost my certainties, my ambitions, my pride, the harshness of fate has dealt us the same hand, he's there, splendid, he's suffering, I feel it, his hair golden in the fires of the setting sun, his figure suffused with a light that transforms his sadness into something sublime, so beautiful that it troubles me, alters my vision, his ravaged beauty, virile, an impression of quiet strength, as if suffering has matured him, a surge, I would like to share his suffering, to feel alongside him the marvelous joy of being unhappy together now, I can't manage it, seeing his suffering holds me back, this will likely be the last chance, why would I give him the means, through memories, to think of me differently, to see me otherwise, just discovering him in that moment, as he was, made me feel regret, I'll hold this against him, surely, blaming myself, thinking about the love that never was, she hadn't wanted that, she preferred to live the breath of the moment in its ephemeral and tragic intensity, she's pale, the intoxication of life exhausts her, its disappointments have carved an expression of torment on her face, to no longer see her distress, the sea shimmers in her eyes but doesn't diminish their glinting coldness, mirrors as frozen as the fires of an iceberg, this woman is mine, for how much longer will I prolong the illusion? take her in my arms, combine our mutual desperation, place my sadness on her lips, name her desire, touch her former pleasures, whimper, hear the wind and the waves beating in our temples with great jolts of pleasure, don't look for me anymore, you will have been nothing but a beautiful animal in my life, that other version of you, that Salomon, he remains a trap for me, he nearly captured my joy, unlike you, he brings a certain savagery to his voice and to his gestures and to his brusque flights of exaltation, an excessiveness all the more pathetic in that it refuses, without admitting it, its condition and its true state, he's the only one who makes me feel weak, willing, in advance, to rejoice in losing myself, in denying myself, all reasons to hate him, because of him I hated you as well, he bears no resemblance to the image I aspired to, he is what I was looking for, existing otherwise than in my gaze, sorry, what's that you just muttered? I can't understand, so I have absolved you, our union only makes sense in the absolute or in the absurd, shot through with the enchantment of twilight, you are not life, dead to everything, you are destined by your very birth to disaster, I can either follow you along the path of crime or I can escape you, but in truth, will I be saved? at no point will I escape your suffering, it skulks around us, in this compact silence more oppressive than your hatred, more cruel than the joy you take in destroying us, the dead float around somewhere inside us, they have untied the strips of cloth binding their limbs, they travel beyond all sensation in a dead universe, you understand? to lean against your chest, to kiss you, tender Wolf, in my memories, speak, don't leave, speak, you have killed me by never having understood what I expected from you

—Sonja

he spoke, my name, a fervent murmur, the silence changed tonality, broke the spell, once again resentment between us, ghostlike, love has fled, leaving a swell of sadness in my heart, piercing, our situation is inhuman, how was Wolf able to bear such tension in our relationship? keep talking, granting yourself the right to direct, to command, to beat, to destroy, to denounce violent words with new words of violence, the stubborn silence of speech, a pelican flies just above the waves, small boats, unmoving in the bay, sound the depths of the water, the sun leans over the edge of the abyss, Wolf contents himself with a smile, his face is as beautiful as the dusk, the tension in his gaze replaced by serenity, you exasperate me, Wolf

—we're going back to France
—when?
—in one week
—for vacation?
—permanently
—the plantation? what will we do with it?
—I am turning over the management to Salomon by proxy
—why don't you sell it?
—I tried, but I didn't find any buyers, everyone's selling
—choose a white manager
—Salomon is a guarantee for the future
—do we have a future here?
—I fear not

the silence has spoken, Sister Theresa, my master seeks joy and love in your voice, the distant heart of the night, solitude, like a sullen bird, regrets as deep as his need for love, he would have sensed your hand on his chest, the shuddering of leaves awakening scattered sensations, the freshness of a sudden smile, the rediscovered soul of things dissipating ancient worries, no, the indifference on your lips did not mutter his name and your cruelty toward me betrayed him, time obliterated, your heat dispersed among the ridges of the hills, attached to little bells that ring with fleeting hope, I will come sit down in that deserted place, paralyzed with suffering and solitude, I will hold out my arm, my brandished fist jostling the audacity of the sun's rays, trying through the light to deliver us from the terrible spell that infuses our life of nightmares, your heart on fire you open the window, like every day at the same hour, the astonished day resuscitates my ancient fears, grimaces, the resentments persist and the anger rumbles, overflowing the usual boundaries of petty squabbles, the punishments you dole out because I'm sulking, why should I laugh if life's misfortunes have ruined joy? you speak when others are quiet, of course, because since your return I have broken my vow of silence, my memory clears the paths of hatred and I say woe unto you, are you threatening me Saintmilia? Sister Theresa, my name is Ti Mèmè N'kedi, stop caricaturing my name, you rebel while the others do exactly as they're told, indeed I have been free for two centuries, I have learned to swear, not to submit, there is not room for both of us in this hospice, Saintmilia, my son conquered this country, Sister Theresa, you lie, he took over my grandfather's plantation, rights confronted pretensions, the years set the scene, along with men's sweat and blood, if time has allowed the executioner to forget, not so for the land that drank the blood, it is the living heart, fervid heart of hatred, spilled blood has a long memory, cries a proverb from the faraway bush, blood cannot be redeemed with good works or good deeds, besides, Sister Theresa, in your country any good deed is lost forever, you open the window, the day floods in, chasing the moisture of dreams from your pillow, your upright specter, rendered transparent by the blue magic of the light, emerges from the abyss of the centuries, attacks the hatred and curses intertwined in a mother's thoughts, every evening my eyes bury beneath my eyelids a past that refuses to die, forests thick with memories, rivers of dreams flowing from the madness of night, the smells of dawn wash over my awakening, our feet drink from the dew, run down unknown paths toward the impromptu of new delights, plunging the vast array of passions into the most distant ponds, all saturated with the low shadow of bamboo and mangroves, don't move, above all don't speak, the waves no longer whisper with the sound of your games or your antics, my fright, the shadow falters, the green shadow carved into rings that rustle and whistle, the shadow unfolds, suspended, deploys its suppleness, my God! a couleuvre-flambeau, the most aggressive species of serpent in Saint-Domingue, there is no venom in its fangs but it is more dangerous than a viper, always lying in wait on some tree branch, it drops suddenly onto your shoulders, coils up, envelops you, strangles you for the pure pleasure of killing, hunts on the orders of Damballah Wedo, that perverse and lecherous lwa with the phosphorescent eyes, it's all right it's all right, the old tune like a warning freezes the blood of the righteous, close your eyes, break with the fascination of its gaze, to be saved, the wind laughs, creaks and squawks in the bamboo, the cunning and ferocity of Damballah runs through our heads, undulates, a dance of seduction, sensual, dance of death, terrifying, the shadow approaches, Wedo, the air moves, real good real good, the green shadow raises its triangular head, the forked tongue close to your face, Sister Theresa, watch out! the cold caress of the kiss, Salomon suddenly appears, he has evaded the shadow, he whistles, Damballah Wedo, stopped in his tracks, ceases his twirling coquetry, what impudent wretch has dared to interrupt the dance of love and death? your eyes terrified, those of Damballah widen, narrow, mere embers that speak his rage

—I can't do it anymore, Saintmilia, my head is spinning already

—don't faint, the climax is coming, take a good look at Salomon, he is your God, Sister Theresa, Agoué against Damballah, the life of a white woman comes between them? no! no! between them there is the friendship of my two sons, they both drank the slave's milk, that solidarity is stronger than death, but woe to us all, to us Negroes, we always pay the rivalry between our lwa with our own lives, in a single movement Damballah turns around, springs forth from his coils, the devastating power of thunder in his tongue, Agoué has anticipated the movement and the ruse, he lowers himself, rapidly holds out his arm, grabs the serpent, and breaks its vertebrae with a single jolt, Damballah Wedo, it's all right it's all right, a little cry, the day becomes cloudy in my eyes, loses its rainbow colors, turns blue, veers into black, not even a shudder, the entire length of its body slowly unfolds, the green

shadow turned gray detaches itself and falls flaccid, the water on Byroth Hill sneezes, curses! Agoué has vanquished Damballah, woe is
me! Sister Theresa, Salomon has ruined our chance at living

—I found out too late, I've fallen into a black hole, the emotion was
too intense

—yes, Mistress, I've prepared you a tea of lemon balm, thyme, and
mint to flush out the bad blood, the master is at the sugar works, I've
sent someone to tell him, he'll be here soon

—am I alive, Saintmilia, truly alive?

—of course, Mistress

—by what miracle?

—you were sinking and the current was already carrying you away,
Salomon fished you out, he had to take you in his arms, forgive him,
Sister Theresa, he knows that a Negro must never touch a white woman,
not even in his dreams, but in the circumstances could he have let you
die? so he took you in his arms and, Mistress, you inadvertently put
your hands around his neck to keep yourself from falling

—it was like a feeling of strange and painful reassurance

—I trembled for Salomon, he was carrying his own death sentence
in his arms, for if a white man had seen the two of you my son would
have been marked for the gallows, he lay you down on the riverbank

—a bed of moss

—as he began to stand up, you held him back, kept him bent over
you, his shadow, dripping water in the sunlight, he gleamed with your
desire

—I opened my eyes and mouth, the taste of the water from his body
on my lips, his shadow sinking into my body, weighty with violent sensations, the rough caress of his fingers, his heaving breath, a slave does
not exist, tell me it was a man who carried me and lay me down in the
thick grass, tell me it was a man bent over me, that his

—he pulled away, my son is no fool! he untangled your arms, Salomon is not a man, he is your husband's property

—be quiet, Saintmilia, don't stir up ghostly memories, don't blame
me for a mistake from which I know I shall never escape, I bit into a
dream as if it were a ripe fruit, my teeth reddened by its juices, my
mouth full of flavors, yet, my tongue bruised, I chew on my bitterness

—Sister Theresa, you hate Salomon, what price has he paid for your obsessions, the fact that he holds behind his eyes the image of your blessed nakedness?

—Salomon

—yes, Mistress!

—I haven't seen you on the plantation lately

—I'm busy overseeing the planting of new cane fields

—for three weeks?

—there are a hundred and fifty acres to clear and plant

—does that mean I can't go on my horseback rides anymore?

—no, Mistress

—so why is it that I've been deprived of them ever since my near drowning in the Couleuvre River?

—I don't know what you're talking about

—don't play dumb, you're an intelligent Negro, you've understood perfectly, are you avoiding me?

—a slave flees into the woods, seeking liberty

—you're no slave

—am I a free man? can I go to Jérémie without your permission, or that of my master?

—you've changed the subject, you didn't answer my question

—it's always the same subject, if you ask me a question, it is up to you to find the answer

—you're becoming insolent, I am too good to you, I'll talk to Wolf and have him whip you

—I shall thank him on that day, for he'll have put us each back in our place

—what do you mean?

—nothing more than what you've heard

—I'm losing my patience with you, saddle up the horses, quickly, we're going to Seringue for the day, have the kitchen prepare us a cold meal, wait! one question, why have you not taken a wife, like the other Negroes?

—I have no right to transmit my chains as an inheritance for my children, I'll start a family when, born of a free father and mother, my sons will be the property of no master

—like Klaus

—yes, Mistress, like your son

where is he hiding? is he alive? sick? a monk? a soldier? having just arrived in Bordeaux in February 1792, I set off for Paris to see him, a former student of the Jesuits he had purchased a position in the Parlement de Paris and was representing the Third Estate in the Estates General, having not had any news from him, I hoped he hadn't been carried away in the series of tragic events that had shaken the old kingdom of France, which had since become a republic at war with all Europe, coalesced against the winds of liberty that blew from Paris toward all the capitals, destabilizing thrones, threatening the privileges of some and the feudal prerogatives of others, as a prudent and wise lawyer, Klaus had probably taken refuge in Brittany in the family castle, unless he'd decided to ride the republican wave, in which case he would still be living in our town house, but he wasn't there, he had left in September, the day after the decapitation of the king, I continued toward Switzerland, to see my family again, invest my money in their watchmaking and cheesemaking businesses, I had managed to save up a nice little sum from the disaster, combined with my savings it made up a lucrative bit of capital that would allow the Schpeerbachs to expand their factories and become leaders in the European watchmaking industry, once my affairs are in order I'll return to France, my heart full with worry but with the secret hope of holding Klaus in my arms, twenty years of separation had changed us both, letters had become more and more infrequent over the years, vaguely hinting at the evolution of my son's ideas and personality, intransigent and libertarian, he had ridiculed my advice to act with moderation and, likely irritated, had stopped responding to my letters, in this period of tumult I feared the worst, so I was eager to find him, unfortunately, destiny had other plans and at Strasbourg, the first and last stop in my pilgrimage to France, I was arrested at the border as a foreign agent, brought before a revolutionary tribunal, released for lack of evidence thanks to the intervention of a concerned friend on the Committee of Public Safety who arranged for house arrest, I briefly thought of writing to Sonja's distant cousins in Brittany and asking Klaus, if he happened to be there, to come join me, by bribing local authorities, we might cross the Rhine into Switzerland via Karlsruhe, but I hesitated as the mail wasn't secure, I risked deepening the suspicions about me, Brittany bordered the Vendée, which was in revolt against the republic, any correspondence with family living in that war zone would have compromised me, the Revolution's spies would sooner or later have accused me of complicity with the enemy, I decided it was safer to wait, dreaming every day of an end to the turmoil, wishing for calm to be restored so that I could continue on my way, crisscross all of France, find Klaus in some inn, hollering and drinking in the virile, bawdy tradition of the Biemmes, I paid close attention to the news from the Vendée, knowing how my son always insisted on the absolute freedom of citizens against the tyranny of power, a moral exigency shared by his ancestors, with the results we all remember, he had surely aligned himself with the Chouans, I scrutinized the most minor military proclamations, the most insignificant gazettes relaying news of events in the most isolated places, I regularly went to the post office to gather information, looking for the Biemme name, hoping to hear Klaus's name randomly mentioned in a conversation among travelers, to know my son was alive, it was pointless, the gazettes and proclamations stayed mute, the travelers indifferent, years passed but, rather than despairing, I latched on to the certainty, perhaps unreasonable, that I would meet Klaus, one day the Terror ended, France had survived and come back to life, moved into the Consulate relieved, breathed, the Revolution had exhausted its last reserves in partisan struggles, but paradoxically the revolutionary spirit remained intact, the French burned with the desire to export and impose their ideals of liberty and fraternity throughout Europe, I was waiting for Bonaparte to stabilize his power through a coup d'état, to put an end to the insecurity and agitation, I got back on the road, but not before having gotten the new authorities to end my house arrest, carrying a travel pass I'd paid a handsome price for (the new regime knows how to talk business, that's a good sign) I left Strasbourg

France running along, landscapes of beech, birch, and chestnut trees, elms and larches, I galloped through Lorraine, dancing, a canal flanked by willows and poplars, on the bridge at Avignon, we dance round and round, parading, the Seine and my loves, always
    —Sister Theresa, you! in Paris!

—Malbrough is going to war, la di di, la di da, ah! yes! I'm here, on vacation for a few days, I smelled your perfume on the square in front of Notre-Dame and I followed the trail

—I'm just back from a fitting for Rochas

—you're modeling now? Air France?

—tired of flitting from one continent to another like a bird, the company's smile on my lips

—you'd rather be smiling in photographs, the face of Rochas

—the fragrance, I am the eternal feminine, gazelle of the savanna, reindeer of the tundra, hummingbird of the islands

—my damnation

—the dream

the first night in the Biemme castle a mask assailed my sleep, I had noticed it on the drawbridge, on seeing me it seemed to awaken from centuries of rest, it grimaced a welcoming smile, it likely followed me, hiding behind the heavy curtains in the salon and the venerable columns in the dining room, and then stealthily down the hallways, I had barely closed my eyes when it struck while yelping like a fox, with diabolical dexterity it tried to flatten itself against my face, I turned my head from one side to the other on the pillow, buried it in the sheets, rolled on my side, a desperate attempt to escape the raging assaults, the idea came to me to stick my fingers into the empty eye sockets, the mask screamed, I woke with a jolt, the room was filled with a green, seemingly lunar light, I was suffocating as if there were hands around my throat, fighting back, struggling, I tried to free myself from the invisible grip, my fingers shone green, burning my neck, an intolerable feeling, come to my rescue, Eternal Lord

—sir, sir, you cried out!

—the mask!

—that's what I thought, it has wasted no time, it recognized a member of the family

—I am not a Biemme

—you might as well be

the castle had been requisitioned by General Hoche's staff, it had served as headquarters for the Army of the West, which had cordoned off the Finistère and the Morbihan regions and thus prevented any resupplying from the north of the retreating Chouan troops, contained just short of the Loire River, barely kept up by the rabble of soldiers, its wood paneling unpolished and cracking, a fine brown dust seeped out of the cracks here and there, the decrepit masonry, overgrown gorse shrubs choking the ditches, grasses and plants invading the crevices of the walls, all attested to the old home's state of abandon, proud of its six centuries of history and calamitous drama, a servant couple, stationed there for generations, took charge of managing the presence of the Biemmes, imposing, dominating the barrens and almost as old as the Armorican Massif, they are the soul of the castle, which survived with and through them, the memory of a family that the devout of the local village always name while making the sign of the cross, they were my last hope of getting news of Klaus

—such a beautiful young man, the fatal beauty of the Biemmes, his gloomy, tormented childhood wandered through the rooms looking for who knows what, as an adolescent, he came for short, infrequent holidays, which he spent holed up in the library, reading or recopying books yellowed with age, we hadn't seen him again until that evening when, at the head of a dozen or so youth about his age, he knocked loudly on the door

—we'll be staying here for two days, only for two days, as we're just passing through

—but where are you going, Monsieur Baron?

—Joseph, my good man, if anyone asks, tell them you don't know anything about it

—understood

—we're awaiting messages from Lorient and Nantes, let us know as soon as they arrive, and now give us something to drink

they spoke loudly, drank heavily, in the middle of the night they ordered me to bring some girls and they reveled until dawn, it seemed like they were in a rush to live, to wring everything they could out of life, settled in the right wing they carried on wildly despite my warnings to be careful, your family, Monsieur Baron, does not solely have friends, better to go unnoticed

—no revolution is going to scare a Biemme

—of course, but

—there is no but, Joseph, let those head choppers come, my friends and I will know just how to greet them

—a pure Biemme, ready to defy the entire world

—and they came, a whole group of them, the Revolutionary Council from Quimper, the Committee of Public Safety from Brest, the commissioners and a troop led by one of the former sharecroppers from the estate, a man named Schmatte, his name suits him

—these are the suspects, arrest them!

—Schmatte dared put his hand on the baron's collar

—how did my son respond?

—instantly and thunderously, he slapped Schmatte with the front and back of his hand, then shattered his head with a shot from his pistol

—mad, mad, Biemme, he is lost

—not at all, taking advantage of all the confusion, he knocked over one of the horsemen, jumped on his horse, and fled at full gallop

—what happened to his friends?

—they were all guillotined, God rest their souls!

on the tomb of the Blacks who had been mowed down alongside Saré, Father Aloïus called for God's mercy, Salomon raised his eyes, surprised, incredulous, we glanced at each other, we heard and understood, did the others gathered there understand the implications of this prayer for the souls of the dead? for the first time a mixed religious ceremony was calling on God to bless the souls of both whites and Negroes, so the Blacks had a soul after all that could be saved by prayers for the whites, that very afternoon the drums called out to each other from one mountaintop to the next, the following morning, the clear eyes of the Blacks met the twin souls of their white masters with derisive greetings

—night heavy with our distress, overflowing with our dreams, I cannot feel my body, the whites have battered it, they have broken the bones of Ogé and Chavannes because, as mulattoes, they refused to be Negroes, Mackandal vomited his breath on the pyre, apotheosis of flames for the liberation of a soul, mischievous mosquito, it thumbed its nose at the planters before flying off to Africa, Sister Theresa, you walked Boukman through the streets of Le Cap and, on a placard, you pinned his hopes, drunk from having borne all the sufferings and miseries of life as a Negro: here is the head of Boukman, leader of the rebels

—Schmatte planted their heads on the ends of pikes stuck between the battlements in the dungeon

—and the crows plucked the hopes for the liberty of an entire people from my eyes, Boukman, goddammit, you are a great Negro, yes it is I, Saintmilia, saying this, I know of what I speak, you struck at the darkness with your fist, the lightning tore through the sky, immense and pathetic, charged with the turbulence and passion of an entire race, you shattered the night, I saw the sky break open, the blood flow in torrents on the faces of the conspirators, they cried out in a single voice: live free or die, a pig was brought out and you, possessed with hope and justice, raised your cutlass, to live free, our voices shaking with emotion, hate and vengeance merged into a single will, or die, a cry, a decision flowing from the plains to the hills, from the valleys to the mountains, to no longer be afraid, an ardent thirst, to be born, to be resuscitated, to rise up, to affirm ourselves, even if the world were to explode, even if the world were to perish, yes to remake the world, the planter's universe capsized in the creature's eyes, the cutlass came down, the pig made no sound, it sank to its knees, fell on its side, as easy as taking the life of a Negro, there was no difference between us and the pig, except tonight there was one, the pig was a white man, no mercy from now on, Boukman brandished a torch, lit the plain on fire, the flames licked at the clouds and the night was nothing but red light dancing between the sky and the horizon, kill, slit their throats, cut off their heads, eviscerate them, ah! the planter, my master, die, blood flows, swells the rivers, eyes overflow with tears, no pity, tears cannot redeem the crime, blood calls for blood, the whites burn for days and nights on end, Sister Theresa, I saw your soul turn to smoke (that made me happy), heard the air suffocating with your perfume, the smell of sugar and fresh blood

—the blood of his friends was not yet dry when your son, Monsieur Baron, sent news, a traveler looking for a place to stay for the night knocked on the postern, fortunately, I was passing by and opened the door, it was pouring rain and, although he wore a coat that was probably made of oilskin, the traveler was soaked, I brought him into the kitchen and I dried his clothes while he ate, once he was sure that I was indeed Joseph, he gave me a letter from the baron for his mother and, at the same time, told me that he had been wounded at Savenay and that, once he had recovered, he planned to leave for England and then to join his parents in the islands

—where is that letter?

—I didn't keep it, I sent it off on the first ship going to Saint-Domingue

—we never received it, Savenay was in late 1793, revolutionary France was holding me prisoner, I heard about the defeat of the Chouans in Strasbourg in January 1794

Klaus was alive, or at least there was a chance he was still alive, outside France, I wrote to my friends still in Port-au-Prince and to business associates in London, New York, Amsterdam, asking them to help me find him, I settled into a long wait at Biemme, taking advantage of my leisure time and forced lack of activity I began major repairs to the castle, fixed up the dungeon and the turrets, demolished the watchtower, which was about to fall down, the hours spent supervising the work ate up my solitude but did not diminish its torments, Sonja, Saint-Domingue, Salomon, Cécile constantly emerged as landmarks punctuating the monotony of my days, the peace of that great residence slowly brought back to its austere beauty surged within me like a deep song (at times I was surprised to find myself wiping away a tear on my cheek, nostalgic dream of a life marked by tenderness and clarity, sadness and vain love), weak palpitation of an adventure ending in complete failure, my hearth shattered, my son disappeared, pointless my life henceforth, tired of waiting, I finally left for Paris, leaving a note for Klaus with my address in Strasbourg just in case, the City of Light was coming alive again, dull and sad under the Convention and the Terror, it was rediscovering joy, pleasure, it was not yet the glory of the old days, but Parisians were taken with a frenzy to live, they danced new life on the banks of the Seine, in the salons, in the town houses, even in the Tuileries gardens, imagine my surprise when I ran into Cécile there, she was pushing sixty but what freshness, rice powder and skilled makeup hid the wrinkles on her face, she looked twenty years younger with a haughty elegance, I might not have recognized her had she not asked her driver to stop upon passing by me in her carriage, I saw her coming, her arms open, I recognized her voice, still youthful and warm

—I thought that was you, there are not two silhouettes like that on earth

—Cécile! what are you doing in Paris?

—I could ask you the same question

—I'm looking for Klaus

—I crossed paths with him in the United States of America, he came back last year with Monsieur de Chateaubriand

—who's that?

—the new god of the lettered public, the darling of all the women, he spent time in exile in England, he returns to us with a celebrated book, *Le génie du christianisme*

—what has that to do with Klaus? don't tell me my son is also a writer now

—not at all, they met one another in London, I fear one or the other of them might be secretly planning a movement against the First Consul

—what do they want?

—to restore the royalty

—but Klaus isn't a royalist, what wasp's nest has he fallen into this time?

—he'll get away scot-free if he isn't unlucky enough to do something irreparable, Bonaparte is a charmer, he has already rallied more than one to his cause, Monsieur de Chateaubriand is still hesitating because, thinking himself better than everyone else, he spends his time, as he puts it, "making his life look smaller in order to place it at the same level as the rest of society," Klaus will certainly come around; those Bonaparte is unable to seduce, he corrupts

—still cynical, you haven't changed, Cécile

—when you have lived as I have, you end up understanding men

—I left you in Saint-Domingue, through what Vodou do I find you now in Paris?

—I didn't rot away in Saint-Domingue for too long after you left, you had predicted correctly, the freedmen aligned with the Blacks, the metropole sent commissioners and troops to force the planters to respect the laws of the republic, Sonthonax and Polverel aligned themselves with the mulattoes and the Blacks against the whites under the pretext that they were the only ones who would save the colony from the designs of the English and Spanish, a certain Toussaint Louverture, once known by the name of Fatras-Bâton, obtained general emancipation of the enslaved from the republican agents, expelled any troublesome whites, even the commissioners, and now governs Saint-Domingue like a king, signing his letters: from the First of the Blacks to the First of the Whites

—Fatras-Bâton, the coachman of

—that's him, yes, the whites derisively call him the old ape dressed in rags, his white and Black partisans believe he's planning to proclaim the independence of Saint-Domingue

—he's pushing it a bit, but do the Negroes have any other choice?

—the reason I'm here is to prevent that infamy, this morning I'm going to see Josephine at the request of my friends, Josephine is a Creole, her parents have plantations in Guadeloupe and Martinique, an independent Saint-Domingue would be a threat

—why are you getting involved in this affair? you have no personal interest

—don't be so sure, Wolf, when I fled the troubles in Saint-Domingue at the time of the Galbaud Affair, I went on to Louisiana, the Americans, a young and entrepreneurial people, have real heads for business, they say time is money, I learned that lesson, time spent doing other people's business is precious, more than you might think, so now I demand to be paid handsomely, if Bonaparte, urged on by his planter friends, ultimately lets himself be misguided by his wife and organizes an expedition against Fatras-Bâton, I'll get a hundred thousand francs in pure gold for my brokerage

—that's huge

—don't make me laugh, it's nothing compared to the millions the planters will amass once again, the cost of sugar and cotton has increased tenfold, enough to increase the appetite of more than one, aren't you tempted?

—there's much more money to be made in Europe

—I agree with you, in the years to come all you have to do is sell cannons and you'll be collecting money in the streets

—in the mud and blood

—did you ever successfully harvest cotton and sugar other than in mud and blood?

—yes, but

—don't look for justifications, Wolf, it's too late, it's soon time for my rendezvous, I'm off, wish me luck

we didn't think to exchange addresses, with her connections, Cécile would have been useful to me, even if only to bring me to Monsieur de Chateaubriand, it took me three days to find and identify him, he and his friends gathered twice a week at Madame Récamier's house, he read his writings to a small retinue of admirers, among whom the women were neither the least fervent nor the least enthusiastic, the illustrious viscount officiated with a stiff, haughty, and prideful tone, feigning indifference and disdain in the face of the women's love, which he considered fitting homage to his beauty and genius, I saw him from afar without managing to get near him, cornered as he was by a gorgeous muse with a generously exposed bosom, he nodded his leonine head from time to time to accept a compliment, welcoming with clear condescension the adoration of a small band of the chosen, all communing in a new religion, *Romanticism*, as the English say, it is meant to be the supreme art of capturing with words the most subtle nuances of feeling, the languid stillness of clouds, the magnificence of forests, he spoke and he spoke, the handsome man, barely finishing one page before they asked for another, annoyed by these flashy formal exercises where the magic of words translated the falsity of emotions, I returned to my hotel, I returned to Strasbourg the following day, where a short letter from Klaus awaited me

> Father,
>
> do not worry, I am alive and fighting with all my strength against the tyrant who has stolen our revolution and turned it to his own ends, I'm married to an Englishwoman, Kathleen, she has given you three lovely grandchildren, all of them boys who one day will come to visit you, they live in England with their mother
>
> affectionately,
>
> Klaus

that was all, an almost impersonal tone, a vague promise, the feeling of a deep wound, a tearing away, as if my son had detached himself from me, the words rang hollow, stripped of life, erected between Klaus and me in order to forever loosen the bonds that I would have preferred remain tenuous but solid, holding on to illusions, I had found my son, but his words told me he was forever lost, the demon of the Biemmes had claimed him, too fond of sadness and suffering he waggled his life at the tip of a bell, in the hopes that the sound might deliver him from his pain, forever enslaved to a destiny from which no one could free him, I would reread his brief letter several times a day, looking between the lines for the traces of a face that, twenty years on, is still that of a baby, expecting that at any moment a noisy past full with cries and squeals interrupted by various commands—are you finished yet, Klaus?—and repeated threats—stop your bawling or you'll get a smack!—Sonja kept me at a distance from my son, keeping him shut up in her bedroom, ultimate space of refusals and frustrations, I didn't get to hear my son's first words, I didn't see his first tooth come in, nor did I get to witness the wonder of his hesitant first steps or to show him the heights of Bellevue, taking in with one sweeping glance the Schpeerbach plantation and the five snaking rivers that make it a veritable corner of paradise, and that is why I found myself waiting in this room, even more worried about the present than the future, the cries of children in the alleyway, a warm, gruff voice, a stifled exclamation, a suggestion whispered in English, listen! here's my herd of children and grandchildren at my door

—Klaus!

—Father!

manly embraces, my son in his virile splendor, we are the same height, with the stoutness of all Schpeerbach men, our heavy gait weighing upon us, rooting us deeper and deeper into the ground with each step, but also the Biemme eagle eye, dominating, predatory, cruel, the angular face of the Bretons and that corsair's profile that is the true mark of a seafaring people, how sweet he is, that son of mine! his eyes smile at me, as if we're experiencing one another in a new way

—how are you, my boy?

—I'm well, Father

—so you're a man now?

Sonja steps forward, holding three little Klauses in her arms, trembling puppies that she bathes in her tender gaze, for the first time I catch a glimmer of tenderness in her eyes, death has softened their cruelty by putting an end to her eternal struggle to always seem tougher than she needed to be, she comes back to me, and I am suddenly overwhelmed by some kind of need for her, an impatience to possess that part of her personality that endlessly escaped me in the past, we are once again face to face, burdened with the violence of our history, standing in a closed space between a son we barely knew and his yapping kids, shhh! you're bothering your grandparents, not at all, Sonja! not at all! I feel neither your presence nor theirs, they remain out of focus, only Klaus is really present, theatrical in his shy, child-like awkwardness, words tumble out, exhausted from communicating a message they were never meant to convey, the basement door creaks in a gust of wind, Klaus! Sonja! they do not answer, disappearing, along with the little pups, into I know not what other life, ah! to straddle the wind, to join them, to leave with them, far, far away from this abode where the future fades away as it waits for the past, to outwit the present I write the story of my life, beseeching my children to forgive me if they find me guilty, Klaus has likely learned the truth, in which case he must have understood that I deserve neither his indifference nor his disdain, in any event these memoirs will neither justify my existence nor serve as a *pro domo* plea in my defense, they are one more testimony added to the long list of stories of the Biemmes, for in truth, they have far more to do with Sonja de Valembrun Lebrun than with me, I am now a defeated old man, at the end of his road, clearing a path to eternal peace, pleading with God to fulfill his final wish, to see my son again and, in the grips of remorse, to forget, I blame myself, more spineless than passionate, for not having known, or been able, or wanted to live in accordance with my conscience and with the divine word, for the love of God, love thy fellow man as you love thyself, Salomon, my brother, will you forgive me for having been neither a good brother, nor a good fellow man, nor a good Christian?

—Sister Theresa, have you alerted the pensioners to the monsignor's visit?

—yes, Mother, and I have already prepared them

—Saintmilia?

—at first she complained but then she gave in

—I want them to be clean and attractively dressed

—it will be as you wish

—today is the Lord's day, we share the lot of the poor

—the monsignor, as well?

—the monsignor, as well

—will it come, Mother, the storm that threatens? will their Agoué show us mercy?

I don't know what to make of these countless images of cruelty that my family left to me over the course of the centuries and that a cassette tape now funnels into my ears, unceasingly, memories and nightmares pursue me, imposing emotions on me that awaken so many echoes that they seem to belong to me, taken apart and then put back together, relived in a strange phantasmagoria, I try to expel them, they come back even stronger, I have no more power over them than I do over my own life, an airplane is my executioner, a daughter of Africa the dream of an impossible love, but the deep voice of this dream is more beautiful than silence, flags flying on the ramparts, banners with their eyes gouged out, fifteen young madmen moving back and forth, keeping watch over the dungeon, alone I am preparing and setting the table for a dinner in the midst of the storm, the sound of the Bordes and the Rochasses, preceded by a whisper in the wind, fill in the hollows and the folds of silence, footsteps scurrying outside, I can feel their haste to get back to the house like a deep fear of thunder, something shifts, lifts me up, I move from my state of silence to a sort of effervescence that allows me to feel the slightest impressions of others, to at last live their joy rather than obsessing over my own misfortune, the vicissitudes of existence true to form in their madness, to slip quietly out of my prison, to be free like Saintmilia, to create and recreate an infinity of dissimilar but coherent universes, to slip along the edges of the abyss while refusing to plunge into it, hesitating, finally, to recognize myself, Sister Hyacinthe, when each of your revelations confirms my fears, the love of suffering and, because uncertain, of expiating, dying, living again, looking past Saintmilia, my gaze plunges into a watery landscape, through the window the sky joins the sea, nature's most marvelous and most painful act, the horizon becomes diluted in an assemblage of blue, gray, and black, higher than the sun, Saintmilia stands at the ready, a shimmering specter, her eyes vacant, all that docility surprises me, an obscure premonition, she is there, immobile, her eyes, ordinarily empty, reflect worlds that rise from the depths toward the light of memory as if rising toward joy, but a sinister joy, I am wary, that woman is not mad, I know her, a dangerous criminal, she murdered her husband in a fit of jealousy, Sister Theresa, why bring this up now? that was my old life, I will no longer catch you playing the innocent victim, go ahead and tell the Mother Superior that a fish named Savale killed your husband, at daybreak, under a full moon, I have nothing to tell and you will not force me to reveal that which memory no longer knows, do you understand, Reverend Mother? her duplicity is unrivaled, she has buried her fantasies in a double coffin, with the help of Toukouma, she showed the whole village her double face of madness and despair, I had surprised her, right at daybreak, she was washing the harpoon she used for the crime in the first waves of the first morning, the bloodstains like so many shadowy spots on our wounded memory

—Saintmilia, what did you do?

—Mistress, on nights of the full moon Agénor cheats on me in the swamps of Nan-Jouissant with Violetta, she arrives, he goes to her, she sings, he drinks in the strange night of her voice Miyan! Miyan! unbearable, Sister Theresa, the sound of their lovemaking lapping in the water, roiling with kisses on the smoldering waves, drumbeat of moans sighs groans shivers a callaloo of caresses sleeping in the hammocks of algae the truth of wronged women in their spasms a concert a harmony of happiness that pained me and you don't know it

—this woman is not mad, she breaks her silence to enter into her truth, the truth of the word, her story tells of love's defeat

—what love, Sister Theresa, that between Salomon and Sonja, you shattered it and your eyes have held on to the pieces, every time you close your eyes, they put themselves back together and become your dream

—those sounds, at night?

—they are the sounds of love, Sonja, I don't understand, are you mad or what? you had Salomon killed and every night you die of love, you die of loving him she rambles on, her voice, unmoving until then, changes place, low in the sky, at the place where it joins the sea, the horizon shimmers, tumult of flames and anger, of thunder and blood, suddenly Saintmilia brandishes her fist, the rage of a gathering storm at the tip of her arm, the window closes by itself, walling in and protecting the calm of my bedroom against the violence outside, I will not know peace, I'm not playing at destiny with Saintmilia any longer, one must not be the death of the other, to close the distance between us, to see her in this hospice, just as I feared, and not as my ancestor's memory claims to recognize her across two centuries of history and several generations, to situate her outside the misunderstandings, to dispel my surprise, to resign myself to abolishing the certainty of fatality, all the while knowing it to be inevitable given the confrontation of our conflicting truths, it is raining, hanging from her fist Saintmilia sings as if the fate of the word were to create the signs within which to enclose our weaknesses and our miseries, with a grand gesture of the hand I sweep away Saintmilia's crazy stories, she promptly rebuilds them, in all their tension, in the form of family histories, they invade my little cubbyhole, ransacking my silence, designating the moment when, beyond all sounds and images, love song, death song, neither Saintmilia nor I would choose to be broken any longer, for different reasons, due to the same suffering, nor would we be mixed up in the same drive for annihilation

—Sonja, my fragrance of nightfall, my fragrance of absurdity and illusion

—oh! you, my doubt

—your lips like the heart of the world

—hatred everywhere, remember how I was wandering around Neuilly, just for a laugh, and all the voices of Neuilly, precautionary, screamed at me: fucking Negro whore! no peddling your wares in Neuilly

they fell upon me, tore me apart like vultures, like vampires they sucked me dry, like men they beat me, raped me, and

—in Neuilly? I don't believe it, maybe near les Halles

—what's the difference, between les Halles and Neuilly it's only the name of the perfume that changes

—of course, you're not a Biemme

—foolish whites

—what are you saying?

—as naked as earthworms

—you're right, using hatred as a fiery beast to sear our memories

—taking apart the days and the hours, and setting dreams on fire with every hour

—have you exceeded your hatred?

—white racism is so idiotic that it obscures the encounter between the races, I cannot hear the smells emanating from the din of the peoples

—who's to blame? foolish Negroes, foolish whites, our eyes never trace the piety of the night

—there's nothing left to do but cry

—don't steal my tears, Sister Theresa, that water is as cool and ancient as rain

—where did you get that idea, Saintmilia?

—don't call me Saintmilia, I am Ti Mèmè N'Kedi, I remember now, you confiscated my name to subjugate it, do you know what it means?

—flower of the savanna, you already told us, didn't you, Sonja?

—then I lied, Sister Theresa, I am not a flower of the savanna, I am the mistress of water, older than my tears and cooler than words

her voice streams from the rooftop, how poignant are the whimperings of hatred! somersaults, threatens, scatters, insults, gives us hell, subjects us to every misery, sends me to the devil, returns the Reverend Mother to her God, her guttural prayers knead the chastity of the Virgin and the lust of Zaka, profane Africa violates the sacredness of Europe, bringing horror to everyday life in the hospice, disarming our fervor, the Mother Superior doesn't know what to listen to and where to turn her head whenever Saintmilia raises her skirts, making as if to piss right out in the open

—have a look, joyless women, life is flowing here, far from your prayers and your gospels, life and love, have pity on them, Zaka, fertilize their wishes and their desires, their prayers and their cries of sensual delight

the priestess scratches the nape of her neck, the most beautiful gray hair of anyone in the community, imagine our distress and our dismayed modesty, as she doubles over in a great bawdy laugh and says to us out of the blue

—what the hell have you come to do in this fucking hellhole? come on, girls, wake up!

she doesn't mince her words, the Reverend Mother, raw and direct as she discourages our Latin

—when you've fought with the infantry in World War I, in the shit of the trenches thanks to a bunch of shitty politicians, you tell yourself that no words live in hell

she reclaims her dignity, the gravity of her face, expressionless, Saintmilia seizes the opportunity, shouts at me, attacks me, vehement, then ironic, all innuendo

—Sister Theresa, isn't love beautiful? between women

—sated carnivores

—the narrow door

—the intoxication of the hours as if time hadn't been given to us only for us to die

—Sister Theresa, what does love taste like?

she laughs, the love within her, the power of the earth, too, strong and vegetal, the madness of these many centuries so sure of her truth and her right, and at last, defiance, I can't breathe, I'm suffocating, anger boils within me, rises, darkens the day, obscurity permeates me, dense, filled with all the irritations accumulated over months of patience, I see red, I wipe my hand across my face, searching for myself once again in the labyrinth of the centuries, my features erased, hesitatingly, I touch a brass mask that is no longer animated by the movement of my eyes, by the trembling of my lips, as a child, it often happened that, annoyed and angry, I'd let all my feelings transfer from my face to my voice, my screams would become monstrous while my face remained frozen, impassive, and my mother, distraught, would hold her head in her hands and weep: the Mask of the Biemmes! the Mask of the Biemmes!

—Sonja! it's decided, we'll board the ship soon, in a few days, are you happy, tell me? what's going on?

my voice sounds rough, the words crashing against each other create a discordant note, emotion strangles them in my throat, transforms surprise into an indefinable feeling, dread, fear, terror

—it's witchcraft

seated in a wicker armchair, overcome by the tranquil enchantment of the twilight hour, my heart finally at peace, for a moment I thought

I might be able to figure out my life and, in a brief instant of regret at having given up on myself, I felt Sonja nearby, new possibilities presented themselves to us, different responsibilities awaited us, a life to begin again together and a love story to reconquer, the sudden intuition of some happiness still remaining to be invented, Sonja shivered, so much hatred in her eyes that they seemed to burn with an inner fire, the blue of the fjords had paled, ceding to the cold and metallic gray of the Breton skies, I blink my eyes, the features of her face have become shockingly rigid, as if a sculptor had fixed, once and for all, all the tragic rigor of fury and hatred, between you and me time has ceased to be, love no longer knows its name, Sonja! she doesn't respond, eyelids shut and dreams destroyed, a few tears spill over, fall silently on her cheeks, despair linked to the certainty of ruin, to flee, to escape the temptation of madness and destruction, to be freed, to scream, to deny the suffering and the misfortune, to undermine destiny with a scream, to live again! silence—I hear silence—light, fragile

—what are the Negroes doing in the workshops? they're usually so noisy, did you send them to the fields?

—they . . . marooned!

—what! all of them?

—almost

—Salomon, too?

the answer takes a while to come, and it's worse than a confession, I don't want to know, I am already powerless against the truth, damn it! Sonja must have read the worry on my face and, like always, she decided to hurt me

—I don't know, he got a few Negroes together and went off in search of the fugitives, maybe that's the best way for him to escape unpunished

—I don't believe a word of it, he'll come back, he won't abandon me, did his mother stay on the plantation?

—you'll find her sitting under the mango tree, facing the window on the other side of the room, ever since her son has gone hunting for the Negroes, she has been waiting for me to appear to demand his return

—why don't you send her back to her hut?

—since you're here, go ahead and try

I crossed the room, walking quickly, Sonja's detached tone, her impassive expression, the cruel light in her eyes is worrying, I open the window onto the spectacle of Saintmilia in the setting sun, she raises her head, brandishes her fist, stands up and, recognizing me, surprised, emphatically removes her faded madras headscarf, bows her head, her hair more vulnerable than the time that has whitened it, she looks old, withered by the elements, such as I have never known her, such as I have never imagined she could be, my faded youth in her eyes, hard and dry from having wept in mourning for others, an anxious expression on her emaciated features

—save my son, save Salomon

—from what, Cécile?

—to save yourself

I'll admit that I didn't understand the correlation between Cécile's vague recommendations, which I'm just now recalling, and Saintmilia's distressed cries, but both spoke to my heart like a duty to fulfill in the face of an obscure and dangerous threat

—explain yourself, Cécile

Saintmilia doesn't hear, she flees, one more shadow or phantom among the first shadows of the night, madras scarf in her hand like the sign of a fate she never ceases to bear, immobile silhouette in the frame of the window, beyond the darkness, I persist in reconstituting the image of a prostrate woman who, carried away by the force of a nameless despair, once threatened me with her fist, weighted with the fullness of a mother's love

—Nanie, give me the moon to eat

—you are too greedy, Wolf, you'll get indigestion

—then sing me a song

—dodo titit

her lullaby voice, song voice, love voice, an ineffable feeling of happiness, so why now has she balled hatred up in her fist and why is she nothing but imprecations? more than a threat, hatred like a curse, that night I understood that I wouldn't escape my fate, I was damned, a massive fire danced, standing in the flames I sneered, horns on my head and pitchfork in my hand, master of a kingdom whose name I had forgotten and whose rites I celebrated with a kind of barbarous fervor, Father Lazenaec appears, his exorcisms transform me into a bleating lamb, repentance and absolution, forgive me my sins, Lord, the night wails in my throat: Eternal One, if I lacked charity, on Judgment Day make it so that

—what happened to Salomon?

—he marooned

—you just told me that he

—what I've said is of no importance

—yes, I want to know the truth

—he tried to rape me

—you're lying, I refuse to believe you

finally the brutality of his reaction! Salomon's savage force hovering over me every night, the passion of his body falling drop by drop on my lips, the mad pounding of my heart, the tension of desire, the solitary exaltation of my senses, I open my eyes, he penetrates my gaze, hot and sensual, he flows into me, devastating, to seize his lips, the silent tenderness of his trembling eyes, the darkness, alive with disturbing images, sensations difficult to distinguish, to identify, separates us and brings us close, I moan, my memory lived like plans for the future, impressions like actions, recollections like a special presence all around and inside me having become awareness of a sort of pleasure that creates itself, gathering itself, absorbing the gasping sounds of the room, the panting of the walls and, beyond that, the chaos of the stars, the chorus of the night, so many joys stretching out their loads of emotions suspended between his belly and mine, between me and nothingness

—things should have happened differently between us, that morning, I forgot to be a Biemme, I didn't dare sow my desires in the orgiastic field of suffering and happiness

—Sister Theresa! be quiet

—the imprecision of the flowering quenepa tree, the insistent burning of the eucalyptus, the penetrating slowness of the essence of vetiver, the air so alive, the abundant fragrance of mango trees, the purple aromas of the flamboyant, the white exhalations of the frangipani and upon us, fat, thick, heavy, the strong smell of love, he took all the scents into his hands, shoved them suddenly into the unknown of my thirst and my hunger, imprinting his mark within me, the steadiness of his gaze, the permanence of his absence

—you're rambling, Sonja

—to die of sadness and resentment, in Salomon's strength there was something like the stench of your own weakness, Wolf: loyalty, he couldn't not desire me

—why would my son have loved the one who was the worst enemy among all enemies?

—from one to the other, the fascination of the forbidden, we were seeking what was at once impossible to find and unprecedented, irreplaceable and taboo

—I don't understand, my child

—Reverend Mother, there is nothing to understand

—so you loved him?

—desired him, yes

—so why do you say that he raped you?

—did I say that? me?

—you even confessed that you wanted to be raped

—I was offering myself, Wolf, it's different, I was offering myself but he shamed me by refusing my offer, I'm asking you to punish his audacity, I will castrate him when he comes back

—you will not geld my son

—remove yourself from my path! Reverend Mother, you're my witness, this woman placed herself between the door and me, she shoved me

—be careful, Saintmilia, you're knocking over the poppet from atop the cake, what will you serve Monsignor the Bishop for dessert?

—pardon for his sins

she steps aside, allows me to pass, traverses the doorstep, enters into the night, Africa in her haunches pulses with the innumerable trickeries of its drums, rounds up the multitude of lwa, the ones who protect or condemn, those who love or hate, those who weep or rage, releases them into the great hall of worship, they jostle one another, push us into a corner, pull out the chairs, their noisy current rolls among the provisions on the table, overflowing, insatiably gluttonous, bellies filled to bursting, the savage hysteria of hunger, Ogoun Ferraille calls for silence

—who played this nasty trick on us?

—me, Sister Yves of the Christ Child

—I didn't ask you to list your titles, you have insulted us by inviting us to eat in such a nameless setting

—the party was not organized for you and, as far as I know, no one invited you

—where are the vèvè that personify us, the distinctive signs of our powers and roles?

—ask Saintmilia, she is hiding within your ranks

—I am not hiding within their ranks, my name is not Saintmilia, I have come from very far away, flying over the centuries, I watched Segu fall, I sang in the gardens of Ifè, I drank the fiery alcohol of the Yoruba, the bull-roarer cried my sufferings in the eyes of an indolent ancestor, listen to me carefully, you all, I convened you here to help me either save my son or avenge his memory, we will celebrate later when the cicadas' chirping announces the end of the season of hate, in the meantime

all night long, Saintmilia spoke through the drum's throat, she had placed it beneath my window, the tree of language remembered itself and spoke of my joys and my fears as a little boy, chasing crab and or-tolan, at dawn and at dusk, my adolescent pleasures, horseman of the days and of sleepless nights chasing forbidden pleasures, by my side a little boy who looks like the night calls me Wolf! Wolf! and, suddenly, calls me Little Master, Little Master, the tree has grown, the grown man roams through his roundabouts all alone but from time to time the stupid little boy calls him Wolf, the new name for solitude and confusion, all night long the tree of language crackled, the tormented voice of the little boy and, like a wound inside me, the painful cry of childhood, save Salomon!

—in the morning, Reverend Mother, Saintmilia, wrapped up in her frail carcass, piled her little goat with bags full of candy and corn cakes, salted codfish and poban bananas, millet with pigeon peas and herring in chili sauce, unworried about the hunger of the bishop who, having arrived late to the ceremony, hadn't even gotten any leftovers from the feast, she launched the food she had prepared for the Marassa into the waves, the little goat spun around, whirled in a spray of foam and sparks before diving in, swallowed up forever in the belly of Agoué

—the bishop saw nothing?

—on his arrival, the lwa just took on the normal appearance of the guests

—Sister Theresa, do you think you can save him?

—I'll try, Reverend Mother, it won't be easy to overturn both history and destiny

—but you must

—I know, I must, if I want to save myself

—Saintmilia, show me where I can find Salomon

—forgive me, Monsignor, for not having waited for you, the girls were restless, they ran out of patience and we allowed them to begin without you

—as if you didn't know where to find him

she took a couple of steps back and, after clearing her throat twice, directed a ball of phlegm at my boots, once dry, it stained the varnish like a spattering of blood, I held back my anger, jumping astride a horse, I took off wildly in search of Salomon, it had rained heavily at dawn, one of those tropical storms, treacherous, perverse, violent, that can destroy your plantation in less time than it takes to say it out loud, Saintmilia's delirium, her ceremonial incantation had troubled the voices of the hurricane, focused on deciphering the messages of my childhood, I hadn't heard the howling of the rain, the wind had blown away the roofs of the women's huts, I thought about the poor things huddled together against the storm, seeking some reserve of warmth in one another's shivering bodies, how many remained in that despicable enclosure? what's happened to my plantation? here I am practically stripped of everything, condemned to abandon that which, in any case, I would no longer have the strength to rebuild, if I have lacked mercy, Lord, I leave my fate in your hands on Judgment Day, I saddled my horse, trusting my instinct, I headed toward the refinery, the muddy and tumultuous waters of the Coin de l'Anse gully continued to roil, passing by Pandier and Byroth, I reached Portail, followed the paved road to Mibalè, turned off to the left, cut over to the path that ran along the hillside, the Couleuvre River, powerful and rebellious, was already invading the fields, cutting off the path at the border between the shoots of sugarcane and the grove of coffee trees, I moved forward with difficulty, I had to dismount, moving through some of the hollows on foot, barely managing not to fall into crevices as deep as graves, until a scree forced me to retrace my steps, clearing my way between huge piles of rocks swept down the slope by the blind waters of the springs at Mibalè and Déranger, tripping with every step, sliding, falling, I let go of the horse's bridle, certain he would be able to make his way back, I was worried about what had happened to the refinery, it had probably been flooded by the waters of the Baliziers River, knowing all the while that it was already part of my past, I still would have liked to have seen it one last time, to fix the image of that "power" that my father's patience and my own had built in the face of nature's fury, if the damage was as bad as it was after the last hurricane, Salomon would have months of repairs and shoring up to deal with, I had already prepared the contract ceding the property to him, accompanied by a letter of emancipation, his first experience as a free man would be to go head to head with nature, how would he make out? Salomon is intelligent, I'm confident in his ability to get by, he has always known how to get us out of the most difficult situations, around these parts we use the term talented Negroes to describe little men who can carve wood and work iron, Salomon is a genius of a Negro, with an inventive mind and nimble fingers

—Alonzo says that Salomon solved the problem of how to transport the sugarcane juice

—yes, he developed a pumping system operated by an ox, thereby freeing up fifty or so Negroes employed to decant the syrup into expensive brass recipients that have to be repaired every year

—and so you end up with fifty layabouts on your hands

—not at all, my dear, I already assigned them to clearing the brush and draining the swamps between Dangluse and Kalem, we'll plant rice there

—Salomon truly is a special Negro

—why do you say that?

—he reads Voltaire and Rousseau, invents machines, here I thought all Negroes were narrow minded and stupid, now I discover one who is sensitive, intelligent, curious about everything, even sailing, do you know he taught himself how to navigate by the stars, he's capable of determining, from one star to the next, the right route to follow and where to find the "fishy depths" without risk of error during his night-time fishing expeditions

—Salomon fishes at night?

—you didn't know?

—no, what does he do with the catch?

—he salts, dries, or smokes the fish and sells them to the ship crews, he's planning to save up enough so that he can buy freedom for himself and his mother

—incredible, Sonja! incredible! buy their freedom? buy it

—is he honest?

—if I was talking about someone else I'd say: as honest as a Negro can be, but with him I'd say yes, without hesitation, honest and capable, certainly more than Alonzo

—so give him Alonzo's position

she laughed as if she wanted to play a practical joke on me, a Black man as a plantation manager, replacing a white, even if he was a lazy Spaniard, that had never happened in the islands, where had Sonja gotten such an idea? but she seemed serious, insisting, a personal request

—what do you think? you aren't answering? I think it's a good idea, just think of all the money we'll save

—give me some time to think about it

—plus, I hate Alonzo, he is too sneaky to be honest

—does that mean you like Salomon?

—he is a wonderful companion on horseback rides

—can you imagine, we are foster brothers?

—he told me

—telling the story of my life to a stranger!

—who? me?

—when it comes to our friendship, our childhood, everyone else is a stranger, we're the only ones who share each other's secrets, we feel a certain modesty, or pride, what do I know? in not talking about it

—he told me everything, I laughed hard about that joke Saintmilia used to play on you, the story of the sun going off to war against the north winds

—don't laugh, OK! that's not a joke, one day at noon we had spent too much time running, playing hide-and-seek in the banana groves at Byroth, we arrived at the plantation bathed in sweat but, just as we opened the gate, the north wind rose up, a squall, and enveloped us in its cold breath, by the time I got into the big house I was shivering, aching, my whole body hurt, wheezing, they called quickly for Saintmilia

—who prepared infusions of herbs and leaves more effective than all the potions from the apothecary, but you thought you would die, you had even seen the devil at the end of the tunnel, he was waving to you to come closer

—he told you that, too? Salomon hasn't kept any secrets from you, I envy your good fortune, my dear, how did you manage to get him to betray me like that?

her forehead darkened, drawing attention to her tanned complexion, she changed the subject immediately, likely ashamed by my indiscreet questions, determined to protect a universe from which she had chosen to exclude me so as to punish me for having been secretive, but here she was asking me, for the second time, to mutilate Salomon in the cruelest, most horrific way, to castrate him, deprive of him of his manly attributes, what could have provoked such a reversal in her feelings, why had Sonja come to hate her marvelous companion, as she had called him?

—the paths of desire, Sister Emilienne, are as impenetrable as those of God

—without a doubt, Reverend Mother

—let us pray for the miracle to be accomplished, Sister Theresa, are you angry with us for having been indiscreet, and having discovered the secret of the cassette and of your destiny?

—not at all Reverend Mother, it was God's will, and today it has earned me the gift of your prayers

—aid for the afflicted

—Lord, have mercy on us

I had lost time scraping the mud off my shoes at Pamboucha, my horse met me there, I got back in the saddle, filled with a sudden worry, I galloped across the town, at Coin de l'Anse the waters of the ravine had gone down, after some hesitation my horse braved the crossing, once I was on the other bank I put my foot on the ground, it was impossible to go via the slippery slope at Côte-de-Fer, I attached my horse to a branch, took care to remove the bit from its mouth so that it might get at a tuft of grass here or there, holding on to the branches of a gum tree I climbed up the shortcut

—no, Sonja! no!

everything was happening fast, a foggy panoply out of which precise memories emerged disjointedly, unburdened of the weight of terror, they gave coherence to the next part of my story, I remember I was screaming, trying to prevent the villainy, to stop fate, a senseless hope, since I had long known the inevitable tragedy, Sonja and I no longer had a choice, but why has fate seized Salomon as the instrument of our ruination? heads, inexplicably present on my plantation at this hour, were looking in my direction, immediately on alert as if they had been told in advance what was going to happen, twenty soldiers surrounded Paret and Sonja, at their feet, lying on his back, tied to four stakes, his members stretched to the limit, Salomon's muscular body, glistening in the sun with what, seen from afar, looked like stripes of shadow, but which I later discovered were the bloody traces of whip lashes, my stomach tightened, his eyelids closed, he already appeared dead, I tripped on a root, caught myself, Lord, deliver us from evil, please let him still be alive

—Salomon! Salomon!

the woods returned my words to me, an echo, his response, my name, joyously, like an exaltation, a child's delight, to lose ourselves beyond the familiar paths, discover the blocked openings of the caves at Degerme, to plunge ourselves straight into the underbrush, deprived of the sun's gaze, rediscovering his voice carried by the wind and childhood fears like life-giving words, he opened his eyes, raised his head, hope turned toward the sound of my footsteps, let it fall again, the effort was too much, I threw myself forward, the dizziness of fear, and at the same time, violence, present and rebelling against the horror I felt, if he dies, Sonja, you will pay, a desire, if not a need for destruction, injustices to crush, a world to reinvent, Sonja leaned over, raised her arm with a cutlass in her hand, to what pagan rite was my wife making a sacrifice that forced her to mutilate my friend, my brother? the circle tightened, the soldiers took up their positions, ready for battle, against whom? I took note of that detail and, long afterward, as I put my memories in order, it will take on a deeper meaning, its true meaning, in the moment there were more important things to deal with, I ran, approaching the group quickly, I cried out again, Sonja turned toward me, her features disfigured with rage and hatred, the ugliness of her soul had risen up into her face, I stopped, taken aback

—if you take another step forward, I'll kill him

he stopped in his tracks, Sister Theresa, slipped on the damp grass, fell, a desperately comic spill, the soldiers burst into laughter, he rose with difficulty as they mocked him, ay! the weight of existence, Salomon's and his own, far too heavy on his shoulders, at last upright, arms outspread, the very posture of childhood, innocent, helpless

—what are you doing? what is it now, Sonja?

that *now* resounded like an admission of impotence in the face of a long past of cruelty, his doubts, his weakness, his silences, his resignation, the world become mad in his voice, in his hand, in his heart

—you hadn't known? they arrested my son in Jérémie, alarmed by the disappearance of the slaves, he had hoped to send a message to you asking you to return as quickly as possible, he spoke of it to Sister Theresa, who gave him permission to travel from one parish to the next, having entrusted him with a note for Captain Paret

—is that true?

—of course! do you think I could possibly have been duped by his ruse? he had come up with a subterfuge to leave the plantation, I pretended to fall into his trap, all the while planning to lay a more surprising one for him

—the slave patrol captured Salomon, Captain Paret claimed he was a maroon, tell them it isn't true, dear Master, my mistress knows the truth, Salomon, too, alas, for my son, that knowledge that is fatal, evidence of darkness, it only counts against him

—make her shut up

—no, I want her to speak

—do you hear this! by what right?

—Captain Paret, is it possible you've forgotten that I am master in my own home?

—you're nothing but a traitor and a smuggler

—I demand that you account for your words

—by the pistol or by the sword?

—by the pistol

—present your witnesses

—not one more step, Wolf, or else

—or else?

—you will be entirely responsible for his death

—I defy you to carry out your threats

I stepped forward trying to look confident, praying to God to have pity on Salomon, to take him under his saintly protection, to enlighten Sonja, to bring her back to reason and avoid the tragedy into which her criminal intention would plunge us all, the blade of the cutlass sparkled

—no! no!

—intoxication like a wound in my memory, bristling of blood and tempers, to know at last the intimacy of the present, Salomon! Salomon! tell me how the dawn wanders

—dawn bubbled over with our hunger

—madness, I don't believe a word of it, my desire has so often wandered in your voice that it is forever withered now, do you understand?

—suffering is consecrated in this cutlass that plunges into the heart of the volcano, will I discover the other side of life there?

—why not the hidden face of love?

—it would only be false joy

—what does bitterness matter, if I hold on to dreams and radiance

—as much as dawn when the mapou tree snows its fire

—they were liberty

—at the cost of what renunciation?

—to emancipate childhood

—to betray, Wolf?

—not faithfulness either and that moment capsized into eternity

—my useless blood, the day in full revolt slips to the edge of life

—faithfulness? still?

—companions in solitude, hide your dreams behind the sun's lowered lashes

—for what salvation?

—to settle on the future, with one blow, why did I not follow along your angry paths?

—you had chosen me, Salomon

—against myself and against my brothers, I put my footsteps into the silence and its detours

—thus shall the earth drink your cry

—unstated, Sonja! Sonja! love, death, my deliverance

—no! no!

I was too far away to intervene, she lowered her arm, the muted sound of the blade plunging unto Salomon's stomach tore me apart, one Black one white, we'd drunk the same milk, both suspended from the same breast, fingers interlaced atop the same belly, our foreheads touching with the same voraciousness, an explosion brutally shatters my shoulder, throws me backward, I lose my balance and fall for the second time, I try to stand, I no longer feel my right arm, or rather I feel it like an inconsolable pain, a red stain begins to spread, my eyes blur, as if through a fog, see Paret take aim, his pistol in hand, simple target practice, the shot fired, the bitter smell of the powder, the sun toppled over beating down on my head, exploded

—Salomon!

it was no longer the cry of a lost child in the woods but a cry of farewell emerged from the depths of his belly, last recourse against death, Salo . . . the blade driven fully in, this time into his heart, cut short my own cry, a ball of rage in my throat, my son, my pain, my blood, my joy, my pride

—grab hold of her and attach her to this post

I struggled, striking out with my hands and feet, scratching, biting, out of control but soon overpowered, the soldiers dragged me along, I am a tree, Sister Theresa, a totem planted right in the center of the courtyard, imbued with the power of the sun, with the invincibility of the day, with the innocence and the excess of nature, restored to my identity and my source, Ti Mèmè N'kedi, that one comes close enough to touch me, her dress stained with the blood of my son, I could feel her hatred and her breath on me

—I killed Salomon

—you're lost, Sister Theresa, Salomon holds on to his vengeance, you spoke when you shouldn't have, in my country when a woman kills the man she hates, for having loved him too much, she shaves her head, a sign of joy that hides her deep sorrow, she goes deep into the heart of the forest, walks aimlessly for days and nights, wanders as much as she wants, weeps for thirty days, lives with her mouth closed, silence as a redemption, on the thirty-first morning, she wraps her waist in a shirt that belonged to the beloved, abhorred victim, spits to the four cardinal points, cries Legba badichon likaba bilagoé, love scampers off, carrying vengeance along in its flight, her face veiled, she doesn't see the path, so she won't come back to haunt the spirit of the deceased to provoke and stir up the rancor of the parents

—I killed Salomon, and now I'm going to kill you as well, vile slave whose milk has soaked the soul of a white man, Captain, pass me the longest horsewhip

I'm laughing, Sister Theresa, who do you think you're going to whip? come, closer, even closer, there, my final gift

—you spit in my face! you dare do that to me

she looked at me, bewildered, disbelieving, the ball of spit, like fetid tears, dribbles down her cheeks, her eyes look through me, moving up the wicked slope of her long, sad story, rediscovering her great-grandfather's indignation flickering beneath the same stain, life re-solders itself beyond the many long years and mucousy life punctures her face with little bubbles of disdain, she took four steps back, the riding crop slashed through the air, a dry sound cut it in half, angrily throwing aside the leather-sheathed handle, Sonja took a lash from the Negro-punishing tree, flung it, a nice move, the strap wrapped around my body, licking greedily at my skin, but my laughter reverberated, shook your shoulders, Sister Theresa, slashed them with a long odor of blood, you blinked your eyes, painfully surprised, but clenched your teeth, gesticulating, frenetic, you cracked the whip again, with all your strength, my snickering countered your skill, for your legs were already bleeding when the leather brushed across my thighs with the invisible scream of the stars

—in broad daylight?

—I had illuminated them again, for the day had been extinguished in your eyes, do you remember that, Sister Theresa?

—I was without strength, paralyzed by the roar of the dogs screaming inside me, mobilizing my last bit of strength I cracked the whip a
third time, it wrapped around Ti Mèmè's neck, stiffened

—you're deluding yourself, the air, furious at having been stirred up
and tossed about against all reason, clotted in your throat, a cracking
sound, no more neck, nothing but veins pumping out the sap of the day,
the blood of the night, the upheavals of a life constantly jostled by the
whip laughter, the lash sarcasm, the riding-crop sniggerings, her head
slips on the grass, rolls around, skids, corrupting the atmosphere but
an atmosphere saturated with laughter, with sarcasm, with sniggerings,
curdling, hardening, I grab hold of the wind, ah! its rebellious power,
my inextinguishable thirst for vengeance, I break away in gusts of wind,
I stretch, I slash, I pierce the atmosphere, the astonished soldiers hear
the rumbling of my voice, totem planted in the soil, voice of the living
earth, and the earth was pain, the earth was sorrow in the heart of an
old woman who was rediscovering her name, suffering in the loins of a
mother who had not been broken by misery, the earth wept, the blood
of crucified Negroes all over the plantations, my son stabbed between
four prayers of madness, along with the repeated violation of my pain,
behold, Sister Theresa, behold, contemplate yourself, I've sculpted
your expression forevermore in the air's own memory so I'll remember

—a mask with empty eyes

—too bad for you

—ha! ha!

—make whatever face you want, no wrinkles will furrow your brow

—ha! ha!

—your bitter laugh like the sound of misery suspended over the
astonished heads of the captain and his men, fear gave them a soul

—sorcery!

—black magic!

—Vodou!

—let's kill the witch

their cries of rage upon me, their horror, an infinite joy

—fire!

the guns explode in their hands, burn their faces, their black faces,
smeared with powder, hideous enough to frighten the day, begging you
for protection, the cold, hard mask, ha! ha! you are losing your way,

ha! ha! erasing the sun with one gesture, Vodou! Vodou! the blackened soldiers took flight, that's funny, a white man fleeing, disguised as a Negro, Boukman on his heels, blessed day, Agoué, the day of your rage, Mackandal rises up, a giant statue spitting fire and flames, distilling poison, Biassou cuts off heads, a tornado, a hurricane, a cyclone, Fatras-Bâton releases the lwa, razing plains and hills, the salt of vengeance sets fire to the cane fields, the blue blood of the Gauls was black that day as it sowed the new furrows of nightmares, liberate our violence, Sister Theresa, we have drunk blue blood and we are intoxicated by it

—I brought about the apocalypse

—you should not have loved Salomon

—Reverend Mother, another one of her lies, I only love

—shhh! I lived the time of a journey, the time of a love affair, don't lift the veil of my happiness by divulging it

—but, Sonja, if I let her continue her lying, she

—will find her fulfillment, you can do nothing about it

I regained consciousness, my head heavy, face dripping with blood, I raised my hand to my forehead, the bullet had grazed my scalp, scraping the skin, a superficial wound but the shock had been intense, I was still shaken up, the sun had become a mask of madness, congealed, hardened, breathing in and compressing the wind, rarified air, oppressive, leaning on my uninjured arm I put my feet on the ground and then, after patient and painful efforts, I stood up, Sonja's body, lacerated by the whip, decapitated (Toukouma had once again done justice), had fallen on Salomon's, both of them naked, in the eternity of their secret

—Saintmilia! Saintmilia!

she passes through the ropes binding her, walks over to my pain, unrecognizable, deprived of her breath she was an opaque blue but, in the clear morning, appeared transparent to me, within her I read my resurfaced past, two young pups hurtling down the hill at Petite-Anse, acrobatic dives from the cliffs at Petit-Fort, two young pups running barefoot and massacring the loose stones on the paths

—Nanie! it hurts

—it's not your fault, Little Master

—death broke my arm

—you couldn't have known

—why did I arrive so late?

—brotherhood was less weighty than your destiny

with these words she left, ethereal, carrying away what had been all of our universe, she followed the path leading to the creek, her footsteps heavy with mourning wandered over the waves, and there she planted her next chapter of daylight and sun, trees, air, wind, birds, and torchlit colors, she vanished

—forever cursed, this plantation that has drunk the blood of my son, damned, until I return to wash his body with my tears and revive my eyes with new hope

—and here I am again

—and here we are again

this morning, when I opened the window, you once again entered into my day with your eternal faded madras headscarf, your demeanor of a little old lady beaten down by suffering whose scowling eyes read right through the suffering of others, your calico dress indecent in the blue light of the morning, it's raining, sickly sun, leftover tears that the lovelorn women of your country have been weeping for centuries, our shared misery, you raise your hand, stretched fully toward the vertigo of the light, toward that part of yourself hidden in the deepest regions of your memory but bursting forth this time into our truth, for the triumph of life or death, the night will no longer bury its joy in your eyes, for the night of history is dissipating, terror was our lot, horror our bed, to no longer think about that crazy time that forked the path of childhood

—come with me

—pray, Lord, for Saintmilia's lost soul

—don't think you can fool me with your kindly airs, in any case, dear sisters, my name is Ti Mèmè N'kedi

—Sonja, free her memories, remind her that we're of the same family through the blood of her milk

—history is not so easily rewritten

—am I the one who stabbed your son? I was not yet even born

—that lie is the worst of them all, death as a reproach to life

—my life belongs to Jesus

—has he redeemed the mask?

—how do you know of its existence?

—I'm the one who sculpted it so that between us it remains what I decided it would be, a sign of recognition and of our destiny

—why must you always lie? is it a family trait?

—like Salomon?

—she annoys me, Sonja, couldn't the Senegalese sorcerers send some powerful magic to counter her nonsense?

—my father is leader of the believers

—are you not the one lying now, and about your feelings

—only to help you raise the mask

—and then I'll know myself?

—yes, in your past, Sister Theresa, and in my truth

—don't lose hope for me, Saintmilia

—really! raise your head, what do you see?

she stretches out her arm, clenches her fist nervously, rejecting once and for all the impossible solidarity I'm offering her, unthinkable charity that my faith commands of me, the common hope that will earn us salvation

—pray, my sisters, for the salvation of their souls

—Sonja, tell her that I cried when I heard the tragic story of her son

—what does that matter to me! will your pity make up for my motherly suffering? Saul, Saul, why do you persecute me?

and as my ancestor had recounted so well, the air was suddenly rarified, gathered up from all over within the fist she brandished

—let us close our eyes, my sisters

—she gained momentum, leapt

—there's nothing left within her that holds on to the memory of my son, neither life nor love nor death nor hatred

—I heard the thunder coming, the accumulated power of the earth, two centuries of despair

—Nanie! Nanie! save her

—the mask between us, I try to shield my face with my hands

—ha! ha! cursed Biemmes! from generation to generation! iron and fire merged together

—I beg of you, Nanie, save my little girl

—my grandfather's voice, sepulchral, risen from the mists of time, Sonja! I'm scared, burn the mask's laugh in a great brushfire

—a Biemme is never afraid, remember that

—I'm a Schpeerbach, do you hear the voice of my ancestor, there, so close but so far away, calling me, claiming me

—Lord, save his soul from the fires of hell

—the mark of metal on my hands, the sulfurous breath of the devil

—Nanie!

—is that you calling me, Wolf? what forest have you lost your way in now?

—don't you see that it's gnawing at her face?

—is Salomon with you? I haven't seen him since he left his heart in the public square, the dogs will devour his joy if he doesn't come back in time to retrieve it

—you're rambling, Nanie, while your granddaughter is in serious danger

—I don't have a daughter, Little Master, the woman at the window is Mistress Sonja, I recognized her, the mask she is wearing has been

—go save her, save her, I tell you, soon it will be too late unless . . . tell me, might your Vodou be powerless against the magic of the whites?

—don't toy with me, Little Master, have you no pity for Nanie?

—you're killing me, was it worth drinking your milk?

—was it worth it to have loved Salomon? Ti Mèmè, save me

—ah! the creeping smell of burned flesh that is not a Negro's

—save her Nanie! . . . my God! it's too late!

—Lord, may her soul rest in peace

—have I made a mistake? that smell of burned milk, but . . . the true smell of my milk, the blood of my blood! and you, what are you on her face, a copper face you dare to steal from my vengeance?

she leaps, the drums howl, a swollen wind, immense and flamboyant, the hospice roars with all the colors packed tightly together, with all the promises of the vast earth lost in the immensity beyond the spray of the sea but present in our skin with its odors of decomposition, villages of shells hanging from the banks of lagoons, villages of feathers, totem villages flattened at the edge of vultures' wings and where the Negroes' manifold heart beats, red, full with the leaven of the waves, she sits astride the slanting rays of light, gallops, the air quivers beneath her hooves, somewhere inside her, as a reminder, the

Uhuru becomes pale, hiccups, a black sun sets alight the madras of her faded hair, her head a crown of flames and suddenly the sea, dying from the ravages of her fires, the slumbering madness in her eyes awakens, boils with all the volcanoes extinguished for so long in her brain, impetuous, knocks, roar of the sulfurous devil the mask melts, volatile stench of hell, all the odors of sin, of theft, of rape, of crimes, of murders, hanging from the neck of the centuries, plunged into the throat of history, all the odors flash, explode, Saintmilia's final joy as if the sun were bursting, Salomon emerges from his night, the past instantly modulated in notes of light, silence strikes, absolute, terrifying, astonished by this audacity life stops, the entire world ceases to exist, and then comes her laughter, arpeggios taken apart in the face of a rejuvenated sun, in that laugh a doubled lament of agony, two souls searching for peace have met one another, and then, as if overcoming her own lament, between the Our Father and the hurried Hail Mary of the nuns, Ti Mèmè N'kedi's dazzling voice

—Salomon, our story has ended, the times where my madness was part of History have ended

then, coming from the deepest heart of the earth, echoing her voice, a concert of joy, harmony of hopes that for two centuries had been hidden in all the wells of misery, pouring into spaces of liberty, reconciled with the dream and the miracle, dancing in the heads of Toukouma and the leaders of the army of shadows, whirling, swelling, piercing the sky with a tall column of cries and songs marching toward the east, at last, at last, the road marked by stars leading to our memory, a continent of bush and savanna, of forests and deserts, of lakes and flowers, landscapes of quiet dawn that are life, from whence comes the sun

in the beginning was Africa

www.ingramcontent.com/pod-product-compliance
Lightning Source LLC
Chambersburg PA
CBHW031931120525
26572CB00023B/235